The
Poisoned
Chalice

A Father Flenn Adventure

By Scott Arnold

Cover:

Interior Design: Jim Brown

Editor: Margaret Shaw/Diane Arnold

The
Poisoned
Chalice

To:
Heather and Sean

CHAPTER *ONE*

Present day...

The thief had been stalking his prey long enough. From out of the shadows he struck with lightning speed. If it hadn't been for Father Scott Flenn, the bandit would have made a clean getaway.

Father Flenn had brought two dozen Alabama Episcopalians with him on a pilgrimage to England this summer. So far, all had gone well—despite Delores Dilwicky being part of the group. Delores was from Father Flenn's parish, and was Saint Ann's would-be socialite. In fact, it was Delores that the thief had been stalking.

Delores was leaning against the statue of the Roman Emperor Constantine outside York Minster, one of the world's grandest houses of worship, eating the first of her sausage pasties from a greasy, brown bag. Unaccustomed in the finer techniques of eating a pasty daintily, Delores set the bag down to rearrange her large, flashy necklace. She'd no more than set her diet soda next to Constantine's foot when the thief darted out from underneath the shrubbery.

Flenn tried to intercept the robber before he made it to the lunch bag on the pavement. Despite being extremely fit—running nearly every day since he had completed physical training for both the Air Force and the CIA—Flenn was no match for this furry fellow. The collie snatched the bag of savory treats and disappeared around a corner toward the city wall.

"Well I never!" Delores declared, watching the dog make off with her sack lunch. "Father, did you see what that mangy mutt just did?"

Flenn stood beside her, trying unsuccessfully not to laugh. "I think someone is hungry," he said.

Delores reached for her soda. "I don't see what's so funny. They ought to have a law about unleashed animals wandering around this cathedral!"

Father Flenn had explained several times that the huge church was called a minster and not a cathedral, but Delores Dilwicky had spent most of the trip ignoring what he and the tour guide had to say. Instead, she'd spent most of her time perusing the gift shops in Canterbury, Salisbury and Lincoln. Today, after touring York Minster, the group had disappeared into various surrounding pubs for lunch and a pint before regathering at the statue to make their way to the Shambles, York's ancient shopping district. Fascinated by the sights and smells coming from a nearby bakery, Delores had wandered off on her own.

"I'm sorry, Delores," Flenn fibbed. "You're right, it isn't funny."

Delores wiped the crumbs from her peach-and-tan blouse. "Well, if you find that mutt's owner, please do something about it! I'm going back to the bakery."

"There isn't time, Delores; we're are all due to meet our guide here in a few minutes." The woman pretended not to hear as she made her way across the courtyard.

Others in the group were already starting to show up, and Flenn could see their guide, David Spate, walking briskly to meet them. Flenn had known Davy from his days in the CIA. Davy was a former spy himself, having worked undercover for British intelligence. But even MI-6 had age restrictions, and the years had finally caught up with Flenn's old friend. These days, David Spate ran his own tour guide company just outside of Manchester.

"I'm sorry, Davy," Flenn said. "I'm afraid we'll be delayed a few minutes. One of our group has run off to the bakery."

Davy glanced at his watch. "Let me guess, that Dillish woman again?"

"Dilwicky," Flenn corrected. "I'm sure she'll be right back." The others were gathering around the statue, chatting, and admiring the picturesque beauty of one of Britain's most visited sites.

"I don't think that woman has missed a bakery or coffee shop since we arrived."

"I'm sorry," Flenn said, "I'm sure she won't be long."

"I'll tell you, Flenn, no offense, but I don't see how you stand it. From my experience, church people are some of the hardest folks to lead on a tour. Give me a group of drunk, rowdy Freemasons any day."

"Maybe you should try *attending* a church someday. It might change your attitude."

Davy grinned, "You know, I think I liked you better in

the old days." The tour director sighed. "Right. Well, I'll just come up with something while we wait. The Shambles have been here over a thousand years, I don't suppose they're going anywhere."

"That's the spirit, Davy," Flenn said as they wandered back toward the group gathering around the stature. "What is it you Brits say? 'Stiff upper lip,' or something like that."

Davy whispered, "Well, *I* certainly never say it." Then loudly to the group: "Right everyone… gather round." Flenn stepped aside to watch for Delores as he listened to his old friend stalling for time. "You may remember from your history books that Constantine was the first Christian emperor of Rome way back in the Fourth Century," said Davy. "You also may be asking yourselves, "Why on earth is there a statue of the *Roman* Emperor Constantine in front of this magnificent *English* building? Well, I'll tell you: "Constantine's father, the emperor of Rome, had made his way to York, or Eboracum, as the Romans called it. He died here, making his son, Constantine, head of the empire. Now, it wasn't exactly following Roman protocol, but…"

"Yoo-hoo!"

Delores had managed to find a street vendor selling fish and chips wrapped in newspaper. "Oh, Father, I hope I'm not late. Do you think Mr. Spate would mind starting over?" She walked past Flenn toward the group, "Oh, Mr. Spate…"

Several members of the group rolled their eyes. Flenn turned away, to give himself a moment, and gazed up at the giant spires of the Minster. Dating as far back as the seventh century, Christians had been gathering on this very spot to seek solace and strength during difficult times. Flenn was doing much the same thing now.

He needed this trip. The past eight months had been grueling. His former comrade and once fellow spy, Zack Matteson, had shown up twice since November, both times seducing him back into elements of his former life with the CIA. Flenn had left that life a decade ago, after a life-altering experience in Edinburgh; *but, try telling that to Zack Matteson!*

Since quitting his work as a spy, Flenn had returned to the church of his mother and had even become an Episcopal priest. This year, he'd arranged with Davy Spate to bring a group from the Diocese of Alabama eager to England to see the birthplace of their denomination. The trip had been worthwhile, with the travelers having seen several important places in Anglicanism's history, including Hampton Court, where King Edward V, the son of Henry VIII, had been baptized. The Church of England had its theological beginnings more so under Edward's brief reign than his lustful father's, who'd been reluctant to change much from the Roman tradition.

"Right, well, if everyone is eager to press on," Father Flenn heard Davy say, "then let's move on to… "

It was Delores who interrupted. "I'd like to go back inside the cathedral." Several in the group wanted her to do just that; so they could leave her there.

Davy and Flenn pretended they hadn't heard, "And, of course," Flenn added, "after the tour you'll be free the rest of the afternoon to do some shopping. There are some wonderful souvenir shops in the Shambles."

That was all it took. Delores said no more about going back inside York Minster. Davy slid up alongside Flenn. "You know, old chum," he whispered, "it's people like her that make me wish you had left me in that cave with Al-Qaeda. At least, I didn't have to pretend to be nice to *them*."

CHAPTER *TWO*

11 years earlier...

The squat man in white robes and a gray turban wiped the sand from his eyes as he stepped out of the Jeep. Four men who'd been leaning against the entrance to the cave immediately snapped to attention. Yasir Kamul turned to his bodyguards and sent one of them into the cave.

Kamul looked the four locals up and down, and snapped to the tallest of them, "This had better be worth my time, or your leader, Asim, will have much to answer for!" Asim al-Aruri had contacted Kamul after he had captured the British dog. Asim had only recently joined Kamul's newly emerging group within Al-Qaeda and knew next to nothing about protocol. He'd been assigned a few men and told to watch the northwest quadrant of Kasir, a nothing village in the middle of nowhere. There'd been little for them to do this past month until, from out of nowhere, a badly disguised English spy had tried to infiltrate their group.

Most of Asim's men were thick as sandstone, but one of them, Abu Batarfi, stood out as having a modicum of intelligence. He was the tall man Kamul was addressing now. "Where is Asim?" Kamul demanded.

"He's inside with the prisoner," Abu said.

"Has the English sheep-dropping told you anything?" Kamul snapped.

Asim had assigned Abu to torture the prisoner to see if he could discover the spy's true identity and find out who had sent him. Asim reasoned it was better to give it to Abu than to any of the other imbeciles; they would likely have done irreparable harm to the prisoner, and that would have not pleased Yasir Kamul.

Kamul oversaw the entire district. Asim was one of a dozen warlords whose duty was to report directly to him, which is why Asim had sent word about the spy after giving Abu a few days to beat the prisoner. Abu Batarfi had a future in Al-Qaeda, of that Asim had no doubt. The tall, Italian-born son of Libyan schoolteachers had become disillusioned with the ways of the West and had traveled here to Pakistan six months ago to join up with Asim's men. Abu had learned much, and no one had more zeal. Abu's green eyes had danced when he'd begged Asim to let him torture the Brit. Asim had smiled with glee every time Abu brought him some tidbit of new information. Finally, after two days of screams coming from Abu's tent, Asim had contacted Kamul and moved the spy into the cave, where they were now awaiting Kamul.

Asim's men had gone to considerable effort to find a generator and lights for the cave, wishing to impress Kamul upon his arrival. Abu had been told to usher Kamul and his men inside as soon as they arrived, but Kamul was cautious. He hadn't become a leader in Al-Qaeda by rushing headlong into danger. For instance, he'd traveled today with only two guards instead of his entire entourage because American drones watched for convoys and vehicles overloaded with men. Al-Qaeda had learned the hard way that it was safer to travel light.

Kamul's guard exited the cave and leaned over to whisper something in his commander's ear. Kamul nodded. "Pick one of these men and stay here at the entrance," he told the man. "The rest of you come with me." The tall man, Abu, motioned to the others.

"Leave your rifles here!" he barked. Kamul trusted no one. "I have all the firepower we need against one British spy. Asim's men looked puzzled by the order, reluctant to give up their weapons. But Abu instructed them to do as they were told.

Abu led the way through the dank and narrow tunnel that had been reinforced years ago by salt miners. The light at the far end illuminated the passageway sufficiently for them to find their way down the long tunnel.

Fifty meters into the cave they saw four men facing them, one of whom was sitting in a chair, his face bruised. Two guards stood behind, both with AK-47's.

Asim was all smiles as he greeted Kamul. "Peace be with you, Yasir!"

Yasir ignored the traditional greeting. "Asim, gather those guns from your guards and bring them to me."

Asim raised an eyebrow. "But, my prisoner... "

"Is now *my* prisoner, as you will also be if you do not do as I say! I do not take chances around people I do not know, and I do not know your men."

Asim stared at the newer AK-74 that Kamul's guard was carrying, and noticed for the first time that Abu and his men were unarmed. "Of course, of course, Yasir, whatever you say," Asim muttered, trying to hide his concern. He took comfort that there was a revolver hidden inside his tunic.

Kamul sat down across from the prisoner. "I understand you are a British spy," Kamul said in perfect English. The man simply stared down at the table. "Judging from the bruise on your face, I assume you did not wish to speak with Asim or his men?"

Asim interrupted. "He told us plenty, Yasir. He is from a place called Jarrow, and he works with British intelligence."

Kamul held up his hand. "I will let *him* tell me, which is what *you* should have done!" Asim swallowed and stepped back. Kamul leaned into the chair. "I know Jarrow. A tiny place, but home of the first English historian, a man named Bede." The prisoner lifted his head. "Does that surprise you, my friend? That I know of such things? Then, it would probably surprise you to learn that I studied at Cambridge. Graduated with a degree in biology. I had plans to go on and become a doctor."

"So why the hell didn't you, instead of becoming a bloody terrorist?" The spy's glare was unmistakable. He would kill Kamul if given half a chance. Kamul's man tightened the grip on his rifle.

"Terrorist?" Kamul nodded. "Yes, that is what you call us," he said calmly. "I must admit, there was a time when I thought the same, until Allah brought me to the truth."

"Don't hide behind God, Kamul. You're an opportunist; you're no more religious than I am! I know who you are… and I know that you never graduated; you flunked out of Cambridge your sophomore year. I also know you couldn't find a job after your visa expired." Fire flashed from the prisoner's eyes. "And I know you left the country because of what you did to your English girlfriend… "

Kamul slammed his hand down on the table. "Lies! All lies, just like the ones your government tells my people all the time!" The rage in Kamul's face seemed to vanish as quickly as it had come. "My studies in biology left me with a certain understanding of human anatomy. I know what the human body can tolerate, and what it cannot. Do not be mistaken, my friend. You will tell me everything I want to know." He turned. "What was that?"

"What was what?" Asim said.

"I heard something; have one of your men check it out," he snapped.

"I'll go," Abu said. Asim nodded, and the tall man disappeared toward the entrance of the cave.

Kamul turned to face the prisoner again. "Where was I? Oh, yes, the human body." He grinned. "We all think we are courageous enough to stand up to almost anything. But pain changes our minds and we find we are not as brave as we first thought." He smiled at the prisoner. "We all have our breaking point, I can assure you."

Kamul motioned to Asim's men. "Put his right hand on the table." It took three of them to pull the prisoner's hand away from his side. Kamul pulled a long knife from underneath his robes. "Do you recognize this blade?" Kamul didn't wait for an answer. "It was taken from a member of your armed forces. It turned out to be very effective on him. He told me what I wanted to know much sooner than I expected." Kamul grinned a second time. "As I said, we all have our breaking point."

The spy struggled to break free, yet Kamul waited patiently for the guards to subdue him. "I have found that it isn't always the largest parts of the body that can cause the greatest pain." He nodded to the men who pushed the prisoner's hand flat against the wooden table. Something as small as the loss of a little finger can cause excruciating… "

"Um… " Abu came up behind them. Kamul turned, as did his bodyguard. "I am sorry to interrupt," Abu said. The guard relaxed.

"What did you find?"

"Nothing."

Kamul turned back to face the spy.

Abu spoke again. "Except… "

Kamul was tired of the interruptions. Asim spoke up. "What is it, Abu?"

"I did find this… " At that point another, shorter man stepped out from behind Abu and shot Kamul's bodyguard. A tiny red dot formed in the middle of the man's forehead. Abu reached underneath his robes and pointed an AK-47 directly at Yasir Kamul. "Unless you all want to join him in hell, I suggest you place your hands on top of your head. Now!"

Asim couldn't restrain his fury. "Traitor!" he screamed, pulling the revolver from beneath his tunic. The stranger shot Asim twice in the chest. Kamul attempted to throw his knife, but Abu shot the terrorist in the shoulder before he could fling the blade and the knife dropped—straight through Kamul's own big toe.

No one else dared move.

The English spy stood up, gathering rifles from where the guard had left them, disabling all but one, which he kept for himself.

"Sure as hell took you long enough!" the spy griped.

Abu smiled, keeping his eyes off the others. "Sorry Davy, my partner here must have stopped for a martini."

The shorter man looked up. "In Pakistan? God, I wish." He looked at Asim's men cowering against the wall. "You two got this? I need to go make a phone call."

"We got it," Abu said.

"Right, give me five minutes," the man said, sprinting toward the entrance.

The spy looked at Abu. "So, what about *them*?"

"Geez, Davy, I don't know. They were going to help Kamul cut off your fingers, so I guess that's your decision."

"Kill them, you fools!" screamed Kamul, reaching for the knife in his foot.

"Touch that," David Spate ordered, "and I will shoot you in a place where you sure as hell won't harm another woman again!"

"I need to remove it!" Kamul cried in agony.

"Yeah, and shove it down our throats. I like it where it is." Abu glanced at Spate. "Come on, Davy, have a heart and take it out."

Spate rolled his eyes. "Fine…" he looked at Kamul, "but if you so much as flinch I'll slice your throat with it."

For all his bravado, Kamul didn't move an inch as Davy pulled out the knife.

"I figured you might twist it first," Abu said.

"Must say, I did think about it." Davy tossed the blade into the darkness behind him.

One of Asim's men finally spoke. "Please, Abu, we never did you any harm. Do not kill us," he begged.

Abu grinned. "What d'ya think, Davy?"

The MI-6 agent put his hand to his chin. "I suppose they could be useful helping load this bugger onto the helicopter."

Kamul's eyes grew twice their normal size. "If any of you assist these men, I will bury you in the sand and let the scorpions eat your eyes!"

Abu looked at the men. "All the more reason you had better give him to us. Then we can all be on our way. I promise you, you will never see Yasir Kamul again." The men readily agreed. Abu had them strip first to be certain no other weapons remained hidden.

They made it to the entrance of the cave just as the helicopter was landing. Two United States Marines stood onboard behind heavy machine guns at the ready. Abu's clandestine partner, the stranger who'd shown up in the cave, was shocked to see five naked men carrying Kamul between them. He pulled the cotton scarf from the front of his face; a lock of jet-black hair fell across his forehead.

Abu brought up the rear as they hauled the Al-Qaeda leader toward the chopper. The British spy held out his hand to the stranger. "I'm David. David Spate. Most folks call me Davy. Glad you showed up when you did."

"Zack Matteson, good to meet you," said the stranger. The two men shook hands as Abu saw to it that their target was secured in the chopper.

Abu put his hand on Davy's shoulder. "Davy here is an okay spy, but he's an even better actor. You should have heard him screaming when I was supposedly beating him."

Davy rubbed his cheek. "Pretend, my arse! You slapped the hell out of me."

Abu shrugged. "Just once… I had to make it look real." Abu glanced at Zack. "He's pretty tough though… " he winked… "for a Brit."

Davy rolled his eyes.

"Is that right?" Zack said. "Well, sorry we cut things a bit close, back there."

"Please," said Davy, "don't say *cut*."

Zack Matteson pulled a small bag of jellybeans from his pocket and watched as Abu shouted orders to the five naked Pakistanis. Obediently, each of them began running into the desert with their hands over their heads.

"Now there's a sight you don't see every day," Zack observed, popping a green jellybean into his mouth. The three men stood silently, watching the naked terrorists running into the desert. Zack put his hand on the tall man's shoulder. "Okay *Aboo-Boo*, let's get out of here."

Scott Flenn turned toward his long-time partner. "Don't ever call me that again."

CHAPTER *THREE*

Present day…

The summer sun barely sets in northern England before it rises again. Father Flenn was jogging along York's ancient city wall at 5 a.m. in full daylight, although only a few locals were doing the same. Flenn loved this city, from the soaring towers of the Minster to the twisty alleys called snickleways, to the miles of city walls, some of which dated back to the Roman era.

He had barely broken a sweat so far this morning. Summertime in England could be at least 30 degrees cooler than back home in Alabama. A native of New Hampshire, Flenn had never grown accustomed to the Birmingham heat, even though he'd spent years in the Middle East. *At least the desert heat is dry*, he often told himself on his runs. *It's the damned Alabama humidity that's such a killer.*

Father Flenn had been the rector of Saint Ann's parish in the Diocese of Alabama for six years. Bishop Tom Morrison had called him to the post shortly after Flenn graduated from seminary. Actually, it had been more Flenn's idea. He'd heard that the little church was unable to afford a priest and was about to close its doors. Flenn had volunteered to shepherd the mission church in exchange for use of the vicarage and the ability to set his own schedule. Bishop Morrison and the parish had readily agreed. As for payment, Scott Flenn had no need of a salary. His family owned Flenn Industries, one of the largest privately-owned companies in the United States. His father, David Flenn Sr., had left both of his sons billionaires.

Flenn's brother, David Jr., had taken charge of the company after their parents passed away. Scott Flenn, or *Flenn*, as he insisted everyone call him, had never been interested in the family business. Instead, he'd joined the Air Force right out of Princeton, and from there had served with military intelligence.

It hadn't taken much convincing for Flenn to be recruited into the CIA. During his 12 years as Zack Matteson's partner, he had served in China, Korea, Pakistan, Iran, Iraq, Libya, Saudi Arabia, and the United Arab Emirates. He and Zack had made some other *"visits"* as well… ones the CIA never sanctioned, at least not officially.

Traveling with Davy Spate on this trip had brought back a lot of memories, none of which he and Davy could talk about openly. Only a handful of people knew about Flenn's background, beyond his family's business and his service in the Air Force. Bishop Tom Morrison was one of less than a half-dozen civilians who knew Flenn's entire story. Flenn had risked telling his bishop, and friend, the strange tale of what had happened in Edinburgh years ago… when Flenn's journey to the priesthood had begun.

Flenn checked his pulse. He estimated that he'd

jogged about four miles this morning, since he'd passed the Monkbar gate twice. The four-story gatehouse was built in the 1300's, around the time of Edward III, and had been one of the main entranceways to the city for centuries. Flenn, who enjoyed dabbling in English history, recalled that Edward's reign was one of the longest in England and had survived both the birth of England's Parliament and the plague.

One more mile, Flenn told himself, and then back to the hotel for a shower and breakfast with his group of pilgrims. After that, it was off to Liverpool where Flenn had originally planned a visit to the cathedral until he'd overheard one of his group last night complain that this trip had turned into an *ABC tour.*

"What's that?" Delores Dilwicky had asked.

"Another Beautiful Cathedral," the parishioner had sighed. After speaking to Davy, Flenn decided to announce at breakfast today that they would cut their time short at the church and include a visit to Penny Lane as well as a museum dedicated to the Beatles. Tomorrow, they'd all board a flight for home in Manchester— everyone, that is, except Flenn. He was taking off for Durham and then to Edinburgh for a much-needed sabbatical. Flenn sighed. He needed the time off, *especially after the last few months.*

No one else was nearby when he saw a young woman who seemed to have fallen. From the looks of things, she was pregnant—very pregnant. Flenn sped up to help.

"Are you okay?" he asked, offering her a hand. The girl didn't respond, only looked away.

"She's fine, but you won't be if you don't hand over your wallet!" came a nervous voice from behind. Flenn turned to see a red-haired kid holding some sort of ancient pistol.

Flenn offered a disarming smile. "Now what's all this about, son?"

The teen's hands were shaking. "Just do it!"

"Please sir," the girl said. "We're desperate. I'm due any day and we've no place to live."

Flenn rarely carried his wallet when on a run, unless he was traveling abroad and needed to keep his passport at hand. "Right, well there's no need to hold a gun on me; I'm happy to help." He retrieved his travel-wallet from around his neck and pulled out a 100-pound note. "Will this do?"

The boy caught a glimpse of the other bills inside. "All of it!" he demanded.

Flenn sighed, then tossed the wallet to him. As the boy reached to catch it, Flenn snatched the kid's wrist with his left hand while simultaneously sweeping the pistol with his right. In less than a second the boy was staring down the muzzle of his own gun.

"Now," Flenn said, "let's talk." He motioned to a nearby bench and made it clear that they were both to sit. Defeated, the boy just slumped over and stared at the city below. The young woman began to cry.

"Strange as it may sound to you both, I'm not going to turn you in," Flenn said. The boy looked up. "And you can keep the money. I just want to know what's going on. You two don't look like kids who go around holding people up."

"It was our first time," the girl sobbed. "Honest, sir, we shan't do it again."

Flenn looked at her accomplice, "Is that right, son?"

"Yeah, whatever," responded the boy.

"Okay, here's what I'm going to do," Flenn said, looking at the girl. "I'm guessing your parents threw you out once they found out you were pregnant and the two of you have been living on the streets, right?" The girl looked away. "Okay, well, you don't have to tell me but here's the thing. I'm a priest. I happen to know the dean at the Minster. I will talk with him and we will find you a place to stay, along with proper care for your girlfriend. Just come around to his office at 10 o'clock tomorrow morning. He'll have found a flat for you by then, *and* a stocked refrigerator."

The boy scoffed, "That's a load of tosh. You're just trying to trick us into coming so you can have us arrested for nicking a hundred quid off you!"

"I *gave* you that hundred quid." Flenn reached into his wallet. "And here's another hundred for you to find a decent place tonight along with some food for your girlfriend."

"I'm not his girlfriend."

The boy turned. "Shut up, Mae!"

"No, Edgar, I think he's telling us the truth." The girl looked at Flenn, wiping her eyes with the back of her hand. "We're sorry, Father; we really are. Edgar's not my boyfriend, he's my brother. We're twins, you see."

Flenn raised an eyebrow.

"Gawd…nothing like that, mister," Edgar said. "Our mum tossed Mae out when she discovered… "

The girl interrupted, "I don't have a boyfriend, well, not anymore. Edgar said he wouldn't stay at home if I couldn't and he's been trying to take care of me."

"I'm sorry. I truly am," Flenn said. "But the offer is still good. Show up tomorrow at Dean Percival Jackson's office. You will get all the help you need, and then some."

"How do we know you're not just going to call the police?" the boy asked, a slightly softer tone in his voice than before.

"I could do that now. I'm the one holding the gun, you know."

"Aren't any bullets," the boy said. Flenn looked down at the weapon and then burst out laughing. He handed it back to the teenager and stood up. "Get rid of this thing; it will only bring you trouble."

The girl stood as well and held out her hand. "Thank you, Father. We're sorry, truly we are. We'll get a hotel tonight and clean up, get some of this muck off. I'll make sure Edgar comes with me tomorrow. Will you be there, too?"

"Afraid not," Flenn said, "but I'll make all the arrangements. Don't give up; good things are about to start happening for you both… I promise."

With that, Flenn headed for the steps down the Monkbar gate and back to the hotel. He said a prayer for Edgar and Mae and made a mental note to call his brother and have $20,000 overnighted to Percival's office, plus a sizeable donation for the dean's discretionary fund.

CHAPTER *FOUR*

Present day...

Father Flenn stood at the bottom of the stairs at Manchester Airport and shook hands with everyone as they prepared to board the 777 back to Atlanta and then home to Birmingham.

"I do so wish you were going back with us, Father," said Delores Dilwicky. "It just seems like you're gone so often lately."

"Doing the Lord's work, Delores, doing the Lord's work." She was referring to the weeks he'd spent on his mission to Honduras a few months back—a mission which had gone horribly wrong. He was staying behind in England, in fact, to recover from all that. Bishop Morrison had insisted.

"Yes, but now you're going on vacation," Delores said. "Seems like you're never around."

"Father Bruce will take good care of you while I'm away," Flenn said, more gently than he felt.

"Yes, but..."

"Remember, Delores, priests are people too. We also need a break from time to time."

The woman pursed her lips. "Just the same, I'm not sure what the vestry will say."

"The vestry will tell him to take all the time he needs," said Martin Billingsly who'd stepped up behind her. "And, Delores, since I'm the senior warden I don't expect to hear any gossip otherwise. Now, let me help you on board." Martin picked up her carry-on bag and hauled it to the top of the stairs.

"Well, I never…" mumbled the flustered woman as she climbed the stairs.

And, let's hope you never do! Flenn thought as he turned to the next parishioner. He smiled and waved at the group and then waited at the airport until he knew their plane was safely in the air. Tonight, he would meet Davy Spate for a drink and then catch the morning train to Durham. His friend, Windsor Tammerlane, was being installed as the new bishop of Durham on Sunday.

He had known Windsor and his wife Pamela for years. *Hoshi and Pam had been college roommates and had remained friends until…* Flenn sighed. The thought of Hoshi brought back the old, familiar pain. He chased her image from his mind and told himself it would be good to see Win and Pam again.

****

The Pig and Pint was nearly four centuries old, with well-worn plaster and timber walls surrounding a large oak bar with bottles of spirits from around the world, along with eight taps of local brew. The pub was dark, yet cheerful and smelled of pork, fried potatoes and ale.

"Davy, that's your fourth pint," Flenn said, "don't you think you should slow down a bit?"

Davy looked up from his glass. "So, not only are you a priest, you're a member of the temperance union, are ya'? I seem to recall a time when you could drink us all under the table."

Flenn winked as he lifted his glass of single-malt Scotch. "Still can."

"Yeah, yeah, tell me another. Love…," he shouted to the waitress, "would you bring my chum a fresh one?"

"Well," Flenn said with a smile, "I suppose so, as long as you're buying."

Davy grinned. "Not on your life… you're the one with all the bread and honey."

"The what?"

The former MI-6 agent looked over the top of his glasses. "Money, Flenn, money."

Flenn sighed. "Why is it, no matter where I go, I end up the one paying the bill?"

Davy grinned. "Cause you're loaded. Besides, I'm just a pensioner these days."

The waitress brought another Scotch. "Tell me," Flenn asked her, pointing at Davy, "does this *pensioner* look like a poor man to you?"

The slight woman with red hair and rosy cheeks smiled. "It depends, love. Poor at what?"

Davy roared with laughter and banged his now empty glass on the table a little too heavily. The couple across from them turned to see what was going on. "Tell you what, dear," Davy said, "go out with me later and I'll show you I'm not poor at anything!"

The girl looked at Flenn. "Aw, listen to your friend now, would you; he's old enough to be me dad!"

"Your granddad more like," said Flenn.

"Although dear," the woman said to Flenn, "if *you* are interested in a drink afterwards… "

Flenn blushed. "It would no doubt be grand," he said, "but someone's got to walk this pensioner home."

"It's your loss, love. My name is Freda in case you want to change your mind."

The two men watched the waitress walk away to fetch another ale for Davy. "My God man, just how far around does that collar of yours reach?"

Flenn just smiled. "It isn't on now."

"Well, it might as well be. She's a real looker, that one."

Flenn sighed. "Yeah, but, well you know… "

Davy straightened, the smile vanishing from his face. "Hoshi?" Flenn looked away.

"Good lord, man, it's been, what, ten years?"

Flenn nodded. "Thereabouts." Freda returned with ale and Davy's fish and chips, along with a large, steaming dish of haggis for Flenn. She winked at the priest before walking away.

"If you're brave enough to eat that rubbish, you can certainly go out with a proper English girl," Davy said.

Flenn lifted a forkful of the traditional Scottish dish. "Something tells me she's anything but 'proper.' And as for me eating sheep's organs, well you MI-6 guys were always soft."

"The hell we were! We could run circles around you creampuffs from Langley any day."

Flenn washed the haggis down with Scotch. "Funny, I didn't see you jogging up on the city wall with me this morning."

"*Pensioner*, mate, remember? And, as for this morning, what on earth were you thinking?"

"What?"

Davy picked up a chip, what Flenn would have called a french-fry, and waved it at him. "You know perfectly well what I'm talking about. Grabbing that kid's gun! You could've been killed."

Flenn leaned back in his chair. "How on earth did you… "

"I may be old, but I still have my ways. Really, Flenn—not only money, but you gave the bloke his gun back!"

"No bullets, and I doubt that thing has worked in years. Still, how did you know?"

Davy shoved the chip in his mouth. "You, of all people, are asking me that?"

Flenn simply shook his head. "I don't play the game anymore, Davy. I don't even dabble."

"You should," Davy said. "You were always good at it. What about your old partner? He still around?"

"You mean Zack? Oh yeah, he's around all right. In fact, I wouldn't be surprised if we turned around and saw him at the next table."

"He's still serving the ol' red, white and blue, huh?"

Flenn wiped his mouth with his napkin. "Zack Matteson will serve his country until the day he dies."

Davy reached for the malt vinegar. "He'd best be

careful," he scowled, "or they'll put him out to pasture the way they did me."

"Sounds as if you still have a foot in the door," Flenn said. Davy simply smiled. "That's enough about the old ways; I'm trying to enjoy my dinner."

Davy pointed to Flenn's plate. "How you can enjoy *that* is beyond me," he said. "Zack? Wasn't he the one that introduced you to Hoshi?"

"Actually, he and his ex-wife, Donna, did."

"*Ex*-wife?"

Flenn nodded. "You ought to know what our work does to families. What are you on now, number four?"

"Five, but I think she's gonna be out the door soon."

The waitress came back to check on them. "Will you be fancying any dessert? Maybe some sticky toffee?" she asked. Davy raised both eyebrows.

"None for me, thank you," said Flenn. "I suspect my friend might, though."

She gazed across the table at Davy and smiled. "Perhaps some yogurt and fruit for you, love?" She winked at Flenn, "The older ones can't seem to handle the *really* sweet stuff, you know."

"Nothing for either of us, Freda," Flenn said, laughing as she turned and disappeared back into the kitchen.

"Can't handle sweets, my arse!" Davy groused. "I know what she meant!"

"Just eat your meal, Davy. Sure you won't come with me tomorrow to Durham?"

Davy finished the last of his cod. "No, thanks. Too many wankers up that way. God, and this Saturday is the

Coal Miner's Gala too! There won't be a sober one in the lot!"

"Not that you'd ever exaggerate," Flenn added.

"You'll see what I mean on Saturday. Trust me, we English can't say a thing about the Irish. The whole bloomin' town will be pissed."

"Suit yourself. But let's be sure to keep in touch. I may need your services again. I'm thinking about offering another pilgrimage next year. You make a great guide… good thing they don't know the real you, huh?"

"Cloak and dagger, Flenny boy. You were pretty good at it, too, once upon a time."

"Yeah, saved your puny hide, didn't I?"

"As I recall, that escapade was planned from start to finish as a joint-intelligence project. By the way, I still say you didn't have to hit me that hard back then. It took weeks for that black eye to go away."

Flenn took a sip of Scotch. "Had to make it look real, right?"

"Too bloody real! I just think you were in a hurry to get back to Hoshi."

"I hadn't met her yet," he said before turning his gaze toward the door.

"*Umph.* There you go again!"

Flenn picked up his fork and played with the remainder of his mashed potatoes. "What?"

"Every time I mention Hoshi, you look away."

Flenn put his fork and napkin on top of his plate and pushed it a few inches away. "I guess I just don't like talking about it."

"That's clear as rain," Davy said. "It's been a long time, Flenny-boy." The waitress reappeared before he could say anything else. Flenn handed her two 50-pound notes and told her to keep the change."

"I'd rather keep *you*, dearie," she said, pocketing the money.

It was Davy who spoke next. "No chance of that, love. This one gave his heart away a long time ago."

Only, Flenn thought, *to have it ripped to shreds.*

CHAPTER *FIVE*

11 years earlier…

"So, you want to have dinner tonight?" Zack asked, opening a bag of jellybeans he'd bought downstairs in the commissary. "Donna's in town."

Flenn looked surprised. "Your girlfriend's in Paris?"

Zack grinned. "What can I say, the woman can't stand to be away from me!"

"Only because she doesn't know you as well as I do." Flenn pushed the dossier away. He was getting a headache and needed caffeine.

"Come on. It'll be fun. Pam and Win are coming."

Flenn raised an eyebrow. "I thought they were on their honeymoon."

Zack nodded. "They are, but you know how sorority sisters are. Pam found out Donna and Hoshi were going to be here in Paris and they've all made reservations at some little out-of-the-way place tonight."

Flenn leaned back in his chair. He and Zack were in Paris because Yasir Kamul had been brought here as part of a joint NATO venture to gather information on an insidious group emerging from Al-Qaeda. "Who's Hoshi?"

"She's a sweet little Japanese girl. She, Pam, and

Donna were sorority sisters in school back in Georgetown. You'll like her."

Flenn didn't need to be a spy to recognize a setup when he saw one. "No thanks. You guys have fun."

"Come on, Flenn, you need a night out." Zack pointed to the papers scattered all over the desk. "Or is this going to be how you spend all your nights in the most beautiful city on earth?"

Flenn gazed down at the paperwork. *A break would be good*, he thought, *even if Donna was prompting Zack to play matchmaker.*

"Do I have your word that you won't leave me alone with this woman?"

"Of course," Zack said. Flenn knew his partner was lying, but the thought of a night out was almost enticing enough to take the chance. "Besides," Zack said, "what's the point of being a spy if you can't enjoy yourself every now and then?"

'Enjoying' himself was not why Flenn had signed up with the CIA over a decade ago. Still, both men could use a night off. He looked at his notes. *This case certainly wasn't going anywhere.*

"Tell you what, if you run down to Costa and get us both a coffee, I'll come with you tonight."

"That's a deal!" Zack said.

Flenn shrugged. "Oh, and one more thing," he said, rubbing his temples and studying a map of Syria. "Make mine a large."

CHAPTER *SIX*

Present day…

The train to Durham passed gently rolling hills of yellow gorse and purple wildflowers. Sheep grazed in nearly every open field, but cows were scarce here, not like back home in Alabama.

Flenn leaned into the seat, looked up at the train's cream-colored ceiling, and thought back. *What a year it had been.* Helping Zack stop an Iranian conspiracy to control the upcoming presidential election, assisting a Birmingham detective solve the murder of a teenaged debutante, helping topple a man in one of the highest offices in the CIA, tracking an old nemesis after he'd murdered a dozen innocent children… *It had been one hell of a year!*

Of course, Zack Matteson had been at the heart of it all. Zack and Flenn had trained together at Langley, and had spent nearly a decade partnered on assignments. Zack still solicited Flenn's help from time to time, usually when he'd found himself in over his head, but Flenn had seen Zack more in the past eight months than he had in the previous five years. This sabbatical was, in part, to get away from all that.

Flenn noticed the acrylic luggage rack overhead. He'd

left his suitcase in a compartment near the door. Habit forced him to turn around and check; it was right where he'd left it. The seat was comfortable—much more spacious in first class than in the cars behind. The pilgrimage group had traveled by bus nearly everywhere, a bit uncomfortable for a tall man who didn't weigh enough to keep him anchored when the bus had hit a pothole. Here on the train though, there was room for him to stretch his legs.

"May I get you something sir?" the blonde steward was wearing a short, red skirt with a gray jacket over a rather risqué white camisole. She leaned over, revealing more than Flenn had expected. "We have coffee or tea, but I can get you something stronger if you'd like."

Smiling at the woman, he said, "Coffee, please. Black."

The woman disappeared but was back seconds later with cup in hand. She made sure to brush Flenn's hand with her own as she gave him his coffee. "Anything else, sir? Anything at all?" Flenn was used to it. He'd inherited his father's good looks. Tall, with emerald green eyes and sandy-brown hair, Flenn attracted a lot of unwanted attention.

He reached for his phone, careful to look only at it and not at her. "No, thank you."

She sighed and turned to wait on the couple sitting in front of him. Flenn checked to see if Pamela had called him back. He'd left a message that he would be arriving on the 10:30 train from York. It would be good to see Pam and Windsor again. *What had it been*, he thought, *three years?* The last time they'd been together was in Dublin when Flenn had been invited to a global meeting on the future of the Anglican Church being hosted at Saint Patrick's Cathedral. The three of them had visited half the pubs in Dublin that week; he could still remember the hangover.

Windsor will make a great bishop, he thought, not for the first time. Windsor Tammerlane was being consecrated as the Bishop of Durham on Sunday, and Flenn had scheduled his sabbatical to be there. *Win tells it like it is.* Flenn thought to himself, and then chuckled out loud. *He'd never survive in Alabama! People hardly ever seemed to express their true feelings in the South.* His secretary, Iriana Racks, had schooled him in the finer points of Southern double entendre. For instance, he'd learned that a Southern woman was permitted say anything she pleased about another woman just so long as she ended each sentence with: 'bless her heart.'

At least the women at Saint Ann's weren't hitting on him anymore. That had stopped his first year when a rumor went around that he was gay. He hadn't denied or validated the accusation, only responded by saying that his private life was just that—private. His celibacy, and the reason behind it, was no one's business but his own

The train pulled into Durham station and Flenn grabbed his bag before stepping onto the small platform. He purchased another coffee from the lone kiosk and pushed through the turnstile.

"Over here, over here!" a woman called.

Pamela Tammerlane hadn't changed much since the

last time he'd seen her. She was still the striking brunette she'd always been, not much different from when she and Hoshi and Donna Peyton used to travel together to Monte Carlo, Egypt… and Paris.

Paris… that was where Zack and Donna had first set him up on that blind date with Hoshi.

"It's lovely to see you, Flenn!" Pam said, giving him a huge hug. "Windsor sends his regrets, but he's so terribly busy right now, with the ordination and all."

"I'm sure he must be," Flenn said, happy to see one of Hoshi's dearest friends. "I can't imagine what it must be like."

Pamela's eyes danced. "Why *you* are not a bishop by now, heaven only knows."

Flenn brushed aside the compliment. "I'm of the theory that those who *want* to be bishop *deserve* to be," he said. "I wouldn't want that headache for anything."

"Well, I'm glad that Windsor doesn't feel that way." Pam led him to her car, a brand new, black Mercedes parked nearby. "I mean, Bishop of Durham… quite impressive, you know."

Flenn nodded. "Absolutely. Durham has quite a reputation. One bishop denies the physical resurrection of Christ, and the next day lightning hits the tower…"

Pam reached inside and pushed a button on the driver's side to open the trunk. "That was decades ago, and it wasn't quite like that. Oh, do you mind tossing your bag in the boot? Not much room in this little thing, I'm afraid."

Flenn laughed. "Well, at least the cathedral didn't

burn to the ground; otherwise, Tom Wright would have never taken over, and what a great bishop he turned out to be! I make a habit of reading everything he writes." Flenn closed the trunk and walked around to climb into the passenger seat. Pamela sat down and instead of using a key, gave a voice instruction to the car and it started.

"I don't suppose you have plans for dinner tonight?" Pamela asked, heading up a steep hill, then turning left onto North Road.

"No, not yet; just unpacking and milling about the condo."

"Flat, dear, *flat*. Here they call apartments and condominiums *flats*. You're staying on Neville street in a row of flats which they like to rent out to the tourists. I must say you're lucky to have found a room at all, what with the festival this weekend."

They made a right onto Neville Street and began a steep ascent. "Yeah, tell me about that. I'm afraid I don't know much about it."

At the top of the hill, Pamela pulled over and parked the car. "It's ghastly, positively ghastly!" She turned to look at him. "But, you mustn't tell anyone I said that. It wouldn't be fitting for the new bishop's wife to disparage the town's annual festival."

Flenn grinned. "'Boot'… 'ghastly'… 'disparage'? Pam, you certainly don't sound like the Jersey girl you used to be!"

"Shh," she said playfully, opening the door and glancing back at him. "You mustn't tell anyone I'm a big fake."

The row of flats ran the entire block, climbing to the top of a hill across from the Bram and Bull, a pub Flenn later discovered was more than 300 years old. Flenn nodded toward the pub. "Looks like a grand place for a drink and a bite to eat."

Pamela shook her head, handing him the keys she'd procured from the landlord earlier that morning. "Ugh. You and Windsor," she said. "Pubs are for the riffraff." She smiled. "Now tonight, we'll treat you to an absolutely grand place for dinner!"

Flenn was surprised at the changes in Pam. He could remember the stories of some of the dives Hoshi, Donna and Pam had frequented back in their college days.

"And here we are," she announced as he opened the front door. "Although we could have found you something much nicer."

"No, this is perfect. Found it online. I specifically wanted something simple with absolutely no internet connections. I'm looking forward to being cut off from the rest of the world for a few weeks. I'm just going to enjoy Durham."

The flat was compact, but functional. The main floor had just the one room—a combination living room with two large chairs, a fireplace and bookshelves loaded with games, puzzles, and books. A tall vase of ostrich feathers sat next to the fireplace. An old copy of *Country Life* lay open across the kitchen table, which was pushed against the wall. On the far end was a kitchen counter, complete with cabinets, oven, and sink, but no refrigerator.

"Um, Pam…?"

"Something's missing, isn't it," she said.

"Not to worry. These quaint places usually have a tiny fridge tucked away behind a cabinet door." She opened one of the cabinets to reveal a white steel door with a small glass window. "No, that's your washer/dryer combination. Careful, these things will absolutely scorch your clothes." She opened another cabinet. "Here you go."

Flenn nodded. "Perfect."

"There's a Sainsbury's market down the street and around the corner. "Our maid says it has just about everything you'll need during your stay." She looked at her watch. "I'm so sorry, darling, but I must be off. I'm seeing people about the church flowers for the ordination in half an hour. I'll just make it if I leave now. See you tonight? We'll send a car around eight."

Flenn smiled. "Looking forward to it, Pam."

"Oh, just one more thing," she said at the doorway. "These days it's *Pamela*." She brightened. "Seems more fitting for a bishop's wife, doesn't it? I hear several members of parliament have wives named Pamela." With that, she disappeared behind the heavy, wooden door.

Flenn glanced around the small room. "Well, there must be more to it than this," he said out loud. He stuck his head through the back door, which was to the right of the kitchen counter, and found a charming walled garden with roses and ivy. A mural of Durham Cathedral was painted on the far wall.

Turning around, he almost fell down the stairs leading to the basement. He flipped a light switch and descended to a quaint room reminiscent of a sea captain's quarters from the 1800s. The chief difference being the tiny 20-inch television attached to the far corner.

He made his way back to the main floor opposite the front door where carpeted steps led upstairs to two small bedrooms, along with a bath. *Better not fall asleep in the basement watching TV,* he told himself. *That's quite a climb to the loo!*

Ignoring Pamela's advice, he found his way across the street to the Bram and Bull for a burger and beer. Four old men were standing at the far end of the long bar, talking and laughing. He sat nearby to eavesdrop on the conversation. This was what he loved most about England, the neighborhood pubs and the people in them. Here was where he could get a real flavor not only of good English food, but of the town and the life of the locals.

Accents in the North were often difficult to understand, but then languages and dialects had once been his thing. Not so much as they had been for Hoshi, though. The way she'd been able to pick up languages was uncanny. In addition to English and Japanese, she was fluent in French, Swahili, and German. It had just come naturally to her. She'd regaled him with stories of how she acted as an interpreter everywhere Donna and Pamela had dragged her. The three of them had traveled all over the world by the time he and Zack had met up with them in Paris.

"Our grand's clobber is positively antwacky," Flenn overheard one of the old men say.

"Well, at least she's not dressed like the back

o'Rackhams!" said another. Flenn was confused but loving it.

"You mean like your new girlfriend?" said a third, laughing heartily.

"I oughta' box yer' ears!" the second man said, though his only movement was to hoist a glass to his lips.

Flenn ordered a steak and ale pie and left a generous tip, along with quiet instructions to buy the old men another round. He had an afternoon to kill, and thought he'd take a stroll around the old city.

Walking down Neville Street, Flenn passed rows of similar flats, stepped around a pungent trash can, and walked past two chip shops. He made a mental note to stop and sample their fish and chips; although he'd be sure to try the one furthest from the garbage bin first.

After turning right at Tesco, Flenn ventured up North Road. He strolled past a bakery, another chip shop, two restaurants, and three markets (along with another Tesco, Sainsburys and an Iceland) all in a row. *Well, he'd certainly have plenty of choice for groceries the next couple of weeks*, he told himself as he made a slight right and headed up another hill toward several upscale souvenir shops, an optical company and more cafes and restaurants, including one that boasted being the most haunted pub in Durham.

The view from Framwellgate Bridge was stunning. Standing on the medieval stone arch, he watched as kayaks made their way gently down the River Wear. A crew of college students, all wearing Durham University tees, looked to be practicing for the next fall-term competitions. He'd already read about those, having been on the team at Princeton so long ago.

Brightly colored flowers were draped from tiered planters along the bridge, beneath streamers of red, gold, and green. Off in the distance, Flenn could hear a brass band—obviously practicing, since they kept repeating the same stanzas over again. Workers were everywhere, sweeping streets, cleaning shop windows and hanging signs from lampposts, all welcoming people to the Durham Miners' Gala.

Flenn crossed the bridge to gaze down at the river's tree-lined banks, where it was said that C.S. Lewis had first imagined the *Chronicles of Narnia.* He had planned on retracing Lewis' steps while he was here, probably after Sunday's ordination.

Above the trees stood the majestic towers of Durham Cathedral. Flenn had thought to visit later, since there would be scores of workers getting ready for both the miner's service on Saturday and the consecration the following day; but since he was this close, he figured he might as well take a quick look around. Besides, there was someone from his past he wanted to greet—someone he'd met long ago—in Edinburgh.

Walking up the hill past the university bookstore and an art gallery, he made his way onto the close, a manicured green lawn surrounded by a square of ancient buildings, including Durham Castle. The cathedral's great Norman towers cast a shadow over the ancient cemetery where Celtic crosses and crumbling stone images of crusader swords sat atop centuries-old tombstones. A few tourists milled about, taking photographs with their cellphones. A young boy was trying to balance himself along the curb with both arms outstretched.

The magnificent church was perched high upon a wooded gorge on a narrow peninsula formed by a loop in the River Wear. Flenn could see why Henry VIII's Royal Librarian once referred to Durham Cathedral as "half church of God, half castle against the Scots."

Well, Flenn smiled to himself, *this is one Scott they won't be keeping out!*

Durham Cathedral had been built around the shrine of Saint Cuthbert. Monks had brought his body here after the Vikings landed at Lindisfarne. Legend claimed that the monks had opened the casket to find the saint's body uncorrupted after a hundred years. They had carried Cuthbert's remains across Northumbria to the safety of Durham, deciding upon the saint's final resting spot after following two women searching for their cow. To his left, halfway up one of the great towers, Flenn saw a gigantic bas-relief of the women with the famous Dun Cow.

Flenn approached the grand north doors where he spotted a massive knocker resembling a lion. Upon closer examination it turned out to be a goblin devouring a sinner. A nearby sign stated that in ancient times, those fleeing from the mobs or the authorities could receive sanctuary from the church if they could manage to make it to the grotesque image before being captured. The church's protection was limited to 37 days, after which the party had to either surrender to authorities or leave England forever.

Flenn reached up and touched the copper door knocker and prayed that he might find sanctuary from the events of the last year as he walked inside the security checkpoint and past two large metal detectors. A thin, silver-haired woman donning a purple robe with Cuthbert's crest smiled at him. "Do you have any questions, sir?" she asked.

Flenn smiled in return. "Not just yet, although I'm certain I will. I just wanted to take a quick look around. I know you have a lot going on this weekend."

"I just hope it isn't like last year," the woman said. "You could smell the beer in here for days after the gala!"

"Oh my," said Flenn. "That could make things interesting on Sunday."

The woman nodded. "Have you come for the bishop's consecration, then?"

"I have," he said, "but I hear the miners are pretty interesting, too."

"Oh, I absolutely abhor the gala," she said with a frown. "Just an excuse for all those Labour Party people from London to come up here, get drunk, and spoil our city!"

"Is it really that bad?"

"My advice to you would be to stay indoors; better yet, leave town for the day."

Flenn smiled and thanked the woman for the advice then walked up to the marble baptismal font, encased by a towering wooden spire that stood at least 20 feet overhead. The wood was ancient, and had blackened with age and the residue of centuries of coal dust. Still, the detail was exquisite and would make any carpenter envious. Flenn thought of Zack Matteson, whose father had been a carpenter. His former partner had always admired quality woodwork. Flenn found himself almost wishing that Zack could see this place as he ambled toward the choir stalls, which pre-dated the English Civil War. Unlike Zack, Flenn was no artisan but he recognized fine craftsmanship when he saw it.

Four workmen, wearing gray overalls and carrying an enormously long ladder, made their way past him and down the aisle to his left. Ahead, Flenn saw the altar and chancel areas where a cleaning crew was working furiously.

From the pictures he'd viewed on the internet he knew the place he wanted to see most was just ahead. At the opposite end of the great church was the tomb of Bede, England's first historian. Flenn made a mental note be sure to visit it later. He had read Bede's *Ecclesiastical History of the English People* twice. It had been written in the eighth century with detailed histories, legends, and myths about the early Christians in England, Ireland, and Scotland. Flenn had practically memorized Bede's account of Saint Cuthbert.

"And here it is!" Flenn said aloud as he saw the blue banner with the familiar gold cross and rounded garnet in the middle. He climbed the steps into the small chapel which had a simple altar on one end, surround by four tall candles and a statue of a man on the left holding his own head. Flenn wondered if it was a statue of King Oswald, whose head was said to be buried with the saint.

Above Cuthbert's tomb was a gigantic embossed image of the risen Christ in a rainbow of colors and surrounded by traditional images of the four evangelists, Matthew, Mark, Luke, and John. It seemed magically suspended above the slab of green marble that covered the tomb. Etched deep into the marble on the floor, surrounded by votive candles, was the word "Cvthbertvs," the Latin name for Cuthbert.

Flenn looked down at the tomb, around which this great cathedral had been built. It remained one of the holiest sites of Anglican Christendom over a millennium later.

"Hello old friend." Flenn whispered as he gazed at the tomb and smiled. "We meet again."

Flenn nearly jumped out of his skin when he heard the voice.

"Why, *hello*, Flenn… "

CHAPTER *SEVEN*

11 years earlier...

"Now, don't you two start talking about us," Donna said as Flenn and Zack both excused themselves to the gents.

Zack winked at Donna. "We wouldn't dare."

Caillebotte's was not the "out-of-the-way" place Zack had promised. It was in the heart of the Rue De La Roquette, the city's trendiest street for all-night revelers. Pewter chandeliers, shaped into an open cube-within-cube design, hung overhead from beamed ceilings. Stylishly displayed modern art decorated the walls around them. Even the restroom was embellished with gold and silver trim with framed abstracts of blue and yellow.

"So?" Zack asked, popping a couple of jellybeans into his mouth. "What do you think?"

"My God, Zack, she's 12!"

"She's the same age as Donna, moron. She's 29."

Flenn shook his head. "And I thought *you* were robbing the cradle! There's no way that girl is 29."

Zack made his way to the urinal which stood underneath a giant fern. "Okay, I admit that she doesn't look it. She's Japanese; they're all tiny."

"No, they're not. I thought you said she was from Seattle."

"She is. Her family is from Japan originally."

Flenn sighed, waiting his turn. "She hasn't said a word all night... "

"You're complaining? Your last girlfriend would never shut up."

"Camille wasn't my girlfriend; we only went on a couple of dates, including that one with you and Donna back in D.C."

Zack washed his hands. "Where she talked incessantly all night long! I'm telling you, Flenn, the quiet ones are dynamos, if you know what I mean."

"God, Zack, don't you ever think of anything else?"

Zack just grinned and walked out the door.

Flenn looked at himself in the mirror. *Even if Hoshi was 29, he was still almost seven years older. What could they possibly have in common?*

He combed his hair, then washed his face. Zack and Donna had been dating about a year. Donna was gorgeous, but other than that, Flenn never did quite grasp what Zack saw in her. As for Pam, she and Windsor both appeared to be content. Windsor had been quiet throughout most of the dinner, although his wife certainly made up for it. Pam could almost outtalk Donna... *well maybe not.*

Flenn stared at his reflection. *Maybe Zack was right; maybe it was time he started thinking of finding a girlfriend.* His mother certainly thought so, although she had no idea of what his life was really like. His father knew about Flenn's work with the CIA, but he had spared her the worry. *In a few years, he'd be 40, and then what? No wife, no kids. Maybe Win and Zack had the right idea. There comes a time when a man needs more than just his work; a man needs companionship and company, someone to talk to...* He smiled sheepishly... *and other things.*

CHAPTER *EIGHT*

Present day…

"How on earth did you know I was behind you?" asked the slender man standing at the entrance to Cuthbert's shrine.

Flenn turned around. "What? Oh, you mean…" The color quickly came back to Flenn's face. "Win! It's so good to see you." Windsor held out his hand, but Flenn surprised him with a hug instead.

"Sorry to startle you, old man; for a moment I thought you were talking to Saint Cuthbert," laughed Windsor. "I have to admit, I wasn't expecting to see you until dinner tonight."

"Yes, well, I went out for a walk and I just sort of ended up here."

Windsor nodded. "Say no more. People often comment that all roads lead to Durham Cathedral." He glanced past Flenn. "I see you've found one of our resident celebrities."

Flenn turned to look at the tomb. "I think *he* sort of found *me*. You might say he's been a personal patron of mine for several years now, ever since I left dad's company."

"Yes. I'm so sorry Pamela and I couldn't make it to your father's funeral."

"Don't be. It was only a year after you and I graduated from Sewanee." Flenn smiled. "I must say, you've done well, Win! You were the first English student to come to the University of the South to major in theology in years, and now you're about to become the first in our class to make bishop."

Windsor smiled. "I always thought that honor would go to you."

Flenn made a face. "Honor? No, those who seek to become bishop… "

Windsor finished the quote, "…*deserve* to be bishop. Yes, yes, I remember Professor Mossi's disdain for all bishops. I think it was because he wasn't one." Windsor looked at his watch. "I'm terribly sorry, Flenn, but I'm due for a fitting of my new rochet and chimere in just a few minutes. I just wanted to say hello. See you tonight, then?"

"Looking forward to it, Win! Great running into you."

Windsor turned, then said in a hushed voice. "No one calls me Win except Pamela when she's upset with me. And, she's definitely *Pamela* now, not Pam anymore I'm afraid."

"Gotcha. I'll be sure to remember." Flenn followed him down the steps from the shrine. "I'll see you tonight."

Flenn walked toward the door and turned left for the café where he ordered a cup of black coffee. On the other side was a large gift shop, where he found a book that interested him. He also found some stationary to take home for his secretary, Iriana Racks. On the walk back to his flat, Flenn noted even more colorful banners and street decorations than before as well as a large sign proclaiming: 'Celebrating the History of Socialism,' and another: 'Welcome Elton Wainwright, Labour's next Prime Minister!'

Flenn stopped on the bridge again to admire the view. "Not that tosser," said one old man to another as they stood staring up at the sign. "What has *Wankright* ever done for Labour? I'll tell you what, nothing, that's what!"

"Now Cyril, he's a damn site better than what we've got now. Wasn't it you who was saying we needed a change?"

"Not him," Flenn heard Cyril say as the two men walked away. "He's all mouth and no trousers, that one!"

"A new world, Cyril, it's a new world," the other man said.

Flenn looked up at the sign. British elections were still two years away. America would have their new President long before then, and so would Russia from the look of things. The former old-guard Soviet had held a tight reign over so-called Democratic Russia for a generation, but the news of his liver cancer had leaked to the Western press just last month.

A new world? Flenn had heard that before. *Doubtful it will be much different from the old.*

CHAPTER *NINE*

Present day…

"So, what you're telling us is that you donate your time to this tiny parish and they don't pay you anything?" Pamela took a sip of Champagne but was eyeing the caviar suspiciously.

Flenn finished off his Scotch and set the glass on the table. "Really, Pam… Pamela… what would I do with more money?"

"Still, it seems that they should be paying you *something*. You boys work awfully hard for your keep. I know Windsor does; I hardly ever see him."

"I'm sure Flenn's arrangements are probably suitable for him," Windsor said, reaching for the caviar that his wife had so far refused to touch.

She cut her eyes toward her husband. "I'm simply saying that the parish has an obligation to pay him. Most people think you boys just work on Sunday mornings."

"Don't we?" replied Flenn, trying to lighten the conversation.

"*Hrumph!* Windsor's gone so much of the time, I hardly ever see him."

Windsor shifted in his upholstered chair.

"Unfortunately, I think that's not likely to improve once I'm bishop."

She handed him her glass for a refill. The light from the Waterford chandelier above made the Champagne flute appear a fiery blue. Flenn glanced around the room at the rich tapestries depicting fox hunts and Tudor monarchs. He thought the décor of the restaurant out of place with the blue-collar pubs and tourist shops surrounding it.

"I'm just saying that they should pay you regardless of how much money you have. Otherwise," Pamela went on, "they will develop a sense of entitlement, and take advantage."

"Darling, can you really see anyone taking advantage of our Scott Flenn?" Win looked across the table. "Sorry Flenn 'ol boy, Pamela has developed a rather dim view of the Church over the years."

Flenn nodded. "I can understand why. Clergy spouses are greatly underappreciated. They often feel they come in second when the needs of the parish come calling."

"To say the least," said Pam.

The waiter returned for their order; Flenn was grateful for the distraction. Pamela ordered first, enquiring at length about how her duck would be prepared. Windsor ordered chicken marsala, and Flenn simply asked for a salad. As the waiter left with their order, Windsor spoke before his wife could. "What are the odds, Flenn, of you and I having known each other so long ago, both receiving a call to ministry, and both ending up at the same seminary at the same time?"

"You'd have gone to Oxford, if I hadn't persuaded you," said Flenn.

"Sewanee was a good fit for me, I have to say, and for Pamela, as well. Frankly, I'm surprised that the University of the South isn't better known in your country."

Pamela nodded, more interested in her Champagne, but still turning up her nose at the caviar. "I must say, I did enjoy our years there." A bit of a commotion was coming from downstairs.

"Probably a celebrity of some sort," Windsor offered. "They tend to show up the day before the gala." The noise increased to the point that other diners began peering over the railing at what all the fuss was about.

"It's *him!*" exclaimed an elegantly dressed woman sitting at the table behind them. "He's actually here tonight!"

"Well, dear," noted a man whom Flenn assumed was the woman's husband. "He *is* scheduled to speak tomorrow."

"Aw, bloody hell!" said another man behind them. "I knew I should've left town yesterday. I hate all this rabble."

"Who is it, Windsor? Check and see." Obediently, Pam's husband stood to see if he could catch a glimpse of the mystery man.

"Can't tell," he said, turning his attention back to his gin and tonic.

"It's Elton Wainwright!" squealed the woman at the other table.

"Good Gawd!" said an unhappy fellow behind them.

Pamela blushed. "I do hope you don't mind, but I did

tell Elton we'd be dining here tonight. He's coming to the ordination, you know."

Winsor glared at her. "He is?"

"Yes, I told you I'd invited him. I thought it would be good for you to have him there. You know the odds are that he'll be prime minister; it wouldn't hurt for you two to kiss and make up."

Flenn cocked his head. "Kiss and make up? I take it there's a story there?"

"Quite." Windsor said as he sat back down.

"Win and Elton had a famous row in the *Times* over the resurgence of Irish patriotism and independence for Northern Ireland," she said. "Elton is all for it;" she added, nodding toward her husband, "Windsor's hellbent against it."

"I am not." Windsor said. "And 'hellbent' is exactly the word Wainwright used in one of his open letters to me. I'm not against the North joining the rest of Ireland… eventually. But the return to violence these past months is not how to go about it. Sinn Féin needs to tone down the rhetoric, that's all. Though why would they with MP's like Wainwright encouraging them?"

"Oh my," gushed the lady at the other table. "He's coming up here!" Sure enough, a tall, handsome man with chiseled cheekbones and thick, silver hair was making his way up the black-and-white marbled staircase toward them, a small crowd of well-wishers behind him.

"Now, be *nice* Windsor," Pam said. "He's obviously here to make peace."

"Make trouble is more like it," Windsor mumbled. "I can't believe you invited him. Politics have no place in… "

"Hello, Father Tammerlane, good to see you again," the tall man greeted Windsor, then nodding to Pamela: "Mrs. Tammerlane, how nice of you to invite me to the affair on Sunday." Pamela blushed again. Whether it was from seeing a member of parliament or the Champagne, Flenn couldn't tell.

"And you, sir, I don't believe we've had the pleasure." The politician extended his hand.

"Scott Flenn. I'm here for the ordination as well."

"*Ahh*, an American. Brilliant! I do hope you will come to the festivities tomorrow, they should be grand!"

"Thank you," Flenn said, "I understand things can get a bit out of hand at times."

The man waved his hand in the air as if shooing a fly. "Just a bit of good, clean fun, that's all!"

"Not so very clean by nightfall," Windsor chimed in.

Wainwright took a breath. "Well, Windsor… I do trust that there is no ill-will between us, in spite of all those articles in the newspaper." He glanced down at Flenn. "Politics, you know. You Americans certainly understand."

"I could not care less about politics," Windsor said in a pressured tone. "And, sir, when has supporting terrorism ever been a proper political stance to take?"

It was Flenn who eased tensions. "You are correct, my lord, Americans certainly have been taking all kinds of political stands here lately. Why, sometimes I don't even recognize my own country anymore. But I'm still hopeful that civility will win out in the end and cooler heads will prevail. It is certainly nice to meet you; will you be joining us for dinner?"

Pamela looked hopeful, but Elton Wainwright declined the invitation. "No, thank you, I still have much to do before tomorrow. Nice to meet you as well. He smiled at Pamela. "Mrs. Tammerlane, always a pleasure." He then nodded to Windsor. "Father."

"My lord," called the woman at the next table, "we are looking forward to hearing you speak tomorrow morning. My husband and I are both huge supporters! We simply cannot wait until you're the next prime minister!" The man behind Flenn stood up and excused himself to the Gents. The politician shook several hands before making his way downstairs to the bar, where several people offered to buy him a drink or asked him to pose with them for a selfie.

The food soon arrived and Pamela ate heartily. Windsor merely picked at his chicken. "You just never know who you'll meet," Pamela said. "That's what I love about Windsor becoming a bishop."

"I thought you said you'd invited him," her husband groused.

"Well... I did, but still and all. I mean, remember that time the six of us were all gathered at the little French bistro when who should pop up but Elton John, right at the next table!"

"Another Elton," Windsor grunted.

"I mean, you and Hoshi took it in stride but I thought Donna was simply going to faint!"

"Actually, I thought I was going to faint," Windsor said with a bit of a chuckle, "especially when Zack asked him why he'd hired that famous keyboardist, Rick Wakeman, to play on 'Madman Across the Water,' and whether the piece had been too difficult for Elton to play."

"Well, you know Zack," Flenn said.

"That wasn't all he asked," Pamela said, taking a sip of Champagne. "Do you remember?"

"Who could forget?" Flenn interjected.

Windsor shook his head. "Imagine, asking a celebrity about his sex life!"

Pamela giggled. *Definitely the Champagne*, Flenn told himself.

Flenn shook his head. "That's Zack, all right—*Mister Tactful*."

Windsor laughed. "No, I don't suppose anyone ever used *that* particular term about Zack Matteson." He picked up his fork with a renewed interest in his meal. "How are he and Donna? We haven't heard from them in ages."

"Don't you remember, dear?" said Pamela. "They divorced a few years back."

"Ah, yes, that's right, so they did," Windsor replied. "Sorry to hear that. Don't they have children?"

"Two girls," said Flenn, looking down at his salad. He didn't notice that his dinner companions had stopped eating and were staring open-mouthed behind him. "I see Zack every now and then. Trust me, he hasn't changed much."

"The hell I haven't!"

Flenn dropped his fork and turned to find Zack Matteson standing behind him.

So much for a peaceful rest in Durham!

CHAPTER *TEN*

11 years earlier…

"No! I'm not going, and that's final." Flenn and Zack had spent the last three weeks at the CIA's Paris office. Zack had been pestering Flenn all day to accompany him and Donna to see the Eiffel Tower tonight. "We've got work to do," Flenn said. "Besides, I've seen it!"

"Only driving past. Come on, it'll be fun!"

"That's what you said about the other night." Flenn protested.

"And it *was* fun."

Flenn poured himself another cup of coffee. "For you, maybe. Besides, what about our assignment? We're still no closer than we were to finding out who this mystery group is."

Zack followed Flenn back to the office they shared. "Your friend Spate still trying to help us track these people down?"

Flenn nodded. "He'll let me know if he finds them. He's set up a meeting with Colonel Zamir from the Afghanistan intelligence corp."

"Zamir? I never liked that guy," Zack said.

Flenn opened a folder on the one desk they both shared. "This group, whoever they are, seems to have infiltrated Al-Qaeda at every level. I mean, look at this." Flenn slid a photograph across the desk.

Zack studied the picture. "Who are these people with Kamul?" Zack asked.

Flenn pulled out a dossier marked *Top Secret*. "Intel says they're the leaders of a secretive cabal. They've grown tired of what they perceive as Al-Qaeda's plodding and are embracing certain methods to hasten victory."

"What methods?" Zack said.

Flenn passed several more photos across the table. Zack looked through as many as he could before finally having to turn away. "My God, these are women and children!"

"Apparently, this new faction has abandoned their leader's restrictions and they're trying to break their enemies through outright barbarism."

Zack looked back at one of the photos. "Not just their leader's restrictions… "

Flenn nodded. "Yeah, they've pretty much abandoned their *humanity* as well."

"Still no name for these barbarians? They've got to be calling themselves something."

"If so, I haven't heard it."

Zack rubbed his eyes. "Al-Aruri never said anything while you were with him?"

"He just thought it was all part of Al-Qaeda, which is what I suppose Colonel Hussain Zamir over at Iraqi Intelligence thinks as well. Various groups go by different names over there, and they're always changing. Davy and I were trying to figure out if it was anything the allies needed to worry about, or if they'd just keep killing each other off."

"And?"

Flenn rubbed his temples. "And… it's something we need to worry about. That's why we wanted to capture Kamul. This new group may be what unifies the rest, if not through ideology then through outright fear."

Zack pulled a bag of jellybeans out of a drawer. He offered it to Flenn, who refused. Zack pointed to one of the pictures. "That was what happened to a warlord's family who tried to resist Kamul." Flenn picked up another photograph only to put it back down again.

"You want to know what I think?"

"What's that?"

Zack grinned. "I think you should come with us to see the Eiffel Tower."

"God, Zack. Don't you ever give up?"

"No."

Flenn shook his head and looked away. "Is *she* going to be there?"

Zack shrugged. "Who?"

Flenn glared at him. "You know very well who! That child from the other night."

"I keep telling you that she's almost 30," Zack said.

"In what, dog years?"

"Why don't you talk to her. She's really quite bright."

Flenn stared at him. "You were there… the kid hardly said a word all night." Flenn got up to refill his Styrofoam cup. "No, absolutely not."

"She's not a kid. Come on," Zack called out into the hallway, "it will be fun!"

"I'm not going, and that's final!" came the reply.

CHAPTER *ELEVEN*

Present day...

The moon was just breaking through the clouds, but the light from the streetlamps, pubs, and flats bathed the city with pale-yellow illumination—enough so that Zack Matteson could still see the questioning look on his former partner's face as they stood outside the Judge's Quarters restaurant.

"Zack, it was certainly a wonderful surprise to see you," said Windsor Tammerlane, shaking hands at the door. "So glad you could accompany us for dinner. I do hope you will reconsider and will come to the ordination on Sunday."

Zack shook Windsor's hand. "I'd love to, Winnie, but as I said, I'm just passing through. I have to be in Lincoln on Sunday. It was great seeing you and Pam. Congrats on the whole bishop thing."

Pamela gave him a hug. "Lovely to see you, dear. I do hope our paths will cross again soon."

"You never know," said Zack.

"Don't ever change, old man," Windsor said, as a valet opened the car door. "It's so refreshing to see people who don't try to be something they're not."

Zack glanced at Pamela. "Is that a compliment?"

She gave a nod, then stared at her husband. "To you it is."

Zack turned to Flenn. "It was nice to see you Flenn. I hope we will run into each other again soon."

Flenn knew from experience that it would be a lot sooner than he'd like. "Well, it's a small world," Flenn said, forcing a smile. The last time he'd been with Zack had been just before Easter. A dozen Honduran children had been murdered by a raging lunatic, causing Flenn to come dangerously close to turning his back on his priestly vows. It was a time he wished now to forget—but then most times with Zack Matteson were like that.

They waved farewell to Zack and drove off to drop Flenn at his flat. He turned to see Zack disappear into a pub next to the Judge's Quarters. Flenn looked at his watch. He gave Zack an hour before he'd be knocking at Flenn's door.

It was ten minutes. Flenn just stared at the door.

"Come on, Flenn, it's me," came the voice from outside.

"That's why I'm not answering," Flenn said, getting up from his chair anyway.

"You know I'm not going away."

Oh God, did he know that! It wasn't that Flenn disliked Zack. Quite the opposite; but their shared history in the CIA was something that Flenn had put behind him. He sighed. *At least in theory.*

"You know," called Zack from the other side of the door, "I could start singing the Irish national anthem at the top of my lungs. I'm sure that would go over well in this neighborhood."

Flenn leaned against the front door. "You don't know the words."

"*Amhrn na bhFiann,*" Zack began to sing, "*Seo dhibh a chirde duan glaigh, Cathrimeach briomhar ceolmhar…*"

Flenn crossed himself. "Your Gaelic's awful," he said as he opened the door. "But not nearly as awful as *that*!" Zack was standing on the stoop wearing a yellow miner's hat festooned with a dyed-green ostrich feather.

"So, what do you think?"

"What do I think?" Flenn stepped aside so that Zack could enter the tiny room. "Trust me, you don't want to know what I think."

Zack looked around the room. "I can go get one for you; they're selling them down by the corner."

Flenn poured himself a Scotch and left the bottle out for Zack. He sat down in the only upholstered chair in the room. "Help yourself, although I'm not sure you need another drink."

"It's a celebration, or haven't you heard? The Miner's Gala is tomorrow!" Zack opened a cabinet to search for a glass, but found the washer/dryer combo instead.

"Top left."

Zack reached up and located what he was looking for. "Well," he said, taking a look around the tiny room, "this is cozy, I'll give it that."

"I like simple things. You know, like how it is when

you're not around." Flenn finished his drink in a single swallow.

"I really wish you'd start liking bourbon," Zack said, pouring himself a glass of the single-malt. "Scotch doesn't go with jellybeans."

"So, why are you here?" Flenn said with a sigh. "And please tell me it doesn't have anything to do with me this time."

Zack grinned. "Nah, you were just a bonus. Like I told Winnie and Pam, I'm here on business."

"It's Windsor and Pamela now," Flenn said. Zack raised an eyebrow. "Her idea. She's not the same party girl she was back in the day."

"Hoshi, Pammy, and Donna," they were quite the trio, weren't they?" Zack lifted his glass. "To the good 'ol days."

"Zack, why the hell are you here?"

"To say hello and enjoy a glass of this fancy hooch, why else?"

"The Tammerlanes may have bought your story, but I know better. What's going on?"

"You know," Zack said, sniffing his drink, "most people never ask me for details once I tell them I'm now an executive salesman for a sewer rejuvenation company. I'm sure England could benefit from such a thing, if there is one. I bet Henry the VIII's crap is still floating around underneath us somewhere."

"Speaking of crap…"

Zack smiled. "Okay, I'm on assignment."

"What assignment?"

"Sorry, classified."

"Bullshit."

"You're an agent," Zack teased. "You know how it is."

"*Was* an agent. You wouldn't have come to me unless you needed something."

Zack set his glass down. "That's not fair; I came to you in Honduras, you know."

Flenn figured he'd carry the scars from Honduras the rest of his life—not from the shoulder wound he had received in the drone blast, but from the senseless murder of a dozen children who'd died in a drone attack meant to kill him. "Well, you certainly didn't come here to save the Queen," he looked at Zack, "or did you?"

"No. Elton Wainwright."

"The MP?"

"There can't be anyone else with that stupid name, can there?"

Flenn raised an eyebrow.

"Oh, I forget, this is England."

Flenn got up and retrieved the bottle, this time not bothering to return it to the counter. "What about Wainwright?" He refilled his glass and offered the bottle to Zack, who did the same.

"Word is, he's going to be the Labour Party's next big thing. Probably Prime Minister in a couple of years."

"So?"

Zack sipped his drink. "So… there are those back home who want more info about the—what is it they say here?— *the bloke*. I followed him into the restaurant tonight. I really didn't know you guys were there." Flenn looked dubious. "No, really. I mean I knew you were in Durham and all… you know me, I always know where you are." Zack smiled. "That's why you think of me as your own personal guardian angel."

"More like my own personal demon."

Zack winked. "Come on, you know you love me."

"I don't love your job. Okay, tell me about Elton."

"Why do you want to know about Wainwright?" Zack probed.

"Curiosity. There's some bad blood between Wainwright and Windsor. Something about the Irish."

"I'll look into it, thanks."

Flenn knew that Zack was thorough; he already knew about the feud. "And?"

"Okay." Zack set his glass on the dining table. "The guy seems to be the real deal," he said. "Loves his country, loves his party, loves serving in Parliament… and loves the women."

"A player?"

"Of sorts. It's cost him two wives so far. It may cost him a third pretty soon if he's not careful."

"Fooling around?" Flenn asked.

Zack nodded. "I guess it's a habit."

Flenn finished his drink and debated whether he should have another. In the end he poured a short one. "Are you really off to Lincoln on Sunday?"

Zack nodded. "That part was true. I'm going on ahead of Wainwright. He's due there on Tuesday, after a round with his mistress on Monday."

Flenn shook his head. "Well, I wish you well on your little fact-finding mission. If you run into any more salacious gossip, I've got a parishioner back home that would just love to hear from you."

"You don't mean that dill pickle woman?"

"Dilwicky. Delores Dilwicky." Flenn looked surprised. "I don't remember telling you about her."

"You did in Honduras. I think I found out about your whole congregation while we were in the jungle. You mumbled a lot. Morphine does that to a person."

"So," Flenn said, changing the subject, "I suppose you're staying somewhere nearby?"

"Well, Piano Man is staying at the Hilton. I can't stay there and risk his security team seeing too much of me."

"Piano Man?"

"My code name for Elton... get it, Elton Wainwright, Elton John?"

"I hope you're not going to ask this guy about his sexual proclivities too?"

Zack winked. "I was drunk that night. Besides, as I said, I already know about Piano Man's girlfriend."

"Oh Lord, I hope it's not a royal," Flenn said.

"Close."

"Don't tell me, I don't want to know."

"No, you don't. Anyway, as for a place to stay, it seems that everything is full up this weekend."

Flenn looked at him. "And you want me to say you can stay here."

"Well, what are old friends for?"

Flenn shrugged. "There's a small twin off the master, but it'll cost you."

"Standard CIA rate?"

Flenn stood and headed for the stairs. "Nope. Just a promise that whatever trouble you get into over here, you'll leave me out of it."

"Scout's honor."

Flenn sighed as he headed up the stairs. "Why is it I don't believe you?"

Zack grinned. "Maybe cause I was never a scout."

CHAPTER *TWELVE*

Present day...

"In conclusion," the handsome, silver-haired politician said. "Labour stood with you then, Labour stands with you now, and Labour will stand with you forever!"

The street erupted in applause and cheers as Elton Wainwright walked off the podium and disappeared to a waiting car parked behind the makeshift stage. Flenn stood in the crowd and watched as a bearded old man wearing a blue shirt and sport coat, sans tie, waved at the crowd and declared an end to the morning-long speeches. A band of pipers in Glen-plaid kilts began to play, and marchers carrying an array of union banners lined up and paraded down North Street.

It would take a while before Flenn would be able to make his way back to the flat. Since the pubs were all crowded, he ducked into Tesco for a cold sausage roll. The smell of alcohol was everywhere, and already he'd seen the Bobbies take several inebriated souls off the street. *What was it he'd once heard in a Baptist sermon?* "The soul can never be inebriated, only the vehicle that houses it. "*Well,* he thought, *there were certainly several 'stoned houses' out today.*

Flenn made his way around a middle-aged woman

who was staggering down the street. Pamela had warned him; still, he'd wanted to see what all the fuss was about.

The speeches had been the usual sort: welcoming all the dignitaries, thanking people for coming from across England, paying homage to the miners who'd lost their lives to black lung, cave-ins, and various other hazards. Wainwright's speech had been the longest. It had been well crafted... obvious the man had larger political aspirations. Wainwright's wife hadn't accompanied him, but Flenn didn't know if it was customary for a speaker's spouse to attend such functions. Based on what Zack had told him last night, the woman might not want to be in her husband's company these days.

Flenn sat down on a nearby bench to eat his lunch and watch people passing by. Young, old; men, women; even teenagers... they all seemed to be 'making rather merry' as Charles Dickens might have said. Police were everywhere, keeping an eye on things. It was likely to end up quite an interesting day in that everyone over the age of 16 seemed to have a bottle of something in hand.

Flenn had given up trying to jog today, the crowds made it impossible; instead, he figured he'd make his way back to his flat for a nap. He'd have to wait for the parade to end, when everyone would likely head to one of the myriad pubs to continue the fun. He thought he'd probably go over to the Bram and Bull for a late afternoon pint himself. Across the road from the Bram was another pub, but he'd decided that a place with the name 'Death Angel' was probably aimed at a different sort of crowd.

He got up and slowly made his way back toward Neville Street. Despite the jostling of the crowd, Flenn felt the pickpocket's hands going for his wallet and immediately turned around to catch the thief in the act.

"Gotcha!" Zack Matteson said, smiling from ear to ear.

"I thought you were on your way to Lincoln," Flenn said, irritated by the prank.

"What did you say?"

Flenn raised his voice over the crowd, "I thought you were heading to Lincoln to follow what's his name. You were gone this morning when I woke up."

"Just wanted to get a good seat for the show!" Zack shouted in return. "Quite a speech, huh?"

"Pretty standard socialist stuff," Flenn said. The bagpipers were fading off into the distance, making it easier to be heard. "I'm heading back for a nap."

"A nap? Boy, your life is exciting! Look around at all these beautiful young women just waiting to fall into a good-looking American's arms!"

Flenn scoffed. "I'm not in the market, remember?"

"I wasn't talking about you."

"Take my advice," Flenn said, "naps are far less complicated."

Zack put his arm around Flenn and gave him a sideways man-hug. "When have I ever taken your advice? I think I'll do a bit more looking around. Your place open again tonight?"

Flenn shook his head. "Not if you plan on bringing someone with you!"

Zack just smiled and headed off across the street toward a group of college-aged women gathered around a man juggling brightly colored tennis balls. "You'll never grow up, will you Zack?" he said out loud.

A big, muscular man with closely cropped hair, reeking of beer, pushed him. "What'd you call me?"

Flenn brushed himself off.

"I'm talking to you!" the man said. "W'at did ya call me? A hack?"

Flenn tried to explain, but the burly man wouldn't, or couldn't, listen. He threw a haphazard punch, which Flenn easily deflected. The drunk came around and tried again and nearly fell over as Flenn stepped aside. The third time, Flenn caught the man's hand, twisted it behind his back and whispered, "why don't you just sit down and clear your head."

"I'll clear you is w'at I'll do!" the man said, trying to break free. Flenn saw a policeman watching from across the street. *Great*, he thought, *just what I need! Get arrested and spend the night in the Durham jail!*

"Hey, chum!" Zack had witnessed the whole thing and had come to Flenn's defense. He bent over the big man. "Didn't you and I go to school together?"

The man tried to focus on the newcomer. "Did we?"

"Yes, yes," said Zack. "Don't you remember your old pal? It's great to see you; how about I buy you a beer?" Flenn released the drunk just as the policeman came within earshot.

"Yeah, I 'member ya', now! A beer, ya' say?"

Zack looked up at Flenn and smiled, then back at the

big man. "Maybe two. We've got a lot of catching up to do!"

The man smiled a nearly toothless grin. "We sur-tain-ly do!"

Flenn nodded his thanks and disappeared into the crowd. He looked back over his shoulder as Zack led the big man, arm-in-arm, into a pub dubbed 'What Ales You?' *It wouldn't take Zack long before he'd manage to lose the guy. Hopefully the college girls would have moved on by then.*

Flenn's nap was for naught; too much noise out on the street. He went downstairs to watch the television and got mildly interested in a documentary about the bird sanctuary on the Farne Islands, just off the coast of Lindisfarne. He planned to visit the islands next week. Flenn remembered his brief time there, and how the birds had reacted to the other man's presence. He had found himself on the innermost of the Farne Islands years ago after having been left for dead.

That was right after he'd lost Hoshi.

Flenn turned off the television, wishing to lighten his mood. Maybe the people out on the streets had it right, maybe today was a good day to go have a drink. He made his way over to the Bram and Bull. Several motorcycles were parked outside the Death Angel, and the noise from inside was deafening. He crossed the street and walked inside the pub, which was considerably busier than yesterday.

The same four men from yesterday were standing at the end of the bar. *As if they've never moved,* Flenn noted.

One of them, a balding man with thick eyebrows,

looked up and smiled as he raised his glass. Flenn ordered a pint and walked over. "We're obliged to ya' for our drink yesterday," the man said. "Budge up mates, let the bloke in!" The others moved to make room for the stranger. "So, whadd'ya think of the gala?" the man asked.

Flenn smiled. "It certainly is quite a celebration."

"Celebration, my arse," said a short, heavyset man wearing a worn-out, red-plaid shirt and twill trousers. "Just an excuse for all those buggers from the South to come up here and give an ear to them daft politicians."

The balding man agreed. "Ya' ask me, there all dim. All mouth and no trousers, I say."

"I dun 'no," said a man who looked to be in his early '60s and the youngest in the group, "I sorta' like that Wainwright chap. He's got his ear to the ground, I say."

The second man spoke, "More like his lips to their bum, hoping for the votes. Come on, Bob, don't be so bloomin' naïve."

The one named Bob shrugged. "Well George, I'm not gonna get argy-bargy about it, I just think he's worth a chance, that's all I'm saying."

"There all as bent as a nine-bob note," the balding man said.

Finally, the man at the far end, by far the oldest of the four, spoke up. "You will have to forgive us, Father, we can go on a bit."

George looked at Flenn. "Father? You a priest, are ya'?"

Flenn looked a bit embarrassed, hoping his being a minister wouldn't dampen the spirit of these charming old guys. "Well, as a matter of fact I am." He looked at the elder statesman of the group. "How did you know?"

"Charlie knows it all, Father," said the balding man. "Catholic or C of E?"

"Church of England... well, the American brand," Flenn said. "I'm an Episcopalian."

"I'm George," said the balding man taking hold of Flenn's hand.

"Good to meet you," said Bob, holding out his hand.

"They call me Murph," the man in the red plaid said. "And I ain't been to church in 30 years, 'ceptin for the 'casional funeral. So, don't get your hopes up!" The others laughed.

"My name's Charlie; I know the owner of your flat,," said the one at the end of the bar, smiling warmly. "I'm the relative newcomer amongst these hooligans."

Flenn reached over and shook his hand. "Your accent, it's a bit different from the people around here."

"*His* accent?" said George. "Cor, that sounds strange comin' from a yank!"

Charlie smiled. "Lived in London until I retired nine years ago."

"Charlie was a professor down at Middlesex," George offered. "He's the brightest of the lot of us!"

"Speak for yourself," Murph said.

"What brings you to Durham, Father, surely not our little gala? I'm guessing the ordination on Sunday?"

Flenn nodded. "Any of you gentlemen going to attend?"

George rolled his eyes.

"Charlie and me are," said Bob, "ain't we, Charlie?"

"If he can pry ya' out of here," Murph joked. "Doubtful, I'll be there, Father. The missus is a Methodist."

"The missus? Right! Don't go lyin' to the good Father here, Murph," George said. "You're still hung o'r on Sunday mornings!"

"Well," Flenn said, taking a quick sip of his beer. "You're in luck, the service isn't until two o'clock."

"He's got you there, Murph," laughed George.

From the end of the bar came a banging noise. They turned to see a burly man with a shaved head and a pointy black goatee wearing a studded, leather jacket. He had just slammed the bar with the bottom of his fist. "I said, give me a beer!"

Not the least bit intimidated, the pretty brunette barmaid wiped the bar with a cloth. "I think you'd be looking for the crowd next door, love," she said.

"All full up," the biker said. "Plus, what's it to you! Give me the damn beer!"

Charlie sighed. "Sorry, Father, I'm afraid it gets like this at the gala."

"Filchers like that, they make me wish I was a young'un again," George said.

Murph nodded sideways toward George. "He used to be a boxer back in the day. 'Gorgeous George' they called him."

George reached for his beer. "Nobody called me that. And if they did, I'd have pummeled 'em. Just like I'd like to do to that wanker right now."

The big man in the leather jacket looked toward the old men. "What are you geezers lookin' at?"

"Nuttin', absolutely nuttin," said Murph.

"Oh yeah, old man? How long's it been since you've been able to get it up, eh?" The big man laughed as beer spilled down his goatee.

"Get stuffed!" George said.

"You wanna' piece of me, geezer?" The biker made his way toward the group. None of them moved an inch, except for George who started rolling up his sleeves. Flenn stepped between them.

"We're all just having a good time," Flenn said to the big man. "How about I buy everyone a beer?"

The biker sized the tall man up, then said. "You his son?"

"No, actually we just met," Flenn said with a smile.

"Well, you'd best watch who you make friends with!"

The man turned to walk away, but George couldn't leave it alone. "Tis the likes of you give the gala a bad name!"

The man was fast, but Flenn was faster. Just as the biker turned back around and lunged for George's shirt collar, Flenn grabbed the biker's pinky finger and bent it backwards. The big man fell to his knees.

"I think it is time for you to leave," Flenn said not letting go of the man's finger until he was out the door. The men in the pub all rallied at the door shouting at the man, warning him not to come back in.

"Strength in numbers," Murph said. "Um, Father, did I hear you say you were buying us all a beer?"

"Ach," George scoffed. "I've handled bigger ones than 'im."

"Forty years ago," added Charlie. George mumbled something and reached for his glass.

"Thank you, Father," said Charlie. "George is right, it's the blokes like him that give the festival a bad name."

Bob nodded. "Pretty slick move there, Father."

Charlie grinned. "I expect the reverend hasn't always worn the dog collar. Military man, Father?"

Flenn nodded. "United States Air Force."

"Chaplain?" Charlie asked.

A voice from behind them said, "Not when I knew him, he wasn't."

Flenn sighed. Without turning, he looked up at the four old men and said, "George, Bob, Murph and Charlie... meet Zack Matteson."

****

Flenn waved at the four old men at the end of the bar, having just paid for their last two rounds. Zack was still regaling them with stories when Flenn stepped out of the Bram and Bull to head back to the flat. No doubt, he'd hear a knock at the door later tonight, unless of course Zack just decided to pick the lock.

He felt the kick in his side before he saw the assailant.

Flenn crumpled to the ground, but managed to roll with it and spring back to his feet. Without thinking, he kicked with his right foot and knocked the burly man back into the wooden door of the pub. Flenn shifted his weight, drew back his hand to deliver the knock-out punch, then caught himself and stepped back.

"I guess we're even," Flenn said to the big man he'd tossed out of the pub earlier. "You okay?" The man scowled as he threw himself at Flenn, but from that distance all Flenn had to do was step aside and the oaf went right past him.

"You've had too much to drink, pal, how about we stop this before someone gets hurt?" The noise brought several of the Bram's patrons out into the street. They restrained the big man, but from across the way it must've looked like an unfair fight, for now several bikers had come out to see what the commotion was all about. Who threw the first punch, no one knew, but soon a street brawl was going on that would have rivaled any saloon fight from the old comedic Westerns back home. Flenn kept trying to intervene, but as soon as he'd pull two men apart , they'd turn and start fighting with two more. He turned and saw Zack leaning against the door frame holding a glass of beer. "You wanna' get in here and help me?" Flenn hollered.

Zack raised his glass, "Nah, I'm good."

"Happens every year!" Flenn turned and saw Charlie standing off to the side. "The two pubs get into a good punch-up, then the police come and everybody goes off for another pint."

"It's tradition," Bob said, standing next to Charlie.

"You see," echoed Zack, obviously enjoying the spectacle, "it's tradition."

Flenn stepped back and watched. No weapons had

been drawn, no one was bleeding; in fact, he saw how the bigger guys from both pubs were pulling most of their punches.

"Well, I'll be… " Flenn said. *Charlie was right.*

Four policemen were making their way up Neville Street.

"Coppers!" someone shouted. With that, the fights all ended as quickly as they had begun as people disappeared into both pubs.

"Yep, every year," Charlie said with a smile.

Flenn shook his head. "Unbelievable," he said, deciding to go back into the pub behind Charlie, Bob and Zack. "Simply unbelievable."

The old man put his arm around Flenn. "Welcome to the Durham Miner's Gala!"

CHAPTER *THIRTEEN*

11 years earlier...

The Eiffel Tower stood majestically against the night sky, illuminated by hundreds of colored lights. Flenn just hoped no one asked him to go up in that thing, not with the March wind blowing as hard as it was. He'd planned to sit it out and let the other three take their chances.

"Come on," Donna said. "It will be fun!" *Where had Flenn heard that before?* But she wasn't addressing him. "Don't chicken out on me now girl!"

Hoshi looked to the top of the tower and backed away. "No, I'll wait here; you and Zack go."

"You heard her, sweetie, let's go," Zack said, pulling Donna's hand.

Donna resisted, "Come on, Hoshi, or I'll let all our sorority sisters know you chickened out!"

"You do and I'll tell them about that party in Rio," Hoshi fired back.

"What party?" Zack asked.

Donna turned quickly and pulled him toward the steps. "Never mind. See you two shortly." They could hear Zack still asking about Rio as Donna led him away.

Crap! Flenn groused to himself. *This certainly hadn't*

ended up like he'd planned. Now he was stuck playing nice guy to the 12-year-old.

She turned around. "I'm going to get a glass of wine."

You sure you don't mean an ice cream? Flenn thought.

"You want one?" Hoshi asked.

With nothing better to do until Zack came back down with his girlfriend, Flenn said, "Sure."

They wandered over to an outdoor kiosk selling beer and wine. She ordered Chardonnay, he asked for a Burgundy. He reached for his wallet, but Hoshi beat him to it. The man in the kiosk asked for her identification. She grunted as she showed it to him.

"I hate when that happens," she said to Flenn as they turned to find a couple of chairs facing the tower. "You'd think I'd get used to it; I mean, I get carded all the freaking time."

"Really?"

"Oh, don't play innocent. Donna told me that you think I look like a kid."

Flenn blushed. *Damn you, Zack!* "No, I only said… "

Hoshi interrupted, "That I look like a 12-year-old."

"I'm going to kill Zack!" Flenn said. "Yep, dead… tonight!"

Hoshi brushed her long black hair out of her face. "So, was that the reason you wouldn't talk to me the other night at dinner?"

"Wouldn't talk to *you*? No, it was *you* who wouldn't talk to *me*."

Hoshi smiled. "I guess I am a little shy when I first meet someone." She took a sip from her plastic cup. "It's just that I know what they're thinking... that I'm short and cute and that I look like I belong on a shelf with a bunch of Kimekomi dolls."

"I'm sure they don't. What's a Kime... kimmy... kimo... "

"Kimekomi."

"Yeah. What's that?"

She raised her glass again. "I thought Donna said you spent a lot of time in Asia?"

"Not so much in Japan, mostly Korea," he said. "That's where my dad's business has its Asia-Pacific headquarters."

She nodded. "Yeah, I hear it's huge."

"Flenn Industries? Yeah, I guess you could say that. So, just what is a Kim... "

She smiled. "Kimekomi."

For the first time, Flenn noticed just how pretty her smile was.

"It's a small doll that Japanese girls like to dress up and place in their homes. Legend says that they were originally made by a great artist wishing to capture the spirit of the woman he loved by making a doll out of her kimono."

Flenn lifted his plastic cup. "Here's to legends," he said.

"So, you don't mind drinking with a 12-year-old?"

Flenn blushed for a second time. "I'm sorry about that; I mean, most women want to look younger."

Hoshi finished off her wine in one gulp. "Yeah? Well, trust me, it has its drawbacks... so does being short."

"You're short?" Flenn grinned. "I hadn't noticed."

She shot him a look. "How could you from up there? What are you, like nine feet tall?"

He smiled. "Yeah, just about." He noticed her empty cup. "How about more wine? This time on me."

Hoshi shrugged. "Why not?"

Flenn went back for the wine and returned with a small bag of popcorn as well. "I'd have brought brie and caviar," he joked, "but this was all they had."

Hoshi's brown eyes lit up. "I love popcorn!" Her hand dove in the bag before he even sat down.

"Me too," he lied.

"Well, that's at least one thing we have in common." She reached back into the bag for more.

Flenn looked up at the tower. "Think they're having fun up there?"

Hoshi laughed. "Donna has fun wherever she goes."

Flenn nodded. "So does Zack. I think that's what attracted them to each other." They both reached into the bag together; their hands touched. This time it was Hoshi's turn to blush.

"Tell me something about yourself, other than you're a 12-year-old Japanese Kewpie doll who likes Chardonnay."

"Not much else to tell, really," she said. *The way the lights caught her eyes made them shine like black pearls.* "My family is from a little hamlet outside Tokyo. My great-grandparents came to America in the '20s. My mom and dad are both doctors; she has a medical degree and he has a Ph.D. in nuclear physics."

"Pretty impressive."

"So," she went on, smiling a bit sheepishly, "I naturally got *my* degree in British history."

"What?"

"I couldn't help it. Somewhere in a past life I think I was an English scullery maid."

"You are kidding… right?"

"Yeah. Not all Asians believe in reincarnation. Actually, I'm an Episcopalian."

Flenn grinned. "Another surprise! So am I."

She turned toward him. "Really?"

"Well, my mom is. I guess my dad is too. His dad was Baptist. But Mom took my brother and me to an Episcopal church in Concord when we were growing up."

"But you don't attend anymore?"

"Nah. Too busy." Another lie. Flenn was agnostic.

"Too bad. I guess we'll just have to tell our kids their daddy is going to hell."

Flenn nearly dropped his wine.

Hoshi laughed. "Well, that's if Donna has her way! She's been wanting to fix me up with a husband ever since we were in college."

"Why? She's not married herself."

"Was." Hoshi frowned. "Only for a year. The guy was a real jerk. Fooled around… lied to her all the time."

Flenn hadn't known any of that. "Zack never said… "

"Oh well, the past is the past. I knew the guy was bad news from the beginning." She sighed. "I can't talk, though, I dated one even worse." She took a slow sip of wine. "Which is why I hate liars."

Flenn looked down at the ground then back up at her as a clown walked by carrying balloons. "Um, Hoshi?"

"Yeah?"

"I have a confession to make… "

"What's that?"

"I don't really like popcorn."

CHAPTER *FOURTEEN*

Present day...

The transformation was remarkable. Flenn wasn't sure that he was walking in the same city as the day before. As he made his way toward Durham Cathedral, he passed smiling couples holding hands, children walking calmly beside their parents, and old men and women strolling slowly by, gazing into store windows.

The most startling change, however, was the street itself. Yesterday it had been littered with confetti, flyers, beer bottles, empty paper cups and assorted trash from the crowd. Today, Sunday, not a sign of that remained. The people, and the rubbish, were all gone.

Flenn had skipped the morning services. He'd stayed up late waiting for Zack, who'd never showed, then decided to sleep in. After a morning jog, he'd had a mid-morning brunch at a café down North Street, then showered and gotten ready for the afternoon ordination.

Pamela had invited him to sit with the family, so he would have an up-close view of Windsor's consecration. Scores of people were already lining up outside the northern door, the one with the massive copper doorknocker where the accused and persecuted once ran for sanctuary.

Flenn wasn't the only one in line wearing a collar as they waited to pass through security; plenty of clergy were attending today. One priest had been asked to step aside, and had his arms held out on either side as a security guard ran an electromagnetic wand around the man's body. Safety was important, but Flenn hated to see armed guards and metal detectors at houses of worship.

"Afternoon, Father," said a man wearing a purple robe bearing Saint Cuthbert's cross. "Are you processing today?" the verger asked.

Flenn smiled. "No, I'm just here to see an old friend get his comeuppance."

The man either missed the joke or was simply not amused. He peered over the top of his glasses. "Name?"

"Scott Flenn."

The steward checked his clipboard and found Flenn's name listed with the family. "Right; here you are. The family has requested that you be shown to where they are gathering. "Margaret!" he called to an elderly woman, also wearing a purple robe. "Take this gentleman to the café please."

Flenn followed the woman inside, then straight across to another door, outside through the cloister, and then into a large room. On the right stood the cathedral's gift shop, on the left, the café, which was closed this afternoon except to family and friends of the Tammerlane's. About 40 people were standing in small groups, chatting as they sipped tea and coffee. Windsor was nowhere to be seen, *no doubt off in a sacristy somewhere,* Flenn thought, *going over last-minute details with the Archbishop of Canterbury.*

"Flenn, darling!" Pamela was dressed in a floor-length royal blue dress with a blue-and-gold lamé shawl. Flenn made his way over and she offered him her cheek. "I can't tell you how much you being here means to us." She turned to her right. "Let me introduce you to some people."

During the next half hour Flenn met the archbishop's wife, the mayor, a representative of the royal family, along with numerous other dignitaries. "And this is Tobias Love," Pamela said. "He owns English Petroleum." Tobias Love offered his hand, then leaned over and whispered something to Pam before heading into the church. When the call came for them to be seated, Flenn gave Pam a hug and headed for the door to find his seat.

The cathedral was packed for Winston's ordination; Pamela and the children were last to be seated. Flenn sat in the pew directly behind Pam. The procession was grand, just as Flenn knew it would be. Banners and streamers waved as they followed the crucifer down the aisle. The children's choir followed the acolytes and thurifer—their voices blending perfectly with the grand choir as they sang, *The Church's One Foundation.*

Numerous deacons, priests, and bishops walked behind the choristers, with Windsor Tammerlane processing near the end of the long line, followed by a host of bishops... and lastly the Archbishop of Canterbury. The immediate past Bishop of Durham was the preacher for the event, and Flenn and Windsor's New Testament professor, Christopher Ryan, recently retired, were also in the procession. Flenn knew that Christopher had been invited to read the Epistle. Flenn remembered sitting next to Windsor Tammerlane at Sewanee for three years in Professor Ryan's class. How odd, he mused, that two friends, from two different countries, and two totally different backgrounds, would end up studying together at the same seminary.

Just how many years ago was that? Flenn pondered as Windsor knelt before the gathered bishops for the laying on of hands. Flenn smiled as he recalled, once again, the old joke at seminary: "Those who desire to be a bishop deserve to be." The priesthood could be difficult enough, and Flenn had absolutely no yearnings to ever wear the mitre.

The bishops all lifted their hands from Win's head, and Windsor Tammerlane was declared a bishop in 'God's One, Holy, Catholic and Apostolic Church.' Cheers resounded from every corner of the ancient church. Windsor was smiling from ear to ear as he hugged his wife and family, then turned to thank the clergy and guests for attending.

Happy for his friend, Flenn watched as the deacons prepared for communion, setting a centuries-old golden chalice upon the altar. Flenn had read that the 600-year-old *Prince Bishop's Chalice*, as it was known, was ordinarily kept in the cathedral's air-tight vault. It was rumored to have originally been used by Thomas Hatfield, a 14th-Century bishop, who, like the other Prince

Bishops, ruled Durham with an authority nearly equal to the king himself. The paten, which would hold the bread for communion, was considerably younger, but also quite valuable. Flenn had seen photographs online. The paten had a symbol of Cuthbert's cross etched into the gold, while the large chalice had no outward ornamentation and pretty much looked its age. Flenn knew that several additional chalices and patens would be used at communion stations throughout the church today. Some 2,000 people had gathered for the ordination, and Flenn assumed that there would be a minimum of five stations in addition to the one at the High Altar where Windsor now stood.

While tradition would have it that the Archbishop of Canterbury would be the chief celebrant at a Eucharist, the Archbishop had properly deferred to Durham Cathedral's new bishop to serve in that capacity. As Bishop Windsor Tammerlane lifted the great cup heavenward and declared the ancient words of consecration, Flenn couldn't help but be caught up in the joy of the moment. Yesterday's drunken altercations were nearly forgotten as Windsor, the chief celebrant, broke the bread and lifted the chalice a second time.

The celebrant always receives communion first, a tradition going back to the Anglican Church's Roman roots. After Windsor, the rest of those serving communion would receive, and then the acolytes and choristers. Next would be the representatives sent by Her Majesty, then Windsor's family, and lastly, the congregation.

As Bishop Tammerlane lifted the chalice to his lips, Flenn remembered the time he and Windsor had sneaked into the sacristy at Sewanee and dusted the chalice with an invisible compound that turned everyone's lips blue. Fortunately for them, no one had ever discovered which seniors had instituted the prank.

He watched Windsor lower the chalice. A look of absolute ecstasy swept over the newly consecrated bishop's face. Windsor didn't move, just stood there holding the golden chalice. And then...

Something was wrong!

Windsor had no more set the chalice back upon the altar when he started to shake violently, his entire body gyrating uncontrollably. The bishop grabbed for the altar to steady himself, then clutched at his chest as he looked toward his wife.

His eyes!

Flenn had seen that look before.

Trickles of blood began to flow from the newly consecrated bishop's mouth and nose. Flenn jumped to his feet and pushed his way through those sitting next to him and sprinted up the steps through the chancel and behind the altar.

"Quickly, someone make him gag!" Flenn yelled.

The archbishop turned as white as the Alb he was wearing as Flenn thrust his own forefinger down Windsor's throat, making him throw up on the marble floor behind the altar. Four doctors from the congregation vaulted up the steps as the verger hurried across and whispered to the choir director.

The verger stepped out and asked the congregation to please remain seated. "Bishop Tammerlane has taken ill and is currently being well cared for," he told the crowd. "I ask for your patience and your prayers." The verger looked to the choir director for assistance calming the congregation. The director lifted his hands, and the choir stood and began to softly sing a Latin hymn acappella. It was the piece they'd prepared to sing during communion.

Flenn stepped back as the doctors took over. Pamela was making her way up the aisle.

"Don't anyone touch that chalice!" Flenn shouted as the chief of security made his way toward the altar. An altar guild member pushed a wet towel into an acolyte's hands and pointed toward Flenn. The frightened girl brought the towel to Flenn, who wrapped it around his hand. Flenn looked at the security guard. "I have to wash immediately. Do not let anyone touch his vomit, and for God's sake, no one go near that chalice. It has been poisoned!"

Were it not for the choir, the entire church would have heard him. As it was, only those at the altar heard, and most stepped back, except for the doctors, one of whom looked at Flenn. "Are you certain?"

Flenn stared at the man; his eyes left no doubt. He turned to the acolyte who'd brought him the towel. "Take me to your sacristy, quickly!"

The sacristy was through a hidden door only meters away. Flenn threw his suit coat to the floor and searched for the piscina, knowing that its pipes would lead straight into the ground and not into a sewer system. He turned the water on full force and kept his eyes and mouth tightly closed as he thrust both hands under the running water.

Two women, the one who had brought the wet towel and another member of the altar guild, came in cautiously, asking what they could do. "Go out there and tell the doctors that the poison may be colocinium. Do it... do it now!"

The frightened women ran and did as Flenn had told them.

Stupid, stupid, stupid! Why hadn't he told the doctors that? It was just too impossible to believe! Not here, not now, not Windsor!

He continued to wash for another full minute, then tore his collar off and ripped off his shirt. He saw no trace of vomit or blood on his torso, but taking no chances grabbed a nearby roll of paper towels, wet them and wiped himself off. He kicked off his shoes, careful not to touch them. Although he saw no stains on his trousers, he removed them as well, dropping them on top of the shoes and then kicking the whole pile of clothes together into a heap in the corner. The women came back just as he removed his boxers. "My God!" one said. The other crossed herself and nearly fainted.

"I'm sorry," he said. "Don't touch those clothes. In fact, you need to exit the building now."

The woman took a long look at him. "You're sure?"

Flenn raised both eyebrows. "Go!"

She crossed over to a tall wardrobe and pulled out an Alb, tossed it to him and disappeared into the nave.

Wrapping the robe around him, Flenn went back into the chancel as the choir and clergy were helping people leave in a calm and orderly fashion. *The British!* Flenn thought. *If this had been Saint Ann's back in Birmingham, people would have been running for the doors.* The thought left him as quickly as it had come, as he turned to find the doctors. Only one of them was attending to Windsor, who lay perfectly still. Flenn knew the reason why.

"Everyone, listen to me!" he shouted in his best 'take-charge' voice. "If I am correct, Bishop Tammerlane was poisoned with a nerve agent which dissipates quickly. However, if you have touched any of his bodily fluids you need to go immediately and wash for several minutes. First, quickly remove any clothing that might have come into contact with Bishop Windsor's vomit or blood. Vestments, shoes, pants, shirts, jackets, dresses. Now is not the time to be modest. Place them all in a pile so they do not to possibly contaminate anyone else. Hurry! Your life may depend on it!"

Three security guards watched in amazement as clergy, doctors, and even the Archbishop of Canterbury, tore their robes and clothes from their bodies and threw them on the floor. Flenn looked at one of the guards. "You, stand watch over these clothes. Make sure no one touches them! You two… take these people to the nearest toilets, showers, whatever is available. Do it fast!"

The doctor attending Windsor refused to budge. "Doctor, please, do as I say."

"I will not leave this man!" the physician replied.

"Are you familiar with colocinium?" Flenn said as

calmly as he could, remaining a good 10-feet from the altar."

"I am. The Syrians used it to kill a double agent in Paris a few years back. I read about it in the papers."

Flenn nodded. "Then you know how dangerous it is. Please, go now!"

The doctor took a breath, "And if you are wrong, we will have abandoned this good man. See here, I do not know you, but I know Windsor Tammerlane. He baptized my little girl. He came to the house when she was sick one night, and he held our hands when we buried her. I will not leave this man!"

Suddenly, the doctor smiled from ear to ear, his eyes grew large, as if he had just seen a beatific vision… then he too began to shake violently.

"Doctor?" the guard inquired. "Are you all right?" The young man started toward him but Flenn grabbed him and held him back.

"It's too late, son, stand back!" The doctor collapsed next to the bishop. Flenn shook the guard. "Don't go anywhere near either of them!" He looked up at the high altar. There, atop the beautiful white linen sat a paten full of communion wafers and a 600-year-old poisoned chalice.

CHAPTER *FIFTEEN*

11 years earlier…

Hoshi laughed as Flenn brushed popcorn off his head and shoulders. "Serves you right," she teased.

"What'd he do now?" asked Zack as he and Donna walked toward them. Donna was grinning from ear to ear.

"Never mind that," Donna said, looking more like she was floating than walking. "Look!" Donna held up her left hand, and there on her finger was a diamond solitaire, sparkling in the colored lights of the Eiffel Tower.

"Oh my God!" squealed Hoshi, jumping up to give her friend a hug.

Flenn raised both eyebrows at Zack, who sheepishly shrugged. "Well, you son of a gun!" Flenn stood to shake his best friend's hand. "So that's what you were planning."

For the first time in as many years as Flenn had known him, Zack blushed. Flenn winked and then gave Donna a kiss on the cheek. "Congratulations!"

Donna and Hoshi sat down while Flenn and Zack went to get everyone a glass of Champagne. "Sorry," Zack said, "but when Donna invited Hoshi, I had to have someone to distract her. I knew Hoshi was afraid of heights, and so are you."

Flenn objected, "I'm not afraid of heights!"

Zack grinned. "It worked out perfectly."

Flenn glanced back at Hoshi, who was laughing along with Donna. "Yes, I suppose it did."

Zack turned toward the girls and then to Flenn, "Ahh, so she's no longer a *little girl,* huh?"

"Quatre Champagnes, s'il vous plait," Flenn said to the man selling wine in plastic cups. "She's actually quite charming."

"Well then, it all worked out after all," said Zack.

"What do you mean?" Flenn paid the man and they each took two cups and headed back.

"I know Donna will ask Hoshi to be her maid of honor, and I want you to be best man."

"Me?"

"Unless I can come up with someone better," Zack teased.

"Quite an honor," Flenn said. "I'll do it… for Donna."

Hoshi looked up at Zack. "Donna tells me you're thinking of getting married at Christmas! In Scotland!"

Flenn raised an eyebrow. "Scotland?"

"Donna's family comes from there, and she's always wanted to get married in a Scottish castle," Zack said. Flenn raised an eyebrow; the Zack Matteson he knew would much rather get married in the office of a justice of the peace than a castle.

"Sounds… grand." Flenn said, hesitantly.

"Why, what's wrong with a Scottish castle?" Donna asked, her smile disappearing.

"Not a thing, sweetheart," Zack said.

Donna wouldn't let it go. "Flenn?"

Flenn shrugged. "Absolutely nothing. In fact, I love it! I can't wait to see Zack in a kilt!"

"Oh, I hadn't thought of that!" Donna said. "Yes! Yes! Absolutely!"

Zack glared at Flenn.

"Um," Hoshi said, "Donna, maybe you should check with Zack about that. I mean, nine months is plenty of time to make decisions about wardrobe for the big day."

"No, it's settled! My honey will be wearing a kilt!" Donna said, "A green and red plaid one, I think." She leaned her head onto Zack's shoulder. "You'll do that for me, won't you sweetie?" Zack shot Flenn an 'I'll kill you later' look.

Hoshi glanced up at Flenn. "Um, I think they decide colors by family name, Donna."

"Oh, who cares. It will be Christmas… red and green it is."

Zack scratched the side of his head. "Gee, hon, I don't know. If colors are supposed to be by family name then maybe… "

Donna waved her hand in the air. "Nope. Red and green; it will be great!"

Hoshi pulled Flenn aside. "Maybe we should leave these two lovebirds alone. Would you mind helping me find a taxi, Scott?"

"Call me Flenn; everyone else does."

Hoshi shook her head. "Well… no, I think Scott suits you better. Calling you by your last name seems so formal."

Flenn shook his head. "You're right, it does sound

formal." He smiled warmly at her. "You can call me whatever you want."

"If you can't think of anything, I have a few things you can call him!" Zack said. "I bet he even knows the one I'm thinking of calling him right now."

"Your best friend! Right, sweetie?" Donna said cheerily.

Hoshi tucked her hair back behind her ears. "Scott, how about we go find that taxi?" she said.

Flenn smiled. "Absolutely. You two okay?"

"We're great," Donna said.

To Zack, he said, "See you tomorrow," then winked… "Not too early, though."

Donna grinned. "Don't worry, he won't be."

CHAPTER *SIXTEEN*

11 years earlier...

"So, tell me again—why are we here? I have a date with Hoshi tomorrow night." Flenn and Zack had arrived in Iraq late the night before and were scheduled to return to Paris on the last military flight out that evening.

Zack Matteson reached in his pocket for a jellybean and brushed the lint off before eating it. "Things are really moving along between you two."

"Yeah, yeah... you didn't answer the question."

"I have no idea. Colonel Zamir just said we both should be at the interrogation this morning."

Flenn opened the door to the small room where Yasir Kamul sat at a table with an Iraqi guard on either side. Hussain Zamir, a colonel in the Afghani intelligence bureau, had yet to arrive.

Kamul looked different from the last time Flenn had seen him. He was thinner, his right eye constantly twitched, and there was an ugly bruise on his left cheek. Flenn chewed on his lower lip. He despised torture of any kind. It seldom worked and usually only produced false information.

"Did I miss anything?" Flenn and Zack turned to see Davy Spate standing behind them.

"I thought you said you'd be watching this guy?" Flenn said, testily.

Davy studied Kamul's face. "Ah, yeah, about that; well, you see, the Iraqis are in charge here. I protested, believe me I did, but… "

Two olive-skinned men in Iraqi army uniform walked purposefully into the room, and the guards snapped to attention. "Who are these men?" one of them asked David.

"They're CIA, Major," Davy said. "Gentlemen, this is Major Samer Wasem."

Wasem raised an eyebrow, still looking at Davy. "And their names?"

Davy responded: "Their names are not important. Colonel Zamir invited them here." A small man wearing a white servant's uniform entered with a tray of pomegranate juice and several Styrofoam cups. Kamul looked up at the delivery man, then turned away as if seeing a ghost.

"I say who attends my interrogations, not Zamir!" Major Wasem glared at the three of them. "Da-vid," he said, "you may stay, but these two will have to wait outside."

Zack objected, "Our government has been working with Colonel Zamir for years. He specifically asked us to be here this morning." The servant left the juice, bowed respectfully to the guards, then wove his way through the small group and out the door.

The major bristled. "And where is Zamir today? He is not here, and I am. I say you leave!"

"And I say we stay!" Zack said just as forcefully.

"Tell you what," said David, breaking the war of wills. "I will share the information with you two after the major is finished."

Knowing he'd just won, Major Wasem straightened and smiled a crooked grin. Flenn just looked at Zack and shrugged. "We'll be right outside the door, Davy."

Zack slammed the door behind them, and mimicked, "*'We'll be right outside the door, Davy!'* Come on Flenn, what the hell's the matter with you, letting the Brits have this before us?"

"I know Davy Spate. He's not like that. He knows we need to find out about this new Al-Qaeda group as much as British Intelligence does. Davy's been with MI-6 a long time, he doesn't play politics; he will tell us everything." He pointed across the compound to where some men were smoking and drinking coffee. "Why don't you go see if you can round us up some coffee, I have a feeling we may be here awhile."

"What, and have you slip in there while I'm gone? No way."

Flenn rubbed his temples. "No, seriously, I'm getting a headache. I need caffeine."

"You know you drink too much of that stuff, don't you?"

"Don't worry, I'll balance it out with some Scotch tonight."

"Speaking of tonight," Zack reached into his pocket for another squashed jellybean, "where are you and Hoshi going?"

"It's *tomorrow* night, and I was thinking of taking her to see that new Johnny Depp movie, the one with Kate Winslet."

"Ugh, take her to see that Will Ferrell movie instead; it's hilarious." They heard a thud and strange noises coming from inside the room. Flenn called out, "Everything okay in there?" The door burst open and Davy Spate ran out.

"Go get the guy who brought that juice!" he yelled. "Do it!"

Flenn and Zack drew their weapons and stepped past Spate. Inside, all four Iraqis lay motionless on the floor. Yasir Kamul was standing, holding a Styrofoam cup in his shackled hands. He looked at Flenn and sneered, then lifted the cup to his mouth and drank. A look of sheer ecstasy flashed in Kamul's eyes, as if he had just seen the face of Allah himself... then, he began to shake uncontrollably as blood trickled from his mouth and nose. A few seconds later, he dropped to the floor and lay motionless with the others.

Zack turned and ran with Davy across the Iraqi base toward the kitchen to find the man who had delivered the poison. Flenn froze in disbelief as he put it all together.

"Zamir!"

CHAPTER *SEVENTEEN*

Present day…

Flenn headed straight to Pamela's home after the Bobbies had finished questioning him. A sympathetic police chaplain had arranged for some clothes for Flenn along with a couple of taxi vouchers. He'd spent several hours at the Durham station not only with police investigators but also with some men in black suits whom he assumed were British Intelligence.

"How was it you knew straight away that Tammerlane was poisoned?" the men in suits kept asking.

"Because I've seen it before. In Iraq when I was serving as an interpreter for some intelligence guy on the base. I think his name was Matteson, Jack or Zack or something." Flenn told them just enough of the truth to be believable. He said that he had been on the base representing Flenn Industries at the time, and that his dad's company had been negotiating a large sale of machinery to the army. Since Flenn was fluent in Farsi and Arabic, he told the investigators that Matteson had asked him to serve as an interpreter at an interrogation gone awry.

"The victims there acted in the same way," Flenn told

them. "First there was this look of euphoria, then they started shaking, and then they began to bleed from the nose and mouth… believe me, you never forget something like that. It was the first time I had ever heard of colocinium."

The police had ordered Flenn to stay in Durham for a few days in case they had any more questions. *No doubt the MI-6 boys would figure out who he was in time, but doubtful they'd say anything about that to the local police.*

He rang the doorbell at the Tammerlane's and was greeted by an armed security guard. "I'm Scott Flenn," he said, "Father Scott Flenn, here to see Mrs. Tammerlane." The guard stared at him suspiciously. "I'm not wearing my collar now; I had to change after the incident this morning."

The guard disappeared, but came back a moment later. "The missus is in the back garden. Just follow the crowd."

Sure enough, scores of people were milling about the massive house. Flenn wove his way through family and friends, all speaking in hushed tones, some appearing quite ashen. He recognized several faces from the ordination service. The mayor was standing in a corner speaking to a man in uniform while Tobias Love was talking to a woman who appeared to be the maid.

The Tammerlanes were outside in the garden.

Pamela was seated in a wicker chair, her two sons standing next to her. Flenn recognized the handsome, middle-aged man speaking to her from the other night. Elton Wainwright squeezed Pam's shoulder and then made his way into the living room where he stopped to speak with the mayor.

"Pam, there are no words… " Flenn knelt before her and reached for her hand. "I'm just so… so terribly sorry."

Pamela Tammerlane's eyes glistened; in one hand she clutched a silk handkerchief. She'd managed to change into comfortable khakis and a soft blue sweater after the service, but she was still wearing the pearls.

"Who, who would do this?" she said, her speech somewhat slurred.

Flenn shook his head. "I've no idea, Pam, but I'm just so very sorry. I'll be in Durham awhile. Please, send for me if there is anything I can do." He rose to allow the next person to offer their condolences. Flenn spoke briefly with Pam and Win's sons, then made his way to the door. Elton Wainwright was winding his way around the room. Flenn couldn't help thinking that even now the man seemed to be soliciting votes.

Outside, Flenn counted seven police officers with helmets, flak jackets, and machine guns. Two squad cars were parked at the end of the street. "Aren't you the priest that tried to save the bishop this mornin'?"

"I just wish that I'd been successful." Flenn walked down and hailed a taxi. "Take me to the cathedral," he told the driver.

"Can't, mate. Closed for the day. Ain't ya' heard? The Russkies done it to us again! Poisoned the bloomin' Archbishop of Canterbury for Chris' sake."

"It was the new bishop of Durham," Flenn corrected, "not the archbishop."

The man glanced in his rearview mirror. "Ya' sure? I heard they got the arch. If ya' ask me, they was after that Elton Wainwright. 'Im's the one they want to knock off, what with 'im gonna be the next minister and all. 'E'll give the Russkies what for, once 'e gets elected!"

"Never mind, just take me to 14 Neville Street."

"Right," the man said, reaching to start the meter. "On me way."

Flenn paid the cabbie with one of the vouchers the police chaplain had given him. Standing in front of the door it hit him—his keys and wallet were still in his trousers at the church! He tried the door anyway. To his surprise, it was unlocked. He opened the door cautiously. Zack Matteson was standing over the stove with his back to him. Flenn smelled beef and onions frying.

"Thought you might be hungry when you got back," Zack said. "Sit down, dinner's almost ready."

"So, I guess you've heard?" Flenn said as he pulled out a chair.

"The whole country's heard, probably the entire world by now. You don't poison an Anglican bishop in the middle of his big brouhaha and expect people not to hear about it." Zack opened the cabinet and got out two plates. "God, I can't believe it, though. Winnie was one of the good guys. We were never close, but Pam and Donna were." He scooped up a spoonful of mashed potatoes and poured some of the mixture from the frying pan on top of them. "Maybe I can find out something from MI-6. Looks like I'll be in town a day or two after all."

"Yeah, I saw Elton Wainwright at the Tammerlanes just now. I figured you'd be in town."

"Never left."

Flenn looked at him, "I thought when you didn't come back last night… "

"You remember those college girls at the festival?"

"Stop," Flenn held up his hand. "I don't want to hear it."

Zack chuckled to himself. "No, you don't."

Flenn sighed. "Who did this, Zack?"

Zack shook his head. "I was hoping you knew."

"A cabbie just informed me that it was the Russians."

Zack turned and handed Flenn a plate, then fixed one for himself. "Nope, not the Russians, not this time." He retrieved a couple of beers from the tiny fridge and set them on the table before sitting down to eat.

"What makes you so sure? Colocinium is pretty hard to come by."

"Not really," Zack said. "It's a byproduct of treating sulfur. The Russians don't like the stuff because it's too unstable and can cause a bigger mess than they prefer. Plus, there's no reason to kill a high-profile cleric in a public spectacle like that. It's not their way."

"Who else has colocinium these days?"

Zack took a swig of the beer. "Don't know. It isn't on the top 10 anymore. I heard Isis used it some more after we left, but it backfired on them one too many times. "*Happy juice,* I think they called it."

"Shelf life's pretty short, as I recall," said Flenn. "That stuff doesn't live in the air very long, only in liquid."

"So, how'd whoever it was get it to Windsor?" Zack picked up a fork and began to eat heartily.

Flenn picked at his food. "Somebody poisoned the Prince Bishop's Chalice."

"That big cuppy thing? You think it was really meant for Win?"

"I'd say so. Our custom is for the chief celebrant at the altar to drink first. Colocinium is so quick it wouldn't be a poison anyone would choose if they were trying to kill an entire congregation."

"So, they were after just one person?"

Flenn tried a bite of the food and found he was hungrier than he'd realized. "Looks like it. Whoever poisoned the chalice would have known that this stuff acts quick. One of the doctors trying to help Windsor also died; maybe he wiped his nose or something, I don't know. Those two were the only ones killed."

Zack thought for a moment. "Who would have known about the celebrant being the first to take communion?"

"Only anybody who has ever paid attention to a church service in England."

"And you say it could have been the archbishop they were after?"

Flenn nodded. "Maybe, but I don't think so. It's pretty customary to let the new bishop act as celebrant. If you're an assassin using colocinium, I suspect you'd do your research."

Zack finished his plate and got up for seconds. "What about that Prince Bishop's thingy?"

"Chalice," Flenn said.

"How could they have slipped the colocinium in it?"

"That's just the thing. It might have been done anywhere. Churches aren't that careful."

"Weren't there services this morning?"

Flenn thought about that. "Yeah, you're right; it would've had to have been after the last service and before the ordination began. That leaves about a two-hour window for someone to slip the poison into the cruet."

"The what?"

"Cruet. It's the glass container that holds the wine and the water before the service."

Zack leaned back in his chair. "So, where were these cruets before they poured the wine into the chalice?"

"Sitting on the credence table. It's a small shelf or table near the altar. Before that, the cruets would have been in the sacristy. The altar guild would have prepared them in there before the service."

Zack picked up his bottle. "I'll check with one of my contacts in London to see if they've found out anything from the cathedral's surveillance cameras."

"Doubtful that they'll have cameras in the sacristy," Flenn said. "I just wish I could get in there, maybe get a feel for things—see if I could figure out how they did it."

Zack put down his fork. "What's stopping us?"

"What, up to the cathedral… now?"

"Why not?"

Flenn stared at him. "Because there will be police everywhere, that's why. The place is cordoned off."

"So?"

Flenn leaned back in his chair. "Can you really get us in there?"

Zack shrugged. "You know me; I can do anything!"

Flenn took a drink and set the bottle on the table. "Turn the stove off and let me go change. These clothes they got for me don't really fit."

Zack finished his meal and put Flenn's leftovers in the fridge. Flenn was back in less than five minutes. "So," Flenn said, as they closed the door and started walking toward Durham Cathedral, "how are you going to get us inside?"

Zack smiled. "I have no idea."

CHAPTER *EIGHTEEN*

11 years earlier...

"How could you have voted for *him*?" Hoshi set her wine glass down on the café table. Judging from how loud she'd just said that, Flenn figured she'd had enough.

"Sweetheart, that was several years ago."

"I don't care how long ago it was; the man was a country bumpkin!"

"Well," he offered, "at the time I thought the old guy was a better choice than either the Republican or the Democrat."

"Give me a break," she said, reaching for the glass.

"Tell you what," he said, setting his own glass down and standing up, "how about we head on over to see the impressionists now. After all, you don't come to the Louvre without seeing a Monet."

Hoshi glanced around but didn't budge. "I don't know," she said, smiling, "I kinda' like it here."

"Come on," he said, leaving a generous tip. "Don't forget, we're meeting Zack and Donna for dinner tonight."

"Aw, do we have to?" she whined. "We've met them every night for the past week. I'd much rather spend the time alone with you, if you know what I mean."

Flenn did.

Hoshi took a quick sip from her glass as she stood. She stumbled in her heels but Flenn helped steady her.

"You okay?" he asked.

"Never better," she said, giggling. She held onto his jacket as she took off one shoe and then other. "I don't suppose I could leave these here and come back for them later?"

"They'd probably end up in the modern art exhibit across the street," Flenn teased. "Here, give them to me."

They made quite the couple walking through the museum, him well over 6-feet tall and wearing non-descript neutral colors so as not to draw attention; her, 5-foot-nothing, barefoot, and wearing a colorful print with a white hairband that kept sliding down her silky hair. Whether out of affection or from too much wine, Hoshi held tightly to Flenn's arm as they made their way past colorful paintings by Degas and Cassatt. Standing by a large painting by Matisse, she reached up and tickled his ear playfully. "I wonder," she said, pointing to a seat nearby, "if anyone ever made love on that bench over there?"

"I have no idea, but we're not about to be the first," he said, dragging her into the next room.

"You're no fun!" she pouted, looking down at her feet. "Hey, where are my shoes?"

CHAPTER *NINETEEN*

Present day...

Zack made a couple of calls on his satellite phone as he and Flenn made their way across the Framwellgate Bridge toward the cathedral. As they walked up the steep hill, Flenn heard Zack arrange clearance with someone. Sure enough, when they'd reached the first police barricade, a middle-aged brunette came to greet them.

"Is one of you Albert Johannsen?" Flenn raised an eyebrow as he glanced over at Zack.

"That's me," Zack said, popping a jellybean in his mouth before pulling out an identification card.

She looked at the card and then at his face. "Thank you for coming. I'm not shocked that the CIA is eager to assist us, I'm just surprised you got here so quickly. We haven't even heard from your embassy yet." The woman held out her hand. "I'm Monica Kettlebottom, head of security for the cathedral. Mr. Morrison told me that you are to have total access."

She handed them each a large, rectangular, yellow sticker. "Please keep these on your lapels at all times; otherwise, you will be escorted away. If you need me, just tell someone in uniform. They'll know how to find me."

Zack thanked the woman as he and Flenn headed

across the lawn. "Johannsen?" Flenn whispered. "Who the hell would believe that?"

"Someone named Kettle-butt," apparently.

"Kettlebottom," Flenn corrected. "It's not that unusual a name here. And why carry CIA identification with a false name?"

Zack smiled. "Why not?"

They walked past two men in blue suits. "And, who's Mr. Morrison?" Flenn asked.

"Doesn't matter," Zack said. "Just someone I know in London." They slowed as they approached the ancient cemetery. He turned to Flenn. "We're here, so now what?"

"Follow me," Flenn said, leading the way through the great sanctuary door and past three policemen who were simply standing around as if they had no idea what to do next. Zack was taken aback by the massive columns holding up the stone-ribbed ceiling. Though he'd traveled the world many times over, Zack had been in very few cathedrals. This one amazed him.

Flenn pointed toward the altar at the far end. The chalice was gone, no doubt taken by hazardous waste technicians to some undisclosed location. "That's where it all happened."

They walked up the aisle as two people wearing orange hazmat suits crawled out from behind the altar. Flenn pointed to an ornate square to the right of the altar which was covered with a lace cloth. "That's the credence table where the wine and water were kept in glass cruets."

"The poison could have been in either cruet," Zack said.

"No. Colocinium has a thick, yellowish consistency." Flenn remembered learning about the poison after the incident in Iraq. "It would have shown up in water. It had to have been in the wine."

Zack nodded. "So, where would the wine have been before it was placed on the table… the *sanctuary*, I think you said?"

"The sacristy. It's the room where everything is prepared before a service. It's where I went to wash after sticking my finger down Windsor's throat."

Zack made a face. "You did what?"

"Doesn't matter, just follow me." Flenn led him past the altar and down the steps to the sacristy. No one was inside. His clothes were still piled in the corner, under an orange Hazmat blanket. Flenn started opening cabinets until he found what he was looking for… six large bottles of tawny port. "Here's where they keep the wine," he said, noticing one bottle was half empty. We need to tell Ms. Kettlebottom about this," he said. "Someone needs to take this bottle and examine the contents."

Zack ran his eyes along the walls, looking for security cameras. As Flenn had predicted, there weren't any. Flenn opened another cabinet beneath the large piscina where cleaning supplies were kept. He found what he was looking for, a pair of rubber gloves the altar guild used when cleaning up the sacristy. He slipped on the gloves to retrieve his wallet and keys from his suit pants, then removed the yellow gloves and left them on top of the clothes, carefully replacing the blanket when he was done.

"We need to tell those guys with the hazmat suits about my clothes. They should be burned with the others they collected, even though the poison would probably be harmless by now."

"People took off their clothes?"

"Only those that might have been contaminated."

Zack scratched his head. "Hopefully no one had a camera with them."

Flenn ignored the comment as he stood in the middle of the sacristy and closed his eyes. He took a few breaths to clear his mind. Zack had seen him do this before. Flenn was trying to reconstruct the events in his mind, imagining the criminal or criminals, following their likely movements, figuring out how it had all happened. Flenn opened his eyes and looked from the cabinet to the piscina, then across to the only door that led into the sacristy. He stared at the door, then looked back at the wine cabinet.

"Something's wrong."

Zack didn't comment, for the same reason he'd remained motionless, so as not to interfere with Flenn's train of thought. Flenn walked over to the door and closed it. He reached down for the knob and turning it, stepped outside the sacristy and closed the door. Zack heard the rattle of the doorknob, then a knock. He opened the door and Flenn stepped back inside.

"That door can be opened from the inside, but it automatically locks when closed. One of the ladies was holding it open for me when I came in to wash. Only someone with a key can get inside."

"So then only cathedral staff could get in here?"

Flenn nodded. "In theory at least." Flenn took another long look around the room then walked to the transept where he stopped in the middle of the church. There were two main entrances into the nave, the sanctuary door and the south door, which led to the cloister, gift shop, and café. If the poison had been brought in by someone from outside the cathedral, it had to have come through one of those two doors. There were likely to be cameras covering both.

Zack intuited what Flenn was thinking. "There are probably lots of side entrances the staff know about. If a priest did this, he could have come through one of those."

Flenn looked at him. "A priest?"

Zack grinned. "Well, you know how you guys are. Maybe someone was angry that they'd not been picked to be the new bishop?"

Flenn rolled his eyes. "Oh yeah, and just happened to have some colocinium in their kitchen and brought it along."

"Well, I don't know what you guys do in your spare time."

"Not funny, Zack. Remember this was Win we're talking about." Flenn walked up the steps to the chancel, or *quire* as it was called here, and stopped in front of a high rectangular inset built around a stone tomb with ten wooden spires. Zack followed.

The son of a master carpenter, Zack couldn't help but

gaze in awe at the tomb of Thomas Hatfield, one of the Prince Bishops of Durham. The ancient woodwork was beautiful. Blue shields depicting three lions decorated either side of the ornate tomb. Above, a stairwell led to what appeared to be a throne directly above the tomb. Zack looked for a way to climb up and take a closer look.

"Zack?"

Zack turned. "What's with the throne? Is that for the Queen?"

Flenn turned to look. "No, it's for the bishop. Hatfield had it built to be taller than the Pope's was back then."

Zack looked at the massive structure and then up at the throne with golden spires directly over it. "Wow, someone sure thought highly of himself."

"Leave the sightseeing for another time; that's not why we're here." Flenn went back to the credence table. "Once the wine was brought out from the sacristy, it would have rested on this table."

"For how long?" Zack asked.

Flenn thought. "The last morning service was at 11:15. It would have been finished by 12:30 or so. The ordination was at 2 p.m., so approximately an hour and a half at most."

Zack checked for cameras covering the altar area and spotted two. He pointed them out to Flenn. "The police shouldn't have any trouble finding out if anyone came up here and poured something into the cruel-thingy."

Flenn sighed. "*Cruet*, Zack. *Cruet*."

"Whatever."

"And just who the hell are you?" A short, balding

man wearing a dingy coat with an ancient tie dangling loosely from his neck, approached them.

"Ms. Kettlebottom sent us." Zack said.

"The hell she did!"

Zack fished in his pocket for his badge. "Albert Johannsen," this is my partner, Sven."

The man glared at Flenn. "*You're* Sven?"

"Ya," said Flenn, cutting his eyes toward Zack.

"I'll need to see your identification," the man said, skeptically.

Now what? Flenn thought, handing the man his wallet as Zack simply stood there smiling.

"This is an American driver's license. Says your name is Scott Flenn."

"Well," Zack said, "what did you expect? That's just his cover. It rhymes, you see. Flenn and Sven. Get it?"

A blonde, well-dressed man in his mid-forties walked over. Zack rolled his eyes as the man asked the detective, "Is there a problem here, Colin?"

"Yes sir, these men…"

The man in the black suit interrupted, "Are exactly who they say they are. Please… carry on."

The dumpy man's face flushed pink. "Yes sir." He handed Flenn his wallet. "Sorry gentlemen, can't be too careful." With that, he was gone.

"Matteson," the blonde man said, "what in God's name are you doing here; we have this!"

Zack looked at Flenn. "Scott Flenn… meet Rip Van Winkle."

Flenn held out his hand, "A code name, I take it?"

"Not at all," the man said with a huff, "and that was a long time ago, Matteson."

Zack shrugged. "I don't know, I think the name still suits you. After all, MI-6 was asleep on that one; the CIA was the one who found the guy."

"The CIA couldn't find their way out of my cat's litter box! You haven't answered my question."

"We're here for the same reason you are," said Zack. "This is my former partner. He's a priest now, for real."

Thanks, Zack!

"We both knew the bishop who was offed. This is the man who recognized the poison."

The British agent studied Flenn. "Oh, you're *that* chap! Now it makes sense. We were wondering about that."

"While you're wondering," Zack said, "could you see to it that he doesn't get any attention from the press?"

"Yes, I see what you mean." He looked Flenn up and down. "Wouldn't want to blow your cover, as you Americans say."

Flenn objected. "It is not a cover; I really am a priest."

"Yes, yes, I'm sure you are." The man turned back to Zack. "Anything *you'd* care to share?"

Zack pointed up toward the cameras. "Check the video feed between noon and 2 p.m. today. You may find your culprit. That's likely when the cornsack was poisoned."

"*Cruet*," sighed Flenn.

"Yeah… *cruet*. There's a half gallon of wine in the sanctuary… "

"Sacristy!"

"Whatever. Oh, and there's a lump of clothes my friend here left by the sink in there when he washed up after trying to save Bishop Tammerlane. You might have those cleaned and pressed. I think they'd look good on you, Rip."

Flenn just closed his eyes and shook his head.

Zack pulled the yellow sticker off his jacket and stuck it onto his counterpart's tie. "Now that we've solved the case for you, we'll be off."

Zack grabbed Flenn by the arm and quickly led him down the center aisle toward the door. Without turning, Zack raised his hand and waved nonchalantly over his head and called, "Tootles!"

CHAPTER *TWENTY*

11 years earlier...

Flenn sat in the commissary drinking his third cup of coffee. He hadn't felt like talking to anyone. The embassy was relatively quiet this morning. A few staffers wandered in an out, but no one spoke to him. The attitude was that if the embassy staff didn't know you, then you were probably CIA, and thus they didn't *want* to know you.

Flenn and Zack had been here nearly a month. During that time, a dozen other agents, all assigned to different missions, had come and gone. None of them fraternized much; not only was it against policy to be seen together outside the embassy, but no other agent could stand to be around Zack Matteson for very long. Invariably Zack's caustic wit kept others at bay.

Flenn and Donna were the exceptions. Donna had claimed to see a precocious little boy underneath Zack's acerbic veneer. Flenn just saw a jackass... but he was a jackass that had saved his life too many times to count, and he was a jackass with a good heart—*You just had to dig deep sometimes to find it!*

At least Zack was the real deal. They had thought Col. Zamir was, too, but he had fooled them all. His ties to Al-

Qaeda were completely off the radar. It wasn't until MI-6 found a link to a Swiss bank account that Zamir's true motives were uncovered.

Money. Six million, to be exact. No doubt Al-Qaeda had been planning to use Zamir for many more years to come, but then Yasir Kamul had been captured. Kamul knew too much and had to be eliminated. Zamir had arranged for a man to slip the poison into the juice, and Kamul had readily taken it... thinking it to be the easiest way out. Kamul would have assumed that Zamir would have eventually found another way to kill him. So, taking the poison and defying the West of their prize was, for Kamul, a no-brainer.

No-brainer?... That's just it! Flenn thought as he sipped his coffee. *We've been convinced that this new group of radicals within Al-Qaeda are witless! They're sadistic, brutal and ruthless... but not stupid. This new movement didn't just come out of nowhere,* he told himself, *but the intelligence agencies had so far been unable to figure out who these people were, what they were calling themselves, and who was behind them.*

"So, here you are!" Zack Matteson sat down across from Flenn with a soda and a fresh bag of jellybeans. He offered the bag to Flenn, who refused. "Shirking work again?"

Flenn ignored the remark as he scratched the back of his head. "Let me ask you something; what would it take for you to kill innocent women and children? No, strike that, what it would it take for you to *torture* innocent women and children to death?"

"Good God, Flenn, you certainly know how to start a conversation!" Zack thought a moment, "I don't know, mental illness maybe."

Flenn nodded. "Yeah, if you're acting alone. But what if you're not alone? What if you're in a group of people doing the same thing?"

"You mean like a dog?"

Flenn raised his eyebrow. "Huh?"

Zack sorted through his bag, pushing aside the licorice jellybeans until he found a green one. "You know, a lone dog sees the cat next door and pays it no mind; but along come two other dogs and they all go chasing after it."

"No, this is more than just pack mentality," Flenn said. "What might motivate a person to abandon their humanity? It was money for Zamir, but what about the average convert to this group?"

Zack shrugged. "I don't know. Desperation?"

Flenn shook his head. "I think it's just the opposite."

Zack dropped a jellybean and reached down to retrieve it from the floor. "I don't follow."

"Hope!" Flenn said.

Zack popped the jellybean in his mouth. "You've lost me."

Flenn made a face. "You're disgusting."

Zack just grinned.

"Okay, let's say that for years you've been farming a dry patch of dust and sand. Along come some folks who say, 'Hey, we can turn everything around; not just for you, but for all righteous people. First, however, we have to show the others that we mean business.' Then they go on and tell that same sand farmer: 'God's tired of our cowardice, he wants us to put things right. It's time to take off the gloves.'"

Flenn sipped the last of his coffee.

"They find the most ruthless people out there, dress them as freedom fighters and then groom them as examples for the rest."

Zack nodded. "So, pack mentality *does* come into play?"

Flenn shrugged. "To a degree, but it is all done for a purpose. They believe, just like the suicide bomber, that they are serving a greater good, and that the ends justify the means."

"And Zamir?" Zack said.

"Zamir was no zealot, just greedy. Probably thought he'd keep providing information to this group for as long as they would pay him, then head to Brazil or some out of the way place where he'd live the life."

Zack stuffed his bag of candy in a jacket pocket and stood. "Well, now that you've got that all figured out, maybe we can get back to work trying to find Zamir."

Flenn stared at Zack. "Zamir isn't the problem here, Zack. It's the guy farming the patch of sand. I'm afraid we're at the beginning of something catastrophic."

CHAPTER *TWENTY-ONE*

Present day…

"There's our champion!" Bob raised his mug as Flenn entered the Bram and Bull. Flenn hadn't felt like fixing breakfast just for himself, and Zack had still been snoring when he left the flat.

Although Charlie wasn't with them, Bob, Murph and George were at the end of the bar sipping coffee. "Hi guys," Flenn said, somehow not surprised to see them here this early. "Where's Charlie?"

"He's with his Missus," said George. "He's the only one of us got one, you know."

Murph put down his cup and turned. "Wait a minute! I got a Missus."

Bob laughed, "Yeah, but she's not your own!"

Murph just smiled. "Well, I got somebody's Missus, 'at's all what counts. Least I'm not alone like you two buggers." He looked at the priest apologetically. "Sorry, Father. She's like me wife. Her husband left her years ago but never bothered to spring for a propa' divorce."

"You don't need to explain, Murph," George said. "The good Father here has pro'ly heard it all."

Flenn looked at the man tending bar. "Could I have some coffee, black, and a couple of fried eggs, please?"

"Better make 'em scrambled," Bob said, "Colin always breaks the yolks!"

"Now Father, dunna' listen to these dead willies," the barkeep said as he poured Flenn's coffee. "I'll just go and make you a proper English breakfast!" As soon as Colin disappeared into the back, Murph reached over the bar to snatch a bottle of Irish whiskey and pour a bit in each of their mugs. "Some for you, Father?" Flenn smiled, but declined. Murph put the bottle back exactly as he'd found it.

"So, you fight off the blokes from the Death Angel on Saturday then rush down to the cat'edrl to try 'an save the bishop! You're quite the lad!" George touted.

"Terrible thing, that," Bob said.

"Reminded me of me younger days," Murph offered, lifting his mug.

"How'd you guys know about me being at the cathedral?" Flenn asked.

"What? Ya' think we stay here *all* day?" said Murph.

Flenn smiled and took a sip of his coffee. "Yeah, I sort of did."

"Charlie and I were at the service," Bob reminded him. "It was a terrible thing."

"How come ya' knew it was p'isin?" asked Murph.

"Lucky guess," Flenn said.

Murph rolled his eyes. "Lucky guess, my arse! Come on, Father, how'd ya' know?"

"Before I was a priest, I worked with special forces in the military." He took a sip of coffee. "I've seen it before with ISIS."

"Good God, ISIS!" said George. "Scum o' the earth, that lot."

"Worse than scum," Murph said, then got up and excused himself to the loo.

Flenn raised an eyebrow.

Bob sighed. "You'll have to excuse him, Father. Murph's nephew was killed over there fightin' that bunch."

"And, here you go, Father," Colin said as he returned with a platter of sausages, fried eggs, blood pudding, two cooked tomatoes cut in half, fried mushrooms and a large bowl of baked beans."

"My Lord, there's enough here to feed an army!" Flenn exclaimed.

Colin laughed as he reached under the bar and brought up three extra plates along with some silverware. "You will be, Father, you will be."

As if on cue, Bob and George reached over and began scooping food onto their plates. "Thank you, Father, very generous of ya'!" George said.

Murph returned from the loo and his eyes grew large as soon as he saw the food. "Ah, took ya' long enough, Colin!" he said, reaching for a plate.

They all turned when they heard the door open. "I thought you might be over here," Zack said. He was wearing blue jeans and a long-sleeved oyster blue shirt. "Ah, breakfast, wonderful!"

Colin handed another plate to Zack. By the time they had all filled their plates there was nothing on the platter for Flenn. "See what I mean, Father?" said Colin. "Not to worry, there's more where that lot came from!" He wiped his hands on his apron and headed back into the kitchen with the empty platter.

Murph reached across for the bottle again. George went around the bar to refill everyone's cup with coffee and pour one for Zack. Murph looked up at Zack and winked. "Care for a growler?"

Zack held out his mug to Murph. "Don't mind if I do. Nice of you to buy breakfast for everyone, Flenn!"

Flenn sighed. "Yeah, isn't it..."

The door opened a second time. "Wotcha!"

Bob, Murph, and George responded in unison, "Wotcha, cocker, fancy a drink?"

Charlie rubbed his hands together. "Coffee, hot and black!" he said, letting the door close behind him. "I thought I saw you two Yanks come in here."

"Fancy a bit more?" Murph asked Zack. Zack held out his cup. "How about you, Bob, a bit more?"

Bob winked. "What is it the Americans say? Fill 'er up!"

Zack tugged on Flenn's arm and motioned toward the far corner. "Would you excuse us, gents?" The four men didn't seem to hear him, too busy joking and trading insults. "I can see why you like this place," Zack said. "Listen, I've gotten the preliminary report on the wine."

"Wow, that was fast," Flenn said. "Rip Van Winkle?"

Zack made a face. "Are you kidding? That guy's a toad. Thinks he's a lot more important than he is. You know, back in Libya... "

"Zack. The report?"

Zack took a sip of coffee. "It wasn't the wine."

"What? It had to be!"

Zack shook his head. "Nope. No trace of colocinium in any of the bottles."

"All that means is that it wasn't in those bottles," Flenn said. "It couldn't have been in the water, it would have stood out. Those were glass cruets. Someone must've discarded the wine bottle."

"Which means we have a rogue altar guild member on the loose!" Zack said.

"Not funny. No, someone came up to that cruet while it was on the credence table and poured the poison inside it." Flenn thought for a moment. "What about the video recording?"

"Nothing yet."

"Damn," muttered Flenn.

"Everything all right, Father?" Colin asked, bringing out another platter of food, even bigger than the first.

Flenn smiled and stood. "Absolutely." Murph reached over with his fork to spear a sausage but Colin moved the platter out of reach.

"No, the good Father here goes first this round," Colin said.

"After all, he's buyin'!" Zack added.

Flenn reached for his wallet. "Put your money away, Father," Charlie said. "This is on me. After what you did this weekend, Durham owes you."

"You're both wrong," Colin said. "This is on the 'ouse!"

"In that case," Zack said. "How about Father Flenn spring for some Irish whiskey for the coffee!"

"Now, why didn't I think of that," said Murph.

CHAPTER *TWENTY-TWO*

11 years earlier…

Flenn was getting a headache. He'd stayed out too late last night with Hoshi and desperately needed more coffee. He slid a photo across to Zack. "Satellite imagery from a month ago, just three days before we captured Kamul. It shows Kamul and some of his cronies outside a known Al-Qaeda camp in Pakistan."

Zack shrugged. "Yeah, so?"

"Look again," Flenn said. "See anybody you know?"

Zack picked up the photo and scanned the faces of people standing near Kamul. "No way!"

Flenn reached for the picture. "Looks like our assassin and Kamul knew each other."

"Which means that Kamul recognized the guy when he brought in the juice!"

"And probably knew exactly what was in it," Flenn added.

Zack leaned back in his chair. "I guess you were right about Zamir."

Flenn looked down at the picture of Kamul and the man who'd organized his assassination. "Whoever these people are, they didn't want him to talk."

"Kamul was willing to die to keep this organization a

secret. What about Zamir? You find anything on his whereabouts yet?"

"Nothing. It's like he disappeared from the planet." Flenn went for more coffee while Zack reached into a bagful of jellybeans as he studied the photograph. He offered the bag to Flenn as he sat back down.

"You know, one of these days your teeth are going to rot from eating those things."

Zack pointed to Flenn's steaming mug. "You have your addiction, I have mine. I could go back to smoking… "

"God no. I hated that smell!" Flenn said.

Zack leaned into his chair. "Speaking of addictions, I see you and Hoshi are certainly attached to each another."

Flenn glared across his coffee mug. "What's that supposed to mean?"

"Nothing." Zack grinned. "Just that you seem smitten."

Flenn swallowed, hoping the caffeine would soon make his head quit pounding. "Smitten? Really, Zack, where do you come up with these words?"

"Well, what would you rather me say… horny?"

"Shut up."

"Seriously, you guys are spending a lot of time together."

"So?"

"That's what I'm asking you. So…?"

Flenn looked away. "She's nice."

"Aw, come on, you gotta' give me more than that."

"What do you want, a play-by-play analysis of the relationship?"

"Just the juicy parts," said Zack.

"Get your mind out of the gutter!"

Zack leaned toward Flenn, lowering his voice. "Was I right?"

"About what?"

"You know," Zack said, "about the petite girls?"

"I won't even dignify that with an answer."

Zack grinned. "You just did!"

Flenn got up and stomped out of the room, taking his coffee with him. Zack reached for the satellite photograph. "Well, well," he said to the walls. "looks like Scott Flenn is finally falling in love."

CHAPTER *TWENTY-THREE*

Present day...

The funeral for Windsor was held on Thursday at Durham Cathedral with more than 1,000 in attendance. The ministry of health had declared the church safe for use much sooner than anyone had anticipated, but security was extremely tight nonetheless.

The Prince of Wales was in attendance, as was the Duchess. Bishops from Anglican communions across the world either sent representatives or came in person. The Presiding Bishop of the Episcopal Church, who'd caused quite a stir a few years back when he preached a rousing sermon at the wedding of one of the Royals, was also there, though he'd not been asked to speak this time. Instead, the immediate past bishop of the cathedral preached a sermon in which he called for prayers for a broken world.

Several members of parliament were present, including Elton Wainwright, who seemed to dote on Pamela, to the point Flenn could tell it was making her sons uncomfortable. Flenn also recognized Tobias Love, the oil magnate, in the crowd of mourners.

A delegation from Sinn Fein was present, all wearing white shirts with green neckties. None of them went up for communion, but neither did a lot of people, Flenn noticed. He had to admit feeling a bit apprehensive himself when the time came, but Flenn drank deeply from the cup anyway, as if to make a statement—if not to the congregation, then at least to himself.

Afterward, a private reception was set up in the cloister for dignitaries. Pamela had taken Flenn by the arm and personally escorted him to the group of archbishops, MP's, and members of Her Majesty's family. As she was re-introducing him to Elton Wainwright, the men in green ties tried to enter the cloister. Cathedral volunteers in purple robes politely explained that the reception was for invited guests of the family only.

"Damn them!" Pamela said, her eyes on fire. "They've no place here!"

"Now Pam," Wainwright said.

"They killed him! To hell with the Russians, the PIRA killed Windsor, and you know it!"

Several people looked at Pam. "I doubt that very seriously. Let me go speak with them," Wainwright said, and was off before she could respond.

"Pam?" Flenn tried to take her hand, but she turned and stomped off. Flenn considered following but decided against it; instead, he watched as Wainwright spoke at length with the Irishmen, shaking hands with each one, before heading back toward Flenn.

"Which way did Pamela go, Father?" Wainwright asked. Flenn wasn't wearing his collar today, and hadn't recalled being introduced as a priest the other night in the restaurant.

"I'm not really sure," Flenn answered. "What did she mean by, 'the PIRA killed Windsor?'" The Provisional Irish Republican Army was known to Flenn; their terrorist activities had been a cause for concern when he'd been in the CIA.

"That stuff is all in the past," the MP answered. "It's all politics now."

"Pam sure seems to think they are responsible," Flenn said.

"Evidently I wasn't the only bloke Windsor had it in for. Even with all our differences, the man loved England. He believed that the Northern Irish should be grateful to be a part of our country. Being from America, you probably wouldn't understand. The roots of the problems between England and Ireland go quite deep. Holding on to the North is still, for some, a way of thumbing our nose at the rest of Ireland."

Flenn raised an eyebrow. "I can't see Windsor thumbing his nose at anyone."

"Oh, he could, Father, he could."

"You mean at you?"

Wainwright chuckled. "Yes… and Sinn Fein."

"Then why are they here today?"

Wainwright shook his head. "Not my fight." He turned just as the Archbishop of Canterbury walked past. "Please excuse me," he said. "Your Grace, may I have a moment?" With that, the tall, good-looking MP was gone.

Flenn watched as the last of the Sinn Fein representatives turned and stared at the crowd. Flenn had seen the look before. It was one of utter disgust.

CHAPTER *TWENTY-FOUR*

11 years earlier...

Airports had never been one of Flenn's favorite places, and he especially disliked being at Charles De Gaulle today.

"You really didn't have to come see me off," Hoshi told him.

"Yes, I did." Flenn leaned over and kissed her. "I wish you could stay."

"You're not the only one with a career, you know," she said.

Flenn shrugged. "Donna's staying," he said, perhaps a bit too plaintively.

"Donna can work from her laptop. I can't."

"There must be other interpreters at the UN; how about talking one of them into letting you stay another week?" He realized now that he was whining.

This time, she reached up to initiate a kiss. "I must say, you make it tempting... " She pulled back. "But I gotta' go." She ran her hands down his jacket, straightening his lapel. "You're still coming to New York next month, right?"

He smiled. "I'll be there; made the hotel reservation last night."

"Well, cancel it," she said.

"What?"

She smiled. "You won't need a hotel. I told you, I have my own place."

Flenn blushed. "I didn't want to presume."

"And that's another thing I like about you."

A familiar voice called to them from across the terminal. Windsor and Pam made their way through the crowd of travelers. "I'm sorry," Windsor called, "traffic was horrendous!"

Hoshi turned to Pam. "I'm so happy for the two of you. Please, you must come see us in New York."

"Us?" Pam said looking puzzled.

"Me, I meant me," Hoshi said, flustered. Flenn thought he noticed her ears turning red. "I mean it Pam, I don't want to lose touch with you just because you've married this handsome fellow."

Windsor grinned.

"Only if you promise to come and visit us in London," Pam said. "Windsor has just taken a job as the education director at St. Paul's. He starts next week."

"Watch out there, Win," Flenn teased, "or they'll convince you to wear a priest's collar one day!"

Windsor's face lit up. "Who knows, maybe."

"Stop putting foolish notions into my husband's head," Pam said. "That's the last thing we need." She looked at Hoshi. "I'll miss you, Hosh."

Hoshi picked up her carry-on. "I'm going to miss you too," she said, a single tear falling down her cheek. Hoshi turned and headed for the gate, leaving the three of them standing together.

"Well, old man," Windsor said, "it looks as if you've made quite the impression."

Pam sighed. "Just be gentle with her, Flenn. She's still pretty vulnerable; her last boyfriend was worse than Donna's ex. That jerk really did a number on Hoshi. Lied to her constantly."

Flenn chewed his bottom lip.

Windsor stuck out his hand. "I pray that our paths will cross again someday."

Flenn shook the man's hand and gave Pam a quick hug. "They will. I'll look forward to seeing you at the wedding."

"Oh, that's right, the wedding," Windsor said.

"Yes," added Pam. "Scotland, here we all come, right?"

As Flenn walked out of the airport to catch a cab back to the office, he made a mental note to cancel his reservation at the Four Seasons.

CHAPTER *TWENTY-FIVE*

Present day…

"Not my fight?" Zack poured himself a Scotch and sat down at the table in Flenn's rented flat. "He actually said that?"

"Yep, that's what Wainwright said."

"Since when has the Irish situation not been of concern to a member of parliament? I mean, even with two decades of relative peace, the wounds still haven't healed."

Flenn shrugged. "I don't know; you're the one following him around."

Zack took a sip from his glass and made a face. "I wish you'd buy some bourbon."

Flenn ignored him. "Makes you wonder just what *is* his fight," he said.

"Mostly the oil companies," said Zack.

"Oil?"

"Well, one company in particular. English Petroleum. They are causing quite a stir these days. Found some deep reserves in Wales a few years back; now they want to build a pipeline across the north. The environmentalists are having a fit."

"Seems like I remember reading something about that; I figured it had all been settled."

Zack scoffed. "Hardly. They've just kept things quiet. Rumor is E.P. has gotten most of the votes to pass it through the Conservatives. Labour is the hold out, believe it or not."

"Why? I mean I can understand the Greens saying no, but Labour?"

"It's complicated," Zack said. "It's not like back home; the environment is everything over here. Whoever is going to be the next P.M. when it all hits the fan is going to get covered in it."

Flenn nodded. "And Wainwright is likely to be the next prime minister."

"Exactly."

Flenn got up to pour himself another Scotch. "What about Wainwright? Where does he stand on the pipeline?"

"Dead set against it. Not surprising, really. He won't get a second term if the thing is passed during his first."

Flenn sat down and raised his glass. "What a mess. Here's to politicians!" he toasted. "May they stay the hell away from us!"

CHAPTER *TWENTY-SIX*

11 years earlier…

The Statue of Liberty had been Flenn's favorite icon of America since he was a kid. He had begged his parents to take him to see it as a child, which they had finally done, but only once. As much as Flenn had traveled the world, it was rather unusual that this was only his second visit to New York City.

Standing on the tour boat with a cup of coffee in his hand and heading toward Lady Liberty, Flenn felt like a boy again. He remembered first learning about the statue in second grade. When the teacher had read the inscription written by Emma Lazarus, Flenn had felt himself drawn to those words. 'Give me your tired, your poor, your huddled masses yearning to breathe free, the wretched refuse of your teeming shore. Send these, the homeless, the tempest-tossed to me, I lift my lamp beside the golden door!'

The words still resonated as he walked with Hoshi around the perimeter. He pointed to the plaque and recited them from memory.

"Would that they were true," Hoshi said with a sigh.

Flenn looked down at her, "What do you mean? They *are* true."

"Maybe in theory, but not in practice," she said.

He held her hand as they walked to the water's edge. "I can't believe you are saying that! Weren't you the one who told me that your great-grandparents came here in the '20's? America is made up of generations of people from all over the world."

"True, but it is also made up of people who have forgotten that." Hoshi sipped her lemonade. "My great-grandparents came here seeking a better life, and they found one in Seattle. But their children, my grandparents, were taken during World War II to a concentration camp, simply because they were of Japanese descent. They lost everything."

Flenn looked up at the statue. "Well, okay, but… "

Hoshi glared at him. "But, what?"

Flenn gestured for them to sit on a nearby bench. "It was a time of war; people were scared."

"My grandparents were scared! So were a bunch of other people at that camp."

Flenn was flustered, "Okay, I agree, it was an overreaction. But we've learned from that." He regretted the words as soon as he'd said them.

"Oh? What was the first thing people did after 9/11? They blamed their Muslim neighbors. Muslims were harassed, beaten even. People suggested that they lock them all up in camps."

"Okay, I never heard *that*," Flenn said, defensively.

"You never heard it because you were probably in Zurich or Paris or somewhere selling Daddy's wares to global corporations. You weren't here to see all the Islamophobia that went on."

"*Islamophobia*? You made that up."

"God, Scott, I thought I knew you. There's no way you're that clueless!"

Flenn could almost feel the quicksand rising around his neck. "I'm not clueless! I've spent a lot of time in the Middle East. Trust me, there is plenty of hatred to go around. America is seen as the great Satan over there."

"Oh? I thought that was Russia. Isn't that what President Regan said about the Soviet Union."

"Trust me, Regan was right," Flenn said.

"Oh my God, you do have your head in the sand!" Hoshi said.

Flenn bristled. "I do not!"

"Yes, you do." She held out her hand. "Give me your wallet?"

"Why?"

"I want to look inside it," she said.

"For what?" He reached into his back pocket.

"Your membership card to the John Birch Society."

Flenn put the wallet back. "Ha, ha, very funny. Only if you show me your membership card to the ACLU," he quipped.

Surprisingly, Hoshi reached into her purse, pulled out her wallet and presented him with a small white card.

"You're kidding!" He looked down at the American Civil Liberties Card. "Nope, you're not." He shook his head. "My girlfriend is a flaming liberal."

"And my boyfriend is a Neanderthal."

They stared at each other until they both busted out laughing. "Guess it's true," Hoshi said.

"What?"

"That opposites attract."

Flenn kissed her. "You're a liberal, I'm not."

She kissed him back, "You're tall, I'm short."

He drew her closer, "You're 12, and I'm an adult…
"Ow!"

CHAPTER *TWENTY-SEVEN*

11 years earlier…

"You're not buying it, are you?" Hoshi pretended to look hurt.

Flenn raised an eyebrow as he gazed at her reflection in the Madison Avenue flower shop window. "No, I don't buy it for a minute. You did not just now see this shop; you spotted it earlier from the restaurant."

Hoshi smiled up at him. "Just one rose, a yellow one. I like them the best." She nuzzled up to him. "Plus, it will look nice beside our bed." Flenn blushed as he reached for his wallet and walked inside.

They strolled down the street toward the hotel with Hoshi holding her yellow rose close with one hand, and Flenn closer with the other. "I still like that I can do that to you."

"What?" he asked.

"Make you blush."

"I don't blush," he said.

"Oh, yes you do! Why do you do that, anyway?"

Flenn looked away. "I don't know. I guess I'm just not used to talking about… *it*."

She laughed. "*It*, as you so romantically put it, is a normal, natural part of life."

"I know, but… "

"But what?"

"I was just born a couple of generations too late, I suppose. I think there should be mystery and romance... "

Hoshi stopped. "Look around you, Scott. There's plenty of romance right here. New York City at twilight—flowers, couples holding hands, a full moon peeking through the clouds… "

He pulled her closer. "You're right. It's just that I don't want people to think that we're shacking up for the week."

Hoshi tickled his side. "Well, we sort of are."

He looked down at the sidewalk. "No, it's more than that." He turned toward her. "A lot more."

Flenn had been struggling all week with how to tell her and when, but he couldn't hold back any longer. "It's why I wanted us to stay at the Four Seasons instead of your place tonight. My mom and dad always said it was the most romantic hotel they'd ever seen."

"And it's great; a lot nicer than my apartment." she said.

"I picked it because I wanted us to have some place romantic before I head back, and I wanted it to be perfect." He sighed. "But I guess there is no such thing as perfect." Flenn looked into her soft, brown eyes and took a deep breath. "I love you."

Hoshi buried her head in his chest, but didn't say a word. He thought he was prepared to just tell her and let the chips fall where they may, whether she felt the same way or not; but now, here, in the middle of New York at twilight, her silence was deafening. He sighed. "It's okay," he said. "I mean I don't expect you… What I'm trying to say… "

"*Shh!*" She nuzzled her face into his chest, then stepped back, silently gazing up at him, her eyes dancing. A single tear ran down her cheek. She wiped it away and smiled.

"I love you, too."

CHAPTER *TWENTY-EIGHT*

Present day...

Flenn rounded the corner and started up the hill to his flat for a bite of lunch. He'd spent the morning jogging and then gone to the cathedral, poking around, trying to come up with some answers. Zack had driven to Lincoln to follow Elton Wainwright. He'd left his number in case Flenn heard any more about the poisoning.

The murder had been splashed over the news all week long, with various pundits and politicians pointing a finger at Russia. *Zack was right; blaming the Russians made no sense. There was no reason for Moscow to interfere, unless Windsor hadn't been the target after all. The archbishop, perhaps?* Yet Flenn couldn't come up with a single reason for the Archbishop of Canterbury to have been the intended target. And no one else would have had access to the chalice; whoever drank from it first would succumb to the poison and warn others.

This had not been meant for the crowd, but for one specific person. Who else could it have been other than Windsor?

Flenn had gone to the cathedral in search of a service leaflet listing all the participants in the ordination. He'd found a copy stuck behind a prayer book in one of the pews. He planned on going back and researching each name on the internet. Colocinium kills quickly. An assassin would have known that; he clearly hadn't been going for mass casualties.

Flenn smelled coffee and stopped in front of the fish and chips shop on Neville Street. *The assassin wasn't just trying to commit murder, he was trying to make a statement! But what, and to whom?*

"There he is!"

Flenn turned to see Bob and Murph coming out of the chip shop. "Fancy a bit o' lunch, Father?" Murph said.

"Hi guys; no, just a coffee before heading back to my place for something light."

"And then a good lie down?" Murph asked. A nap was the furthest thing from Flenn's mind.

"Will you be at the pub later?" Bob asked. "Charlie's having a bit of a procedure this afternoon, so he won't be there, but we will."

"Hope he's okay," Flenn said sincerely.

Murph shook his head. "Cancer, though you'll never 'ear 'im blart on about it."

Bob shook his head and lowered his voice. "He's dyin', Father. Docs give him six months, a year tops." Flenn was surprised, and saddened, to hear the news; he'd grown fond of all the fellows at the pub.

"Aye," Murph said. "He's a class act, that one. Why ol' Charlie wants to hang out with us three gaffers is beyond me."

"But we're glad for it," Bob added.

Murph nodded. "Aye."

"So, see ya' later, Father?" Bob asked, trying to lighten the moment.

Flenn shrugged. "I don't know. If not, I'll catch up with you tomorrow." They shook hands and Bob and Murph headed down the hill and around the corner. Depressed to hear the news about Charlie, Flenn decided to make his own lunch and made his wayup to his flat, where he made himself a cheese and onion sandwich and turned on his laptop. He typed in a few commands and found an interactive map of Durham Cathedral. As he ate, he went over every entrance, doorway, and stairwell on the map. *The killer had to have been seen by someone. Zack said reports showed no sign of poison in the wine from the sacristy. If the wine hadn't already been tainted in the bottle, then the assassin walked up to the credence table and somehow, with dozens of people getting ready for the service, had managed to pour the colocinium inside the cruet. The cameras had to have caught the killer on video!*

Flenn thought of calling Zack to see if he'd heard anything more, but figured that he'd be the first one Zack would contact when he had news.

There was a knock at the door. "Coming," he called. He looked through the peephole. *What's he doing here?*

He opened the door and the man Zack had dubbed 'Rip Van Winkle' entered the flat. "Can I help you?" Flenn said.

The man walked past him and sat down. "We need to talk."

CHAPTER *TWENTY-NINE*

11 years earlier...

"We need to talk." Flenn's gut tightened at the words; he nearly spilled his coffee on the phone. Their week together in New York had been intense. Things were moving along rapidly. *Maybe that had scared her; maybe things were going too fast.*

"What's wrong, Hosh?"

"Nothing's wrong," she said cheerily. "Why do you think something's the matter?"

"Because," he said, "when a woman says, 'we need to talk,' it usually means she's breaking up with you."

"Are you kidding? No way, mister. You're not getting rid of me that easily."

"Thank God," he said... and he meant it. He was 36 years old, but had never felt this way about anyone before. And now, here he was about to head into Syria on another undercover mission to see what he and Zack could find out about this new Al-Qaeda group, and all he wanted to do was fly back to New York to be with Hoshi.

"So, what is this thing we need to talk about?"

"The ambassador's wife is ill and he's heading back to Japan, so I've suddenly got two weeks off, and plane fares to Istanbul aren't that bad right now... "

"Seriously? That's great news!" Flenn said. "I mean, not about the ambassador's wife, but, really, you can come?"

"Well, your job doesn't seem to let you come back to the States very much, so I just thought… . Of course, if you'd rather not see me… "

"How soon can you get here?" Flenn asked, excitedly.

"Day after tomorrow soon enough?"

Flenn found it hard to concentrate the rest of the day. *He was supposed to fly out tomorrow to meet with Davy Spate and coordinate some last-minute details, but he'd just have to talk Zack into doing it for him.*

This job wouldn't be nearly as complicated as the last one. He and Zack would be posing as arms dealers to one of the men they'd managed to identify from the photographs with Yasir Kamul. Once they'd lured him in, Davy would swoop in with a team to capture the man. *This time there would be no servants delivering poisoned pomegranate juice!*

At some point, he'd have to figure out how to tell Hoshi about what he really did for a living. So far, he'd let her believe that he worked for his father, managing overseas interests for Flenn Industries. He'd even let her continue calling him Scott, though he'd never really liked the name. His father had been called "Flenn" as far back as he could remember, and he'd always admired his dad. David Flenn was the only other member of his family who knew the truth about what he did for a living. His mom would have worried herself to death; she very nearly had when he'd been in the Air Force. *And, didn't she already have enough to worry about with her cancer just barely in remission? Maybe it was time to tell his parents about Hoshi*, he thought. *Maybe then his mom would quit asking him if he was gay!*

Flenn couldn't remember ever feeling this way about anyone. There had been a girl in high school he'd had feelings for, and a couple of romances in college, but he had been all business since entering the CIA, and seldom dated. Zack, however, had more than made up for Flenn's deficiency in the romance department.

Donna was about to put an end to all that.

Flenn was happy for them. Zack had been starry-eyed since he'd first met Donna. Flenn had teased him about the age difference, but here he was dating someone the same age, who looked even younger. Flenn had noticed people staring at them on the streets of New York whenever they ventured out to see a Broadway play or go out to eat. Granted, there hadn't been much of that during his visit. They'd chosen to stay in most of the time.

Flenn felt himself blush. He was doing that a lot lately. *He'd have to get over that, and soon. It wouldn't do to have a blushing arms dealer negotiating with a Syrian warlord!* Still, Flenn found his thoughts working their way back to that apartment and to Hoshi's small, but agile body. *Very agile!* he thought, then blushed again.

CHAPTER *THIRTY*

Present day...

Flenn stared at the tall, dark-haired British intelligence agent who had just seated himself at his kitchen table without an invitation. "Just what is it that you and I have to talk about?"

"I did some checking," said the man Zack called Rip Van Winkle. "Seems like you're the real deal after all. A priest from Alabama, friend of the Tammerlanes, here for the ordination. Your experience in Iraq explains how you knew about the colocinium."

"Okay, so again, why are *you* here?"

"Where's Matteson?"

"I have no idea," Flenn said.

"Do you know if he went to Lincoln?" It was more of an accusation than a question.

"Zack isn't in the habit of telling me his business. In fact, he never told me your real name, just your code name."

"It isn't a code name. Did Matteson tell you why he was in Durham?"

Flenn shook his head. "You know how you guys are. Look, I'm no longer in the business, so I really don't know what it is you're after."

The man leaned forward. "Why is Matteson tailing Elton Wainwright?"

Flenn was annoyed. "Clearly, that is a question better asked of Zack." Flenn stood up. "Now, if you'll excuse me."

The agent didn't budge. "Why were you at the cathedral this morning?"

"Like you said, I'm the real deal. Priests and churches, they kind of go together... you know, like bangers and mash, fish and chips... "

The man finally stood. "Things aren't like the old days; the CIA and MI-6 aren't on the best of terms lately, thanks to you Americans."

"Hey, don't blame me for that debacle; not my circus anymore."

"We're still a bit touchy about the CIA sending agents," he said, looking directly into Flenn's eyes, "or former agents, snooping into our business." He headed toward the front door. "I am genuinely sorry about your friend. But this is *our* affair. We'll take care of it without any assistance from overseas."

"Be sure that you do," Flenn said.

"Good day to you, sir. I'll be around."

"Thanks for the warning." Flenn slammed the door before the man could reply.

What the hell was that all about?

Flenn finished his sandwich and thought about the odd conversation. Finally, he grabbed his keys and made his way down the hill to hail a taxi to the train station. *It was time to find out more about this Rip Van Winkle.*

****

The Cope and Mitre wasn't one of York's busiest pubs, which was why Davy had suggested meeting there. Flenn had called him earlier in the afternoon from a red telephone kiosk at the train station.

"Rip Van Winkle, that jackass?" Davy sipped at his ale. "Sure, I knew him. Name's Beamish, Bernard Beamish."

Flenn nodded. "I can see why they'd change his name."

Davy grinned. "Interesting story how he got it… "

"Another time, Davy. What can you tell me about him?"

"He's a tosser, that one. No people skills, what-soever." Davy finished his ale and ordered another pint. "He's a decent enough agent, though, I'll give him that, especially where the Russians are involved. From what I hear, he helped solve that thing down in Salisbury a couple years back. If he's in Durham, they must think it's the Russians again."

Flenn reached for his Scotch. "Not what Zack thinks. Frankly, I can't figure out why anyone would want to kill Windsor Tammerlane."

"Well, it'd have to be a major player," Davy said. "Not just any bloke can get their hands on that stuff. They'd have to have a major lab and experts to handle it." The waitress brought them both a plate of steak and kidney pie, then went off to fetch Flenn a second drink.

"Zack didn't seem to think it would be all that hard to get, but you knew more about that stuff back then than we did. How many people would you need to make it?"

"Well, not so sure about how many. I suppose one chemist could do the job, if he knew what he was doing. It's not something you could whip up in the kitchen sink, though. It would take some really fancy equipment, even by today's standards."

"Would there be traces?"

"Sure, if they were sloppy. The stuff can only be made into a liquid or a paste, and only in small amounts."

"A paste?"

"Yeah, but that day in Iran it was a liquid in the juice to hide the color. Stuff has no taste, no odor, but it doesn't last as long."

Flenn thanked the waitress for bringing another single-malt. "This Beamish fellow, you think he knows anything about colocinium?"

"I'm sure he does, though nobody's used it in years. Anyway, he's a real tool, I'd stay out of his way if I were you."

Flenn adjusted his napkin. "May not be possible. He wants to know why Zack's in town."

"Matteson? Here in York?"

Flenn shook his head. "Durham, well, all over, I guess; he has some other investigation going on. Just happened to be in Durham when all this went down."

Davy gave a low whistle. "That's not good."

Flenn raised an eyebrow.

"Goes back to how Beamish got his code name," Davy explained. "He and Matteson were working the same side of the fence on a thing at the Brussels airport awhile back. It was a horserace to see who'd make it to the terrorist's apartment first, the CIA or us."

"I seem to remember Zack boasting he and his team caught that guy."

"Yeah, that's just it," Davy said. "Beamish was all set up to take the bloke, you see, but Matteson slipped some knock-out drops into his coffee that morning. They found Beamish slumped over a bench at Bruxelles Central, and the CIA got all the credit.

Flenn chuckled. "Yeah, that sounds like Zack."

Their food arrived and Davy ate hungrily. "Oh, I almost forgot," he said halfway through the meal. "I did run upon someone else you know just yesterday."

"Oh, yeah?"

"The kid who tried to rob you up on the wall last week. He's working at the Minster! I saw him pushing a broom on the steps before the place opened."

Flenn winked. "You just coming home at that hour, were you?"

"You remember that bird from the pub the other night?"

Flenn's mouth fell open. "No way!"

"You know me, I hate to kiss and tell; but, as I was coming home, there the bugger was. I stopped and talked to the kid. Not such a bad chap—told me he was looking out for his sister who is due any day." Davy smiled. "It was a good thing you did, Flenn."

"Well, at least something good has happened since I arrived."

CHAPTER *THIRTY-ONE*

11 years earlier…

Omar Rashad was anxious to complete the deal; so much so he'd come out of hiding to meet with the two Dutch gun dealers at their hotel. Rashad had brought along a security detail, two of whom were standing behind him.

"I need stingers, six of them," Rashad told the tall man, who raised a single eyebrow, "and I need them right away!"

"Mr. Rashad, as we told you, surface to air missiles are expensive. They are also very hard to come by."

"I do not care how expensive they are," Rashad said loudly. "I need them by the end of the month!"

The two white men leaned closely together and spoke quietly with one another. The shorter of the two men nodded, then looked back at Rashad. "They are three million dollars."

Rashad smiled. "Not a problem."

"Each."

The Syrian's eyes narrowed. "Do not take me for a fool, Hans. I can take my business elsewhere!"

The man he'd called Hans leaned back in his chair. "But you cannot, or you would be elsewhere. We only have three available; I will have to arrange to steal the other three from the Ugandans… which is why they are so expensive. We will lose men in that raid." Zack never seemed to have trouble making up fanciful stories, although he *was* having some trouble maintaining a Dutch accent.

Rashad hadn't noticed. "I do not care about your men. I will give you one million for each Stinger."

This time the tall man with sandy brown hair spoke. "You may not care about our men, but we do. I'm sure, as a great leader, you know the value of troops who will give their lives for you. We stand to lose much if our Ugandan raid goes badly."

Rashad thought about what the tall man had said. His backers had deep pockets and they had instructed him to come back with the launchers, no matter the cost.

"However," the tall man said, "there may be room for negotiation. If you will allow my associate and me to step outside the room for a moment to discuss this?"

Rashad couldn't hide the gleam in his eyes at the prospect of not only going home with six surface-to-air missiles, but also having out-negotiated these infidels. "Of course," he said with a wave toward the door. "Just do not keep me waiting long; I am a busy man."

"As are we Mr. Rashad, as are we." Flenn and Zack stepped into the hallway and watched as a team of eight heavily armed MI-6 agents quietly hurried down the hall. Davy Spate was in the lead. They had been watching the 'negotiations' from a nearby room.

"They're all yours, gentlemen. Have fun!" Flenn said as he and Zack moved out of the way, lest a stray bullet pierce the wall. They needn't have worried. Rashad and his men were taken completely by surprise, just as Rashad's two other men downstairs had been.

After disarming the Syrians, Davy came out into the hallway. "Thanks, chaps! Maybe this one will turn out to be the prize for us."

"Just don't let him near any pomegranate juice this time," Zack said, pulling a small bag of jellybeans out of his pocket.

"Security's tight on this one;" Davy responded, "tighter than I've seen in years. I don't suppose the CIA is any closer to figuring out who these blokes are?"

Flenn shrugged, "Unfortunately, no closer than you guys."

"You know that we share all our intel with you," Zack added.

"Yeah right," Davy said as the Syrians were led into the hallway, hands bound behind their backs and mouths taped. Rashad glared angrily at Flenn.

"Just remember," Flenn called out as the Brits headed toward the stairwell with their prisoners, "you promised us a seat at the interrogation."

"Complete with popcorn!" Davy called back.

The mention of popcorn made Flenn think of Hoshi. She was back in New York now. The ambassador's wife had improved a few days later and he had returned to the U.N. early. *Just as well*, he told himself, since the meeting with Rashad had finished up quicker than he had thought. *Still, the three days... and especially the nights... with Hoshi had been incredible. After the interrogation, he and*

Zack were both due some R and R. They could fly to the States to surprise the girls.

"Are you okay?" Zack asked as they headed for the elevator.

"Yeah, why do you ask?" Flenn said.

"Cause you're blushing."

CHAPTER *THIRTY-TWO*

11 years earlier…

"I wish you didn't have to go." Hoshi watched as Flenn gave the taxi driver his suitcase. "Seems like you just got here."

"I did," Flenn said, "but four days was all Zack and I could arrange. Flenn reached out to hold her. "I'll call as soon as I land."

"Don't you dare, I'll be asleep!"

Flenn smiled. "What, I'm not worth waking up for?"

Hoshi reached up and whispered, "You were this morning." Flenn blushed.

"I promise, I'll get back to New York first chance I get."

"Great; then maybe we'll have time to go back to the Statue of Liberty next time."

"And get into another fight like last time?"

"Yep," she said, hugging him goodbye. "And then have fun making up again."

Flenn climbed into the taxi and headed for JFK. His flight was in two hours, just not to Paris as he had told Hoshi, but to Cairo where he was going to connect with Zack. A joint mission with the Mukhabarat, the Egyptian intelligence forces, had been slated for two days from today. It was rumored Zamir had finally been found hiding in the Sinai. Flenn had been slipped the coordinates last night by an agent at a flower stand where he had bought Hoshi a yellow rose. The coordinates for the Al-Qaeda camp had been written on the receipt, which Flenn had slipped into his pocket.

From what he'd been told, the last time the coordinates had been called in to the Mukhabarat someone had warned the insurgents before the strike. This way, there would be no intermediaries. Flenn and Zack wouldn't give the Egyptians the coordinates until the day of the raid. Flenn sighed. *There would be casualties on this one*. An air strike had not been an option, at least according to those who made such decisions. This would be entirely a ground offensive. The intelligence communities wanted Zamir. There was still so much to find out about this new group, and Zamir's capture was top priority. Ordinarily, Flenn didn't worry about dangerous missions. He'd always figured that when his number came up, there'd be nothing he could do about it. He imagined that somewhere out there was a bullet that would one day find him. *At least, he hoped it would be a bullet, not something sharp and slow.*

But now, Flenn had something more to live for, something he had never had before. Something soft and warm, kind and compassionate, smart and sexy. Someone who was as beautiful on the inside as she was on the outside.

Now he had Hoshi.

At some point he would need to tell her about what he really did for a living. He'd have to clear it first with his superiors, even though Zack hadn't before telling Donna. But that was the way Zack often did things. Zack didn't like answering to anyone. The CIA gave agents permission to tell their future spouses only after they had been thoroughly vetted. Knowing Zack Matteson, he probably hadn't even told their boss back at Langley about the upcoming wedding.

Flenn boarded the plane, but not before calling Hoshi once more.

"I love you," she had said right before hanging up. "Be careful."

Easier said than done, he thought.

CHAPTER *THIRTY-THREE*

Present day…

Flenn arrived at his flat in Durham on the noon train after spending the night in York. That morning, he'd gone by to see the Minster to thank Dean Jackson for hiring Edgar, the kid who was trying to help his pregnant sister.

It was just beginning to rain as he made his way up Neville Street. Flenn hadn't jogged this morning, so he'd decided to walk from the station for the exercise; he increased his pace to make it to the flat before the rain intensified. From the toothpick on the floor, he knew immediately that someone had been in the flat while he was gone. It was an old trick: Leave a toothpick on top of the door so that it will fall to the ground if the door is opened. He'd starting put it up there after the fight between the pubs, just in case the big guy still held a grudge.

"Hello?" he called, thinking that Zack Matteson might answer back.

Nothing.

"Hello?" he said again. He flipped the light switch and went downstairs. The cushions were askew. He lifted one but didn't see anything. He climbed the stairs to the bedrooms. If he hadn't been so meticulous about how he made his bed in the morning he might not have noticed that it had been re-made.

He went downstairs and looked through the kitchen cabinets and ran his finger across the top of the counter, then underneath the fireplace mantle. He finally found what he was looking for on top of the lamp. The filial had been replaced with a tiny video camera.

"Ah, there you are!" Flenn said into the device. "Well, well, Mr. Beamish, I presume. I'm not sure just what you are expecting to find here except a naked priest fixing coffee in the morning, but if that is what turns you on, no sense in waiting until tomorrow!" Flenn proceeded to remove his clothes and to make a pot of coffee. He pulled out one of the shorter ostrich feathers from the cannister by the fireplace and placed it behind his ear. He then positioned a chair directly in front of the eavesdropping device and slowly sipped not one, but two mugs of black coffee. "Well, I suppose you've seen enough," he said at last, "and I'm certainly wide awake now." He winked at the camera. Good day, Bernard."

Flenn stood up, unscrewed the camera, went outside on the verandah and tossed the device over the wall.

"Um, Flenn?"

Zack was standing just inside the front door, his eyes open wide, as was the door. "Is this some new Episcopalian ritual?"

Flenn snatched the feather off his head and grabbed his underwear and trousers. "Just a little show for your friend, Beamish."

"Ahh… huh?"

"He came by yesterday and must have returned when I went to York to ask Davy Spate about him. He bugged the flat."

"Beamish came here?"

"Wanting to know why you were in town."

Zack plopped down in a kitchen chair while Flenn finished getting dressed. "He knows why I'm in town."

"I'm just telling you what the man said." Flenn pulled the polo shirt over his head.

"He knows we're checking out the candidates for prime minister. They do the same with our presidential candidates."

"Then why is he asking about you?"

Zack looked toward the refrigerator. "Got anything to eat?"

"Zack?"

"Okay." He sighed. "He probably just wants to know if I've figured out who Wainwright is sleeping with. They like to keep that stuff under the radar over here whenever possible."

"What? Have you ever read *The Sun*? There are more scandals in that paper every day than… "

"I know, I know. That's exactly what they're trying to prevent. I think MI-6 likes this guy. Like I told you, except for chasing skirts Wainwright's probably the best choice they have coming up."

"Chasing skirts? Since when did you get all Phillip Marlow? And, what's with British intelligence trying to shape the election?"

Zack rolled his eyes. "As if *we* never did that."

"Not in our own country."

"Okay, I give you that much."

Flenn raised an eyebrow. "So, do you know who the mystery woman is?"

"Look, I've said too much already. Just let it go for now."

"Must be quite a lady."

"Just drop it," Zack said

"Sure, whatever. So, how come you're back in town?"

Zack checked his watch. "I told you, I go where Wainwright goes, and he's back in Durham. Looks like he'll be staying for a few days."

"Let me guess, you need a place to sleep?"

"Nope, got one."

Flenn cocked his head. "Oh? Where are you staying?"

"Here."

Flenn rolled his eyes. "Okay, just check the bed upstairs for bugs, and I don't mean bedbugs. I have no idea how many of those things Rip Van Winkle left lying around."

"He's British, they don't think about the bedroom," Zack said, then added: "I wasn't kidding about food; you got anything?"

Flenn shook his head. "Nothing quick. I finished off the cheese for lunch. Wanna go over to the Bram and Bull?"

"You buying?"

Flenn frowned. "Don't I always?"

CHAPTER *THIRTY-FOUR*

11 years earlier...

"My God, Scott, what happened?" Flenn had tried to hide his bandaged left arm from the computer camera but had forgotten about the mirror directly behind him. Hoshi had noticed his arm right away.

"It's nothing. The doctor says I'll be fine." That was the truth. "I slipped on some oil and fell on a piece of rebar sticking out of the ground." That was the lie.

Hoshi's forehead furrowed, "Oh, poor baby. Does it hurt much?"

It did. Fortunately, the bullet had gone clean through. Zack had pushed him out of the way as soon as the guard had seen them coming. The Mukhabarat had taken several casualties, as had the terrorists. In all, 12 people had been killed and several more injured, including Flenn. *Alas, Zamir had not been in the camp.*

The injury had prevented Flenn from attending the intelligence briefing, but Zack said that the Mukhabarat had already found out plenty from their prisoners.

"Udon!"

Flenn raised an eyebrow. "What?"

"Udon," Hoshi repeated. "Eat plenty of Udon soup.

177

It's good for what ails you; at least that's what my grandmother always said. "My mom calls it Japanese penicillin."

"I'll remember that," Flenn said.

"I wish I could come nurse you back to health," she said, sweetly.

Flenn smiled. "You'd look cute in a nurse's uniform," he said, and immediately blushed.

"Just don't go playing doctor with anyone else but me, mister."

"Oh yeah, what are you going to do about it?" he teased.

"I may be thousands of miles away, but did I ever tell you what my Aunt Yoko used to say?" Hoshi did her best Japanese accent, 'Dynamite come in small package!'"

Flenn laughed. "Well, your aunt was right. I've seen dynamite."

"You haven't seen anything," she said, "until you've seen me mad."

Flenn found it hard to picture. "I can't imagine it," he said.

She raised one eyebrow. "Believe me, mister, you don't want to!"

They talked for nearly an hour, until his laptop buzzed and he saw a private message coming in from Zack.

Flenn sighed. "Honey, I'm afraid I've got to go. See you in a couple of weeks?"

"I can't wait," she said. "I love you."

"And you know I love you," Flenn said.

"You'd better, or that hole in your arm won't be the only thing you have to worry about!"

Flenn smiled as the screen went dark.

CHAPTER *THIRTY-FIVE*

Present day...

Zack's eyes said it all. "Didn't I tell you, lad?" Murph said. "Colin's a good cook, but Valerie here makes the best steak and ale pie in the entire North of England!"

Zack nodded, "It is out of this world!"

Scott Flenn reached across the bar. "Here, let me try it."

Zack pulled the bowl out of Flenn's reach. "You eat your salad. Why anyone would order a salad in a pub is beyond me."

"Aye, plumb daft, if'n you ask me," Murph said.

"I have to admit, Father," Charlie said from his place in the corner, parked in front of an untouched pint. "A salad isn't likely to hold you over for very long."

Flenn smiled. "I'm a runner, Charlie; gotta' watch my girlish figure."

"You go right ahead, Father," Murph piped up, "I'm gonna' watch Valerie's!"

The woman laughed and went back to the kitchen. "Ah, Murph, aren't you sometin', now."

"Sorry, gents, but I gotta' 'ed off to the netty," Murph left his perch and headed to the back.

"This time, put wood int' 'ole," said George.

"Put wood in the hole?" asked Flenn.

"Means close the door," Charlie explained. "Murph tends to forget."

"Ach, would you look at 'im," said George. "Murph's not 'eadin' to the loo, 'e's off to chat up Val."

"Good luck, I say," said Bob, "course it never worked before."

"Cause she likes the looks of me instead," George offered.

Zack smiled. "Val's a looker, I'll say that. And one hell of a cook."

Flenn glanced down at his salad.

The door opened behind them and two men with dark hair and darker suits walked into the pub, looked around the room, then chose a table in the far corner.

"Now that's somethin' you don't see every day, do you George?" said Bob in a hushed tone.

Zack and Flenn stared at Rip Van Winkle and his associate. Zack gave a silly grin to his British counterparts. "How about it, Flenn? Want to go say hello to those gentlemen?"

"I'm fine right here," Flenn said, eyeing Zack's pie.

"Well, I think I'll just go let them know how welcome they are." Zack said, standing up. He picked up his pie and strolled over to the table.

"You know, Father, you can order one of those for yourself."

"Thanks, Bob. I will tomorrow, that is if I manage to get a good run in first."

Murph returned from the kitchen. "Who're the dandies," he asked, cozying back up to his pint.

"Friends of Zack's," Charlie explained. Flenn cocked his head. "Kind of obvious, Father," Charlie said.

"Look like dibble to me," said Murph. Flenn raised a questioning eyebrow. Murph explained. "Coppers, police. And from London too, the likes of 'em."

"What're the police doin' with 'ol Zack there, Father?"

"Not sure, Bob." Flenn said honestly. "Not sure I want to know, either." They all laughed.

When voices rose from across the room, George set down his beer. "Look there, mates. The suits are givin' the Father's friend down the banks!"

"Father, ya' want me to go over there and sort all this out?" asked George.

"No, Zack can take care of himself."

"Still, I don't fancy them," said Murph, "Come on lads, let's go sit near 'em and see what they're ramblin' on about." George got up and followed Murph, beer in hand.

"Be right along," Bob said. "Gotta' go to the netty; I'm bustin' about now."

Charlie grinned and shook his head. "They mean well, Father," he said, lifting his glass but barely touching it to his lips.

Flenn watched Murph and George pretend not to be listening to the conversation two tables over. "I know; they're good guys… all four of you are."

Charlie looked away.

Flenn took a breath. "So, Charlie, what's this I hear about you being sick?"

"Ach, the lads have been wagging their tongues, have they?" Charlie picked up his beer and gazed into the amber liquid as he swirled it slowly in the glass.

"Like you said, they mean well. Anything I can do?"

"Not unless you brought along a cure for stomach cancer." Charlie shook his head, then looked up and smiled. "Don't worry about me, Father. I'm an old man whose lived his life. Made some mistakes along the way, a couple of really big ones lately, but hoping the good Lord will understand when we say hello in a few months. Just hope it's not in passing on my way to somewhere else." He looked away. "It's the family, you know. Especially my granddaughter, she's quite fond of me. It'll be worse on her."

Before Flenn could respond, the two men in suits stood up and stormed out of the pub. Zack made his way over to the end of the bar with Murph and Charlie right behind him.

"What'd I miss?" asked Bob, coming from the back, still fumbling with his zipper.

"Only ol' Zack here givin' those doylems a proper dressing down!" Murph put his arm around Zack, looking like the manager of a prizefighter. "Don't know what ya' said chum, but I 'eard 'ow you said it." Murph was grinning from ear to ear. "Put them in their place, 'e did!"

"Everything okay?" Flenn asked Zack.

"Course 'tis," answered Murph. "Those beauts were givin' 'im down the banks, but Zack here let 'em both know this ain't gettin' the babby a frock and pinny!"

Flenn looked at Charlie. "Zack let them know they were wasting time," Charlie explained.

"Well, sounds like that deserves a fresh round on me," said Zack, distracting the lot from talking any more about it.

Flenn raised an eyebrow. "What? You're buying?"

"No more for me," said Charlie.

"How about a clean glass this time," said George, winking at Valerie.

"I'll have whatever George is having," Flenn said, glaring ruefully at his half-eaten salad, "along with a bowl of that steak and ale pie!"

****

Flenn reached above the door frame and found the toothpick he'd balance there still in place.

"The old methods are still the best, huh?" said Zack as he went to check the other toothpick above the patio door. "Doubtful Rip Van Winkle would have scaled the garden wall to get in the back door, but better safe than sorry," he said, confirming that the other toothpick was still in place.

"So," Flenn said, after starting the coffee and sitting down in the closest chair, "what was that all about?"

Zack kicked off his shoes and sprawled in the upholstered chair next to the fireplace. "Not much, really. Beamish is pissed about your little porno, I'll say that much."

Flenn grinned. "Served him right, bugging my flat. What'd I ever do to him?"

"Not you he's interested in."

"So, you want to tell me who the mystery woman is?" Flenn asked.

"Not particularly, no."

"I don't get it; why would MI-6 care about the exposure of an affair, even if it is the guy whose leading in the polls to be the next prime minister. This isn't the '60's with JFK chasing women everywhere and the press turning a blind eye. I don't think anybody cares anymore."

"Apparently, they do over here," Zack said.

Flenn looked through the small window onto the walled patio. "I guess people still like things nice and tidy, building walls around themselves so that they can only see what they want to see."

Ever ready to nettle his friend, Zack piped up. "Isn't that what you religious types do? Build walls so that things like science and facts don't bother you?"

Flenn knew Zack was trying to push buttons but took the question seriously. "Some do, fundamentalists in particular, but things like faith and science are not mutually exclusive. I think science and religion are at their best when they hold hands."

When the coffee was ready, Flenn poured them both a cup. "Milk's in the fridge," he told Zack.

"Aw, come on, I just got comfortable. How about you get it for me?"

Flenn opened the tiny refrigerator and added milk to Zack's mug. He started to hand it to him, then pulled it back. "First, who's Wainwright's mistress?"

Zack shook his head. "Trust me, you don't want to know."

"He's not fooling around with our President, is he?" After President Ripley resigned two years ago, and the subsequent resignation of the Vice President, Speaker of the House Diane Claxton had been forced to step up to the top spot. She clearly wasn't comfortable with the position, and after being diagnosed with cancer she had refused to run in the upcoming election.

"President Claxton is set for a nervous breakdown, not an affair," Zack said. "Now give me that."

Flenn handed him the mug. "So, what did Rip Van Winkle want with you? He didn't seem too happy when he left the pub."

"That's because I told him to go…, " he looked at Flenn, "Never mind."

Flenn leaned back on the counter and stared at his friend. "What are you not telling me, Zack?"

Zack smiled. "Plenty."

"What is it with you? Usually, you want my help."

Zack shook his head. "Not this time. Trust me, you don't want anything to do with this."

"I'm more interested in getting to the bottom of who poisoned Windsor. Any word from your contacts about the video feed at the cathedral?"

"Not yet," Zack said. "I don't suppose you found out anything from Spate when you were in York? He was the one who carried that whole Yasir Kamul investigation to its end. One of the first times either the Brits or the CIA had heard of colocinium or ISIS, you know."

Flenn topped off his coffee and sat back down at the kitchen table. "As a matter of fact, I did find out something. Davy said colocinium doesn't last but a few minutes in liquid form, so it couldn't have been in the chalice very long. Since it deteriorates so quickly, it couldn't have been intended to kill a massive amount of people. Just Windsor, apparently."

Zack sat up. "Wait a minute, what did you say?"

Flenn began repeating himself. "Since it acts so quickly, I don't think… "

"No, before that."

"What? That colocinium doesn't last in liquid form?"

Zack sat straight up in the chair. "Yeah, that. What other form does it come in?"

Flenn wasn't sure why the interest. "Davy said it can be made into a sticky paste. Why, is that important?"

Zack stood up. "Is there a library around here?"

"Are you kidding? This is Durham. It's a college town; of course, there's a library."

Zack set his coffee mug on the table. "Which way is the university?"

"Why?"

"I'll tell you later. Which way to the university library?"

Flenn grinned. "I didn't think you could read."

"Come on," said Zack, "which way?"

Whatever the hell Zack was up to, he wasn't sharing. "Up by the cathedral, on the Palace Green. I don't know how late it's open, though."

"It's a university library, it'll be open." Zack set his

mug down, and headed out the door. Flenn stepped outside and watched him walk down Neville Street and disappear around the corner.

"What the hell was that about?" he said out loud.

CHAPTER *THIRTY-SIX*

11 years earlier...

"It's about time you got here!" Zack and Donna sat across the table from Pam and Windsor. "We'd just about given up on you two!"

Hoshi went around the table to hug the ladies while Flenn shook Windsor's hand. "Great to see you Win!"

"What about me?" Zack said, pretending to look hurt.

"I'm sorry, Win, did you just hear a voice?"

Zack said, "Okay, that's one." Flenn made his way over to Pam. "So good to see you, Win and Donna again, Pam."

"That's two!" said Zack.

Flenn kissed Pam on the cheek then gave Donna a hug. "Just six more months," he said to Donna. "Are you sure you still want to marry this guy?"

"Three!" Zack said. "That settles it; Flenn's buying!"

"Of course I am. Dinner's on me tonight."

Zack rolled his eyes. "Oh, now he acknowledges me."

Flenn grinned, "I have to look at your ugly mug every day."

"You guys see what I have to work with?" Zack said.

Donna interjected, "Hoshi, let me just warn you now, when you get one of these guys, you get the other one."

Hoshi laughed. "I've already figured that out." The waiter took their drink orders. Zack asked for a bourbon while Donna had a beer. Pam and Windsor both ordered wine and Flenn a Scotch. Hoshi just ordered a soda.

"You're not having a drink?" Donna asked. "Back in college, this girl could drink Pam and me under the table! Bring her a white wine," Donna told the waiter. Hoshi turned to the man and shook her head no.

You feeling okay?" Flenn asked. Hoshi smiled and nodded.

"I'm fine."

It was Windsor who spoke next. "So, how was your flight?"

Hoshi smiled. "Not bad. Eight hours from New York to Glasgow. Scott was waiting for me at the airport with a dozen yellow roses."

"*Hrumph*," Zack said. "How come you never give me roses?"

Hoshi winked at Zack. "If you're doing for him the things that I am, then I think Scott and I need to have a talk!" Flenn turned as red as the blood moon which was rising over Scotland tonight.

Halfway through the hors d'oeuvres, the conversation gravitated toward the wedding. Donna's sister was to be the matron of honor, and Pam and Hoshi were to be bridesmaids. Flenn was best man.

Donna huffed in exasperation, scattering feathery bangs off her forehead "He still hasn't selected the other groomsmen."

"I don't need any," Zack said.

Pam and Hoshi both stared at him. "Yes, you do, honey," said Donna. "My bridesmaids need someone to walk down the aisle with."

Zack looked past Pam, "Windsor, how about it. Want to be a grooms-thingy?"

"Groomsman!" Donna corrected.

"Nothing like putting a guy on the spot," said Flenn.

"I'd be honored," offered Windsor.

Zack smiled. "Well, there you have it, all settled." Pam and Hoshi exchanged a look.

"No, it's not!" Donna said.

"Sure it is. Flenn can walk Hoshi down the aisle, and Win can his wife."

"Flenn will walk my sister down the aisle," said Donna. "We still need someone for Hoshi."

"Why can't Flenn walk with Hoshi?"

Flenn jumped in before this turned into a full pre-nuptial quarrel. "Because I'll be kicking your butt for arguing with the bride, that's why! The best man always walks the maid or matron of honor down the aisle."

He turned to Donna. "You'll have to excuse Zack. He hasn't been to many weddings."

"How can I, traipsing after you all day?"

"Consulting work, isn't it?" Windsor said.

"Flenn Industries sends us all over the place," explained Zack. "We never know where we'll end up, or for how long." He and Donna exchanged a quick glance.

"Must be tough working for Scott," Hoshi teased. "I know how mean he can be."

Zack laughed. "This guy? He's a cream puff."

"Gee thanks," Flenn said. "By the way, you're fired."

Donna giggled.

"After dinner, Windsor and I would love to walk you down the Royal Mile," Pam said. "It's one of Edinburgh's highlights."

"It really is!" Donna said. "Zack and I were there this afternoon. How about you guys; wanna tag along?" she asked Hoshi and Flenn.

"We'd love to. I've never been," Flenn answered.

"You didn't go this afternoon?"

"Flenn and I were busy," Hoshi said. Flenn turned beet red; Zack looked at his friend and winked.

Windsor changed the subject. "Yes, well, the Royal Mile runs from the castle to the palace where her majesty resides whenever she is in Scotland."

"You'll love it, Hoshi!" Donna said. "Lots of quirky shops and bookstores."

"Bookstores?" said Flenn, glad to be talking about something else. "Sounds nice."

"Afraid they're all closed right now, but perhaps we could check them out in the morning before we go up to the castle and meet with the wedding planner," Pam offered.

"Sounds like a plan to me," said Flenn. "Just remember that Zack and I have to head to Paris tomorrow night."

"Work, work, work!" Hoshi complained.

"Get used to it, Hosh," Donna said. "Besides, we three girls are going to have a night on the town tomorrow night… just the three of us." She glanced at Windsor. "Sorry, Winnie."

"Enjoy yourselves, dear," Windsor said. "I'm going over to Saint Giles for Evensong."

"Wow, that's exciting!" Zack said, sarcastically. Flenn kicked him under the table. "Ow!"

Pam shrugged, "That's my Winnie. If there's a church open somewhere, he'll find it." She looked across the table at Flenn and Hoshi. "So, shall we all meet in front of Holyrood Palace at eight?" Everyone agreed. "Maybe we could still go for a stroll after dinner."

Hoshi smiled, but said, "I think we'll just meet up with you in the morning."

"You don't want to go for a walk with us?" Donna said.

Zack cut her off. "No, they're 'busy,' remember?" Zack jumped. "Ow!"

CHAPTER *THIRTY-SEVEN*

Present day...

"What the hell was what about?" Charlie asked Flenn.

Flenn turned to see Charlie on the street behind him as he stood on the sidewalk watching Zack head for the university library.

"Hi, Charlie. Sorry, it's Zack; he just got a sudden notion to go to a library."

"Hmm... doesn't seem the library type." Charlie smiled. "I should know, I helped run one for a long time."

"That's right, you were a professor down at Middlesex, right?"

"Actually, my full title was Professor of Medieval History and Dean of Antiquities. We shared a lot of tasks back then."

Flenn was impressed. "How on earth did you end up here?"

"Well, now my title is simply *pensioner*. It's cheaper to live in Durham; plus, there's the university. When I'm not sitting with Murph and the gang, or in some damned doctor's office, I muddle about over at the school—that is, if I'm not off to visit with my granddaughter."

Flenn opened the door wider. "You want to come in for a cup of coffee?"

"Actually, I would," Charlie said. "There's something I want to see if you can help me clear up."

Flenn cocked his head just as his cell phone buzzed. It was a text from Pamela Tammerlane.

I need to talk with you. It's urgent! Can you meet me at my home right away?

"I'm sorry, Charlie, can it wait? Apparently, there's been some sort of emergency with a friend of mine. Can we talk later?"

Charlie gave Flenn's arm a friendly squeeze. "Sure, Father, sure. No problem at all." He nodded toward Flenn's phone. "I hope everything turns out all right." Charlie flashed a warm smile and then made his way down the hill as Flenn turned to lock the door. By the time Flenn had l made it down to the corner Tesco market, Charlie was nowhere in sight. Flenn caught the first taxi that came by and gave the driver the Tammerlanes' address.

Windsor and Pamela's home on Bishop's Gate boasted a beautifully landscaped front garden with a series of stone steps leading to a large, gray-brick Tudor home. Flenn knocked on the massive red door only to be greeted by the maid, a large woman with dyed blonde hair who smelled of cigarette smoke.

The spacious oaken-floored foyer led to an even larger chandeliered vestibule with a pearl-white, split stairwell. Flenn hadn't gotten a proper sense of the grandeur of the house when he'd been here the first time. He was directed through French doors on the left to a grand dining room where two bay windows flooded the room with natural light. A large antique table was centered in the middle of the room. A chestnut-brown buffet ran alongside the far wall. *Seventeenth century, from the looks of it*, Flenn thought. At the opposite end of the table sat Pamela, staring into space, her face ashen-white. A laptop computer rested on the table next to her. She didn't look at him when he entered the room.

"She's been this way off and on since yesterday," the maid whispered to the priest.

"Mum?" the maid called.

Pamela sat motionless.

"Mrs. Tammerlane? Father Flenn has arrived," the woman said a bit louder. She waited for her employer to lift her head before leaving the room and shutting the doors behind her.

"Scott?"

Flenn rushed to her side. "Yes, Pamela, it's me. What's going on, dear? Are you all right?"

"Scott? Where's Hoshi?"

"Pam, I'm right here." He put his hand on her shoulder. She jerked as if having suddenly been transported back from another galaxy, then looked up, seeing him for the first time.

"I'm so sorry. It's this damned medicine the doctor has me on, I just zone out every now and then. Thank you for coming."

"Of course," he said, taking a chair next to hers. "What's going on, Pam?"

"Pam?" She nodded her head. "Yes, it might as well be *Pam* again. No use putting on airs now."

"It's just me, Pam. We've known each other for years, remember?"

She smiled faintly and patted his hand. "I do right now dear. No telling what I'll remember five minutes from now."

"Maybe that medicine is too strong for you. Why don't you try taking half a dose?"

The old Pam seemed to surface for a moment. "So, you've a medical degree now? A billionaire, a priest, and a doctor?"

Flenn smiled. "Don't need to be a doctor to tell you're on too much medication."

Pamela sighed. "I suppose. Let me be brief, I don't know when I may drift off again. Zack Matteson... is he still in Durham?"

Flenn was surprised. "As a matter of fact, he is. Why?"

She nodded approvingly. "Good. Very good." She seemed to be maintaining her focus for the moment. "Is he still with the FBI, I mean the CIA?"

Flenn raised both eyebrows. "What?"

"Don't be daft. Donna drank too much one night. She told us all what you and Zack did for a living. You're obviously no longer a spy, but what about Zack?"

Flenn stammered, "I... I... "

"Please, no denials. I can feel this stuff trying to steal my thoughts again. "Is Zack still with the CIA?"

"Why?"

Pamela pulled her dress away from her bosom and

reached inside to retrieve something. She handed it to Flenn. "I received this in the post today."

Flenn unfolded the piece of paper. A typed message read:

Tell him he will be next unless...

"What is this? Tell *who*? Unless *what*?"

"That's why I need Zack," Pamela said, wiping away a tear. "I want you to give this to him." She looked up at Flenn. "Please. You don't need to be involved, but I don't know how to reach Zack except through you. This is life or death, Flenn."

Flenn reached out for her hand, but it went limp; she was slipping back into the abyss from which she'd temporarily awakened. "Pam, you need to give this to the police! If someone is in danger... "

"No!" Her eyes re-focused for a second, and it looked as if fire was blazing through them. "No police—only Zack! Tell him I think I know who sent me this."

"Who, Pam?" Flenn stuffed the paper in his shirt pocket.

She didn't answer. "Pam?"

Pam either wouldn't—or couldn't—respond. Flenn sighed, then stood to go in search of the maid. He found her in the kitchen, standing over a granite countertop, chopping carrots. A restaurant-style coffeepot was behind her.

"Would you care for some tea, Father?"

"No, thank you. But, I wouldn't mind a cup of that coffee."

"Oh, Father, you wouldn't want that. It's hours old."

Flenn shrugged. "That's never bothered me before." The maid poured him a cup; he declined the cream and sugar.

"You say she's been like this since yesterday?"

The maid went back to chopping. "Yes. This is the longest bout I've seen her have."

"She's had others?"

The maid rolled her eyes, then nodded.

Flenn took a sip of the stale coffee, then retrieved his phone to summon an Uber. "Well, I suppose it is understandable that her doctor would have put her on something after Windsor's death."

"Is that what she told you?" the maid asked. Flenn sipped more of the coffee and waited, afraid to hear what she was about to say. "She's been on those tablets a lot longer than that," the woman said with a huff.

Flenn didn't respond, except to write down his cell phone number and give it to her, along with the empty mug. "Call me if I can be of any help; thanks for the coffee," he said, then went outside to wait for the car to arrive to take him back to the flat. He took out the piece of paper. *Just who is it that is going to be next?* he wondered. *Who is the person Pam is supposed to tell this to, and why Zack instead of the police?*

And, though he felt guilty for thinking it, *just how many people did Donna tell back then?* He sighed. *If only Donna had kept her mouth shut, Hoshi might still be his.*

CHAPTER *THIRTY-EIGHT*

11 years earlier…

"Aw, do you have to go?" Hoshi said. "I'd much rather spend the time alone here with you, if you know what I mean."

Flenn did.

They had spent the morning walking the Royal Mile until it was time for everyone to meet with the wedding planner at Edinburgh Castle. They'd all parted after lunch at a nearby pub, and then Hoshi and Flenn had returned alone to their hotel room.

"Couldn't you call in sick tomorrow?" she asked, hopefully. "What would one more day in Edinburgh cost you? After all, your dad owns the company." Zack and Flenn were supposed to meet up with Davy Spate in the morning for Omar Rashad's interrogation. Rashad had been brought to a special unit where French and British investigators had already begun their work. Hopefully, he would lead them to Zamir.

"You told me you like romance," Hoshi said. "Well, Edinburgh certainly has a lot of that." Flenn put on his jacket, feeling for the ring he'd bought last week while in Tel Aviv. He had flown there just for that purpose—to find an engagement ring worthy of the woman he loved.

He'd thought of proposing to her last night in front of the monument to Sir Walter Scott, but there had been too many people around. *Definitely in Paris*, he told himself.

"Hoshi, we've been over this. I just can't. I'm supposed to meet Zack at the airport in in a couple of hours. Besides, you're supposed to go out with Pam and Donna tonight, remember?"

Hoshi leaned back in the bed, the strap of her burgundy lace camisole falling seductively off her left shoulder. She patted the pillow next to her. "I'll be happy to cancel... if you will."

Flenn bit his bottom lip, his chest expanding until it collapsed in a heavy sigh. "I... I can't. Besides," he said, more to himself than to her, "you'll be in Paris in a few days. We'll have plenty of time together then."

He bent over to give her a kiss goodbye. She reached up and grabbed hold of his tie to pull him closer. "Okay, mister, I'll let you off the hook... *this time*." She wrapped her arms around his neck. "Just don't make a habit of it. All work and no play makes Scott a dull boy." She stroked the back of his head as she kissed him lightly at first, and then harder. He felt himself falling into the softness of cotton, silk... and Hoshi.

Well, he told himself, *he did still have a couple of hours.*

CHAPTER *THIRTY-NINE*

Present day…

Flenn waited up for Zack past midnight before turning in. He checked the next morning, but Zack's bed hadn't been slept in, nor had the toothpick been moved from above the door. His morning jog went slowly, especially going up the steep hills where his quadriceps complained with every step. *Just one of the problems of getting older,* he told himself.

Flenn saw Murph heading toward the Bram and Bull.

"Morning', Father," Murph called, *no doubt thinking of a way to distract Valarie so he could add a taste of whiskey to his morning mug.* "Sorry to hear about your friend," Murph called. Flenn was all the way to the North Road before Murph's words registered. *Had something happened overnight to Pamela?* He said a prayer for her, deciding to finish his run early in order to find out.

He turned right onto Crossgate and did the loop again before stopping at the Bram and Bull for coffee and to check with Murph. Flenn stood outside the pub and felt his pulse. Not as high as he wanted, but at least he'd made himself run this morning. Healthy habits were easily broken and difficult to take up again. He promised himself not to miss another day.

"Cheers, Father!" Bob said.

"Mornin'!" Murph echoed.

"Ayup!" Murph said, coming back from the loo, zipping up his trousers.

"Hiya, love," Valerie said cheerfully. "Wotcha' fancy?"

Flenn smiled. "Got any bangers and beans this mornin'?" Flenn said with his best Yorkshire accent.

"Ach, would you listen to him now?" Valerie said. "Soon, you'll be a proper bloke!"

"Brilliant!" said Bob, smiling.

"He's too posh to be one o' us," Murph teased.

"Nah," Val said, "just give 'im a fortnight I say. 'Bangers and beans,' now that's a propa' breakfast!"

"Wotcha!" George said as he came through the door.

"Wotcha!" Bob and Murph responded.

"Tea, Val," George said as he took his regular spot at the end of the bar.

"Sorry to 'ear about your friend, Father," George said as Valerie handed him milk for his tea.

Crap! He'd forgotten about Pamela. He needed coffee, fast!

"Yeah, too bad. Not to worry, mate," Murph added. "I hear the constable's going to be right as rain, right as rain. Don't know how long Zack'll have to stay a guest of her majesty, though."

Flenn shook his head. *Zack?* "Wait a minute, I'm lost. What?"

"Jail," said Bob.

"Zack's in jail?"

"You ain't 'eard?"

Flenn shook his head. "What happened?"

"Wotcha!" They all turned to see Charlie walking

through the door. Everyone but Flenn called out, "Wotcha cocker, fancy a drink?"

"Coffee, and make it strong!" Charlie said rubbing his hands together. "Mornin', Father. Sorry about your friend."

"Apparently, everyone is sorry about my friend. Everyone but me. What's going on?"

"You don't know?" Charlie said. "He hit a policeman last night."

Murph grinned. "Knocked the copper out cold, 'e did!"

Flenn's jaw dropped, though not so much in surprise as in timing. *He needed to show Pam's note to Zack.* "Where is he now?" Flenn asked. "I suppose I'll have to go bail him out."

"*Pshaw,*" said Murph. "The bluebottles ain't likely to let 'im out anytime soon."

"It's true, Father," added Charlie. "Hitting a police-man is a pretty serious offense."

Valerie heard the conversation as she brought in his breakfast. "Ya' talkin' 'bout the Father's friend, are you? Not likely 'e'll be seein' the light of day anytime soon. Father, ya' be wantin' some coffee with that?"

"Please! And make it strong, I hadn't expected a shock like this one."

"Well, here comes another one!" Bob said, staring out the window. Murph joined Bob at the window, as did George.

"Well, ain't 'e a jammy dodger," said George.

"How on earth?" Charlie said as the door opened and none other than Zack Matteson stepped inside, wearing what he'd had on when he'd left for the library last night.

"Hi Val, hope I'm not too late for breakfast!" He looked

at the five men staring at him, their mouths open. "You guys okay?"

Flenn spoke first. "We heard you were in jail." Zack sat next to Flenn, grabbing a sausage from Flenn's plate.

"I was. They don't serve much of a breakfast, I must say."

"Food there is something awful," agreed Murph, sounding like he'd had first-hand experience.

"How'd you bust out?" asked George.

"A friend explained it was all a misunderstanding. Val, could I have some tea with this, with milk if you don't mind?"

"Careful Val, that one's a dangerous man," George teased, "You know what they say about blokes who just got out of prison and the ladies."

Flenn tried to spear the last sausage, but Zack got to it first. "Not him, he's like that all the time."

Valerie smiled and winked at Zack. "Here's your tea, love. I'll be back with some more breakfast, Father."

"Great!" said Murph, reaching over the bar as soon as she was gone.

"Yeah, me and Bob wouldn't mind a bite there, Val!" George called toward the kitchen. "Oh, and don't forget Charlie!"

"I wouldn't mind some more, either," Zack hollered. "Oh, and some fried eggs while you're at it."

Flenn reached for his wallet. "Here we go again," he muttered under his breath.

CHAPTER *FORTY*

11 years earlier...

Hoshi wasn't happy with the green dress or the blue. Scott had liked the yellow one, but she thought she looked awful in yellow. "Wear the black one," Donna said as she searched for her lost earring.

"Black?" Hoshi said. "Really? Is this a fancy place we're going tonight?"

"*Places,*" Donna corrected, looking through every drawer. She and Hoshi had moved into the same room after Zack and Flenn had left for Paris. "We're going all over Edinburgh; going to do the town the way we used to."

"We're not kids anymore Donna," she said putting her hands on her hip. "I still don't see why you won't tell Pam and me where we're going."

Donna went into the bathroom to search for her earring. "'Cause it's a surprise, that's why," she called. Hoshi tried on the black dress, looked in the mirror and immediately took it back off.

"Did you tell Pam where we're going?"

"Nope."

"Must be expensive," Hoshi said.

Donna came out and started looking on the floor by

the bed. "What do you care, you're marrying Daddy Warbucks soon."

"Don't call him that. And I could care less about his money."

"Yeah, right," Donna said.

Hoshi put on the blue dress for the second time in five minutes. "I love Scott for who he is, not for what he has."

"There's a joke there, but I'm not touching it," Donna said from halfway under the bed.

"And, for your information, he hasn't proposed yet!"

"He will, Hosh, he will," Donna said.

Hoshi looked down at the floor where only Donna's legs were sticking out from under the bed. "Ew! Don't you know they never vacuum under there?"

"I've got to find that earring! Paul gave it to me."

"Your old boyfriend from college?"

Donna crawled out from under the bed. "So?"

Hoshi's mouth fell open. "You're still wearing jewelry that your ex gave you?"

"It's pretty... see?" Donna pushed back her hair so that Hoshi could see the one that she had managed to find. "Plus, it brings back memories," she said running her hand over the bedspread.

Hoshi took off the blue dress and reached for the green one. "Aren't you supposed to be making memories with Zack?"

Donna pulled back the covers. "Well, Zack's not here."

Hoshi couldn't believe what she was hearing. "Donna!" she scolded.

Donna smiled. "Well, Paul and I had a good time together. What's the harm in that?"

"I can see that Pam and I are going to have to keep an eye on you tonight!" Hoshi said, taking off the green dress and deciding to wear the yellow one, in honor of Scott.

"Aha!"

"You found it?"

"Underneath the pillow!"

Hoshi picked up the phone. "You know what that means?"

Donna gazed at the earring. "That I still have my memories?"

"No, that housekeeping didn't change the sheets! I'm calling them right now. I'm not sleeping here until they're changed."

"Why?"

"Ew," was all Hoshi said.

CHAPTER *FORTY-ONE*

Present day...

Flenn paid the tab and left Valerie a healthy tip. He and Zack took their coffee over to a vacant corner. "So, what's this all about, Zack? Why were you in a fight with a cop?"

"Last night, after the library closed, I stopped by the Vicar's Closet for a drink. How was I to know it was a gay bar? Anyway, some drunk guy grabbed my... well, grabbed me, so I decked him."

"Don't tell me," Flenn smirked. "The drunk guy was a cop?"

"Too bad I couldn't make it to the cathedral to claim sanctuary, huh?" Zack teased. He went over to Valerie to ask for a shot of whiskey in his tea. He winked at Murph, who grinned in return

"So," he said, sitting back down next to Flenn. "There you have it."

Flenn leaned back in his chair. "Not quite. How'd you get out?"

"Van Winkle."

"You're kidding me."

Zack glanced at the four guys at the end of the bar, laughing at something George had said. "Nope. Beamish showed up this morning and pulled some strings. I got an earful, believe me." Zack reached into his pocket, but came up empty. "Know where a decent candy store is around here?"

"Listen," Flenn said, "I got a call yesterday from Pam. Somebody's threatening her."

Zack bit his bottom lip. "Did she say who?"

Flenn shook his head. "She was messed up on something… according to the maid, it's been going on awhile."

"Pam?"

"Yeah, I know, hard to believe, huh? You think you know somebody."

Zack was silent.

"Anyway, she gives me this note that says she is to tell someone that they're next unless they cooperate."

"Someone?"

Flenn nodded. "Didn't give a name, but I got the feeling that whoever wrote it assumed Pam would know whom they meant."

"Did she?"

"I dun'no. She zoned out after that, just totally went somewhere else."

"Him or her?" Zack asked.

"What do you mean?"

"The note. Did it say tell *him* or tell *her*?" Zack took a slow sip of coffee while he tried to remember.

"Him. It said, 'tell him.'" Flenn raised an eyebrow. "Why? Do you know something?"

"Not about that note, no, but I did find out about the video feed from the cathedral."

Flenn leaned in. "And?"

"You're not going to like it."

"It wasn't one of the clergy was it?" Flenn leaned back, "What priest has access to a selective poison like that? Couldn't have been anyone with the altar guild. I checked, they're all just sweet little old ladies."

Zack took a sip of coffee then set the mug on the table. "Flenn, how sure are you about how that wine would have been handled?"

Flenn shrugged. "What?"

"Could there have been anyone else other than the little old ladies that had access to it?"

"Procedure is pretty much the same in all Anglican churches. The wine gets poured into a cruet and the cruet is set on the credence table for the priest or bishop to use. In some places an acolyte helps set the altar, but you're not going to tell me that a kid did this?"

Zack sighed.

"No! A kid? How?"

Zack rolled his eyes. "Of course not."

"Then who?"

"That's just the thing. Nobody. Beamish said they were working on the same theory. The wine sat on that... whatever you call it... "

"Credence table."

"Yeah, credence table. It sat there for an hour prior to the service. Nobody came near it."

"They must've," Flenn said, not believing what he was hearing. "What about during the service itself?"

"Beamish said no. He'd watched the video himself."

"He wouldn't be trying to throw you off the scent, would he? You know, after what you did to him in Brussels?"

"How'd you know about Brussels?" Zack asked. "Oh yeah, you talked to Spate."

"Well, do you think Beamish would do that to you— mislead you, I mean?"

"In a heartbeat." Zack finished his tea. "But I made a call, and my source confirmed it."

"Come on mates, quit waggin' your chins down there and come join us!" George called.

Flenn turned around and smiled, holding up a finger to signal just another minute. "Look George! The Father's givin' ya' the finger!" Everyone laughed at Murph's joke.

Zack got up. "There's more. I'll tell you later; right now, I gotta' go take a shower and clean up, then get back to the library. I have an idea what I'm looking for now."

Flenn nodded. "I'll come with you."

"No. You stay here with the guys. I need some time to work this out in my head."

Reluctantly, Flenn agreed. "Okay, but there's one more thing. Pam asked for *you* specifically."

Zack seemed disinterested.

"Apparently, Hoshi wasn't the only one Donna told years ago about us being in the CIA." Still, no reaction from Zack. Flenn raised an eyebrow. "Old news?"

"Yeah, you might say that."

Flenn sighed. "Sorry, Zack, but I still wish Donna had kept her mouth shut all those years ago."

Zack understood why.

"So, what does Pam want with you? Why not the police?"

Zack shrugged. "Who knows? Look, I gotta' go. I'll catch up with you later." He motioned toward the end of the bar. "The guys are waiting."

Flenn frowned as he reached into his pocket. "I don't know what it is you're not telling me, but here, let me give you the keys to the flat."

Zack grinned. "Since when did I ever need keys?"

CHAPTER *FORTY-TWO*

11 years earlier…

Pam arrived on time and the three women headed out the door of the hotel to hail a cab. "Why all this secrecy, Donna?" Pam asked. "I feel as if I'm doing something naughty."

"Good!" Donna laughed. "Tonight is girls' night! It's the three of us against Edinburgh!"

"Poor Edinburgh!" Hoshi said, getting into the spirit of things. Donna had refused to reveal the places she'd managed to find for tonight, just that they would all have a good time. The first stop was a loud and raucous pub where a local band blared out rock and roll hits from the '90's. Donna ordered a Mai Tai and Pam a Chardonnay. Hoshi asked for a soda.

The music and atmosphere brought back memories of their college days together. Since college, the three had traveled together whenever they could… usually ending up in a place like this. Tonight, they were *starting* their evening in a rowdy bar. "Um… this promises to be an interesting evening," Hoshi said as she and Pam surveyed their surroundings.

"You haven't seen anything yet!" Donna promised.

The next stop was quieter. A small, elegant restaurant

tucked away at the top of the Royal Mile, just across from the castle. It was in the same spot where women were tried and hanged as witches in medieval days. Bathed in candlelight, rich tapestries hung from oak-paneled walls. Chairs, upholstered in burgundy and gold, were evenly spaced around tables immaculately set with sterling silver and crystal. A bottle of Champagne awaited them as the head waiter sat each lady in turn.

"How on earth did you hear about this place?" Pam asked.

"Actually, Flenn told me about it," Donna said.

Hoshi was surprised. "Scott?"

"He said the food here is divine."

"Forget the food," Hoshi said. "Look who just came in!" The three women turned to see a couple ushered to a table in the far corner.

"Who's that?" Donna asked.

"You don't know?" Pam said, incredulously.

Hoshi whispered, 'Jesus Christ Superstar,' 'Cats,' 'Phantom of the Opera'?"

"You're kidding! I'm going over there for his autograph."

Pam grabbed her arm. "You'll do no such thing!"

"Aw, come on… " Donna said.

Hoshi giggled and poured Champagne for the other two. "What?" Donna said, "aren't you having any?"

"Yes dear, have some," Pam echoed.

"Nah," Hoshi said. "I don't really feel like drinking tonight."

Donna downed her first glass and poured herself

another. She looked at Hoshi as the waiter came to take their order. "Live it up, girl! We're out to celebrate! Whoo-hoo!"

The celebrity couple glared at them and Pam lifted her menu to hide behind it. Hoshi just laughed. "Well, girls, we've been to Rio, London, Cameroon and Beijing… all those cities survived us. I suppose Edinburgh will, as well."

Donna picked up her glass as she looked the handsome waiter up and down. "The night is young, Hoshi, the night is young!"

CHAPTER *FORTY-THREE*

Present day...

Flenn found what he was looking for on the last aisle; A bottle of onion chutney. It tasted great on a toasted ham and cheese sandwich, which was what he was planning on fixing himself for lunch. He picked up a can of coffee, a six-pack of ale, ingredients for tonight's salad, and a small pack of chocolate candy. *Chocolate here is so much better than back home. No soy or corn syrup; just milk, sugar, butter, and cocoa,* he thought. He saw a package of jellybeans and added it to the cart for Zack.

He rounded the corner from Tesco and started up the hill. He could see someone standing in front of the door to his flat. "Down here, Charlie!"

"Need help with your things?" Charlie called as Flenn drew closer.

"No, it's just the two bags. You might check the door and see if Zack left it open, though."

Charlie did, but the door was locked. Flenn offered him one of the bags so that he could retrieve his keys. "You have a few minutes for an old man, Father?"

Flenn smiled. "For you, Charlie, I've got all day."

"Won't take all day; just need to get something off my chest, that's all."

Flenn set the groceries on the table. "Can I interest you in a cup of coffee? There's still some in the pot."

"Thank you, no. I've had my fill for the day."

Flenn poured himself a cup. "With or without Murph's stolen whiskey?"

Charlie laughed. "Oh, he's been doing that for years. Val and Colin know all about it."

"And they don't mind?" Flenn put the beer in the tiny fridge.

"Murph's a special case. He lost his wife and child in a fire thirty years ago, back when he ran the pub across the street."

Flenn turned. "Murph ran the Death Angel?"

"It wasn't called that back then; it was the Angel's Den. That's what Murph called his little girl, *Angel*. They lived upstairs, over the pub. One night, Murph forgot to turn off the stove before going to make a night deposit at the bank. By the time he got home, the fire department had put out the fire, but the fumes had overcome Peggy and Angel. I wasn't here then, course, but what I was told was that the previous owner of the Bram, Harry Makepeace, took Murph in.

"Harry was great; helped Murph get the place fixed back up and ready to sell, he even helped Murph find another place to live after some time passed. Harry died about eight years ago. Val's his daughter."

Flenn sat down at the table. "Wow, you just never know about someone's story, do you?"

Charlie nodded. "Oh, and just so you know, Murph has paid for his mornin' whisky many times over doing odd jobs around the pub. I think it gives him peace of mind to still be hanging around a pub."

Flenn smiled. "And you, why do you hang around?"

Charlie gave a wry smile, then chuckled. "Oh, I don't know. I guess I had my fill of all those intellectual types— the tweed suits, the pâté and Brie socials." Charlie scratched his head. "Murph and the gang aren't trying to impress anyone. They're just three blokes who are who they are, and they accept just about anyone that comes through the door. My wife and I live next to Bob, that's how we found our way here. He invited me for a pint right after we moved in. We've been gathering up there nearly every day since. I guess we'll continue to do that until… " His voice broke.

Flenn put his hand on the man's shoulder. "I'm sorry, Charlie."

"Don't be. I've led a good life… for the most part."

Flenn cocked his head slightly to the side. "For the most part?"

"That's the reason I'm here, Father." Charlie shifted in his chair. "Did you ever do something that you thought might be a wee dodgy, sure though that no harm would come of it, only to find out later it might be worse than you ever dreamed?"

Flenn shrugged. "I'm not really sure I know what you just said."

Charlie's eyes were moist. "You know that saying? What is it now? Oh yeah, 'The road to hell is paved with good intentions.'"

Flenn frowned. "I've heard it. Just don't believe it."

Charlie raised an eyebrow. "You don't?"

"I think intentions are everything. Scripture talks in several places about how it's what's in the heart that matters."

Charlie nodded ever so slightly. "You believe that do you, Father?"

Flenn smiled. "If that weren't the case, we'd all be in pretty big trouble."

"I might be in trouble already… or, may have caused some."

Flenn leaned closer. "Care to share the details of whatever it is that's bothering you?"

The old man thought a bit. "Not just yet, Father. I've got some things to work out in my mind first. Truth is, I don't know if I did what I think I did or not."

"Okay, now you've lost me." Flenn smiled. "But I'll be here when you get it all worked out. I'm heading over to the Farne Islands tomorrow, but I'll be in Durham for another week after that."

"The Farne Islands, you say? Ach, Father, you're going to love that! My son and his family live over on the coast." Charlie smiled. "The old man spent his last days there, you know."

Flenn raised an eyebrow. "The old man?"

"Saint Cuthbert. That's what some call him up here in the North. Of course, he was only 53 when he died."

Flenn grimaced. "Fifty-three's looking younger to me every day!"

"Wait till you get to be my age," Charlie said with a

grin. "Just be sure to wear a hat and a jacket when you go to the Inner Farne."

"Cold out there?"

Charlie grinned again as he stood up. "Can be, but that's not the reason. You'll see."

"You sure you won't stay and talk some more?"

Charlie shook his head. "Maybe soon. Let me think on things. Just thought I ought to talk to a priest." He winked at Flenn. "A man in my predicament wants to be sure he doesn't upset the Almighty, you know." Charlie walked out the door and down Neville Street.

Flenn shook his head. *What the hell was that all about?*

CHAPTER *FORTY-FOUR*

Flenn made his way across Framwellgate Bridge carrying a small umbrella under his arm since the forecast called for afternoon showers.

Tourists were going in and out of the specialty shops and making their way up to Durham Castle as if nothing had happened here last Sunday. Flenn stopped at the cathedral's entrance as a middle-aged woman in purple robes greeted him. "First time here, Father?" He'd felt compelled to wear his collar this afternoon for some reason.

Flenn thanked the guide but explained that he'd been here before. "I'm meeting someone this afternoon," he said. She smiled warmly before moving on to an Asian couple examining the massive baptismal font.

He closed his eyes, remembering the horrific scene as it had unfolded at the high altar. *Windsor had died in his arms, and for what? A terrorist plot badly planned? Someone furious over social changes in the Church?*

He felt somebody brush by him. Flenn opened his eyes to see three men in green ties heading toward the cloister. They reminded him of the Irishmen from Sunday. *What was it Pam had said? Something about Windsor being openly critical of the Provisional Irish Republican Army.* Flenn decided to follow them.

He exited the large wooden doors into the cloister as they made their way into the café. He crossed by the gift shop, ordered a coffee, and sat at the table next to theirs pretending to be fiddling with his phone as the men had their tea and scones in silence. *Probably nothing,* he told himself. He looked at his watch. It was nearly 3 o'clock.

Flenn headed back into the church where he made his way along the right side of the high altar and up the steps to Cuthbert's shrine. He knew 'the old man,' as Charlie called him, wasn't really here, but it was comforting to be this close to what was left of his mortal remains.

His appointment was one he'd made for himself. Four months ago this very day, at 3 p.m., a dozen children had been murdered on a mountaintop in Honduras. Flenn had come here to pray for the lost children and their parents. Holy Innocents' school was even now under construction at San Jose de la Montaña. Flenn had seen to it that not only the school, but adequate housing for the villagers was being constructed in memory of the slain children.

As he knelt in silence he prayed for Pam and her family, and that Windsor, as the prayer book put it, would go from "strength to strength" in God's kingdom. Lastly, he prayed for Charlie, for the courage to face the days ahead and the wisdom to see his way through whatever it was that was bothering him lately.

It was nearly 4 o'clock before Flenn left the shrine. Evensong would begin at 5:15, but he wanted to see if he could catch up with Zack first. He wanted to find out about whatever it was that Zack was working on at the library.

The rain was falling gently as he crossed the deserted Palace Green. Flenn chuckled at himself as he realized that he was the only one dumb enough to be outside in the rain. He walked past a tea shop and made his way down Silver Street which led to the bridge. The rain was coming down harder now. He assumed anyone with any sense was hovering over a mug or a pint right now in a dry, warm pub.

The sound of the rain on the pavement masked the footsteps behind him.

Flenn didn't hear the assailants until they were right on him. Before he could react, he felt himself falling head-long over the parapet into the River Wear! The current swept him under the bridge, where he managed to grab hold of a piece of protruding rebar. The water was cold, but he stayed hidden under the bridge for several minutes. The last time he'd been thrown off a bridge, he'd been shot at by two men with Kalashnikovs. Besides, he didn't need to see who had thrown him into the river. He knew. It had to have been the men with the green ties.

Finally, he let go and allowed the current to carry him toward the shore. When the water was shallow enough, he stood and waded onto the Riverwalk. Soaking wet, he made his way down the path toward the steps which led up to the bridge.

"Going somewhere are you now, Flenny boy?"

The three men from the café stepped onto the path in front of him. He noticed they'd pocketed their ties. "Or, should I say Father? The CIA should be ashamed, dressing you up as a priest!"

Where had he heard that voice before?

"What, don't you remember me?" said the big man in the middle.

Flenn wiped the water from his brow. "You were at the ordination."

"Yeah, fancy meeting you there. I suppose you thought I'd still be in prison."

Flenn blinked. "Connor O'Malley?"

The man grinned. "So, you do remember. Seven years they locked me up, all account o' you!"

Flenn had helped capture an arms dealer smuggling guns into Northern Ireland right before the Good Friday peace accord was signed in Belfast. O'Malley had been one of the IRA's point men. "Well, I see they didn't teach you any manners while you were there."

O'Malley sneered. "They taught me plenty. Like never travel across a bridge alone." The other two men laughed.

"And how to lace wine with colocinium?"

The men exchanged glances. "Colo-what?" O'Malley said.

"No reason to play dumber than you already are, Connor. What I can't figure out is how the PIRA got its hands on the stuff."

O'Malley turned red. "We don't kill clergy, not even English ones."

"Funny, I don't recall *jumping* from that bridge."

"If I wanted you dead, Flenn, you'd be dead. This is just my way of saying hello." O'Malley rolled up his sleeves. "Oh, and don't worry... I'm told a few weeks in hospital can do a lad a world 'o good." O'Malley signaled the other two, but before they could catch hold of Flenn's arms for the beating he intended to give the American Flenn kicked O'Malley in the groin while simultaneously poking the man on his right in the throat. O'Malley collapsed to his knees, as the other man fell, gasping for air.

Unfortunately, the man on Flenn's left caught him with a good left hook. Flenn rolled with the punch, then came up swinging. The Irishman landed a couple of good punches himself, but Flenn knocked him into the water where he tripped on a fallen branch and got caught in the current.

"Help!" he yelled. "I can't swim!"

Flenn looked down at O'Malley. "You swim?"

The Irishman was holding his crotch and rolling in the mud. "Not bleedin' now I don't!" Flenn glanced at the other man who was in no shape to rescue his mate.

"Hell, O'Malley, I've already been in there once!"

"So, you're already wet! Besides, you owe me," the Irishman said. "Seven year's worth, Flenn."

Flenn trotted down the path to a bend ahead of the drowning man. He waded out halfway then swam the rest until he was able to pull the man to safety. O'Malley limped toward them.

"We even?" Flenn asked, narrowing his eyes in warning.

"For now, I guess." O'Malley checked on his man

then gingerly sat down on the riverbank. "Do I need to get Sean to hospital?"

"You mean the one up there? No, but he'll have a sore throat for a while." Flenn glared at Connor O'Malley. "So, you didn't have anything to do with Windsor Tammerlane's death?"

"Swear to God, Flenn! I don't do poison, anyways. That's women's work."

"Then what were you doing at the ordination?"

O'Malley reached into his pocket. "Careful!" Flenn warned.

"Just me inhaler, Flenn." He took a puff from the device then shoved it back in his pocket. "Sucks to get old."

"So, what's your beef with Windsor?"

"Tammerlane's been goin' off about me lads lately. We were just there to make our presence known. Nothing else, I swear. I never meant him any real harm."

Flenn was dubious. "What were you doing in the cathedral today?"

O'Malley pointed to the man still lying on the shore. "Jonathan here lost his phone."

"It wouldn't be that hard to throw all three of you in the river, Connor."

"What do you think I was doing?" Connor O'Malley sniped. "I've been trying to find you! I figured you'd show up again...eventually." He shook his head. "Look, we didn't do it. Until I'm ordered otherwise, the peace accord still stands between us and the Brits. I just wanted to find you, that's all."

The rain let up as Flenn looked down at the big man, now nearly as wet as he was. "Call me stupid, but I believe you," he said. "Just go back to Belfast. There's been enough trouble here already."

"Make you a deal," O'Malley offered.

"Yeah, what's that?"

"You quit pretending you're a priest, and I'll leave." He grinned. "At least I can go home remembering the look on yer face as you went over that bridge!"

CHAPTER *FORTY-FIVE*

11 years earlier...

Hoshi and Pam stood outside the restaurant waiting for Donna, who'd excused herself to the powder room. Hoshi knew what she was really doing.

"I got it!" Donna said holding up a piece of paper as she rushed outside.

"You didn't just go ask that man for his autograph!"

Donna smiled triumphantly as she stuffed the paper in her purse. "Okay, Pam, I didn't. But I seem to remember a certain star-struck girl back in college chasing after Stevie Wonder's autograph!"

Hoshi giggled. "And Bon Jovi! Don't forget Bon Jovi!"

Pam rolled her eyes. "I was a kid."

Donna grinned. "And you still are, at least for tonight... let go and act like one!"

"Where to next?" Hoshi asked.

"Ahh, well this one is the *pièce de résistance*," she said. "You girls, follow me."

Pam cocked her head. "What, we're not taking a taxi?"

"It's not far, just down the hill and over a couple of streets," Donna said as she headed off toward an alley. The shops were all closed now, but they could hear music and laughter coming from the pubs they passed. The Royal Mile was enchanting at night; it seemed to Hoshi to be the very heart of the old world, with its towering spires and centuries-old markets and historical landmarks. Even the names on the directional signs were charming: *Cannongate, Castlehill, Lawnmarket, Abbey Strand.* They stopped to watch a juggler who smiled when Hoshi tossed a few coins into his basket. Across the street a bagpiper began to play. Anywhere else, Hoshi might have covered her ears, but here it seemed magical.

Conversation was impossible now. The sound of the pipes resonated for a couple of blocks, masking all the noise around them… including the footsteps of the man following them.

"Are you sure you know where we're going?" Pam asked Donna as they turned off the Royal Mile and headed down an alleyway.

"Trust me," Donna said.

"We would, dear, but you've had about six drinks so far tonight," Pam said.

"Only six… so far, that is!" Donna tossed back. "Come on, girls, let's move along."

"I would rather you didn't," said a man's voice from behind them. Hoshi, Pam and Donna turned to see an unshaven, balding man with an ugly scar running along his right cheek.

"Oh dear!" exclaimed Pam.

"Just give me those purses, loves. No one needs to get hurt," the man said. "Come on now, I'd hate for one of you lovelies to spend the week in hospital. Mind you, I don't want to do any slicin', but I surely will if you don't hand 'em over!" Hoshi gasped as the man waved the knife toward her belly.

"Give him what he wants, Hosh!" Pam said.

"Here," Donna said, holding out her purse, "I've got something for you," The man moved to snatch it, but just as he did, she grabbed his wrist and bent it sharply backward.

"Ow!" he hollered, dropping his knife. Just as quickly as she had grabbed his wrist, Donna took his forearm, turned her back, and bent over slightly, throwing him easily across her shoulder. He landed with a thud on the cobblestones below. Two security guards, who had stepped out the back door of a pub for a smoke, ran to assist the women. When they got there, they found the ladies didn't need their help at all.

"Ach," said one, "it's ol' Jimmy."

"Thought he was still in jail," said the other. He looked at Hoshi, Pam, and Donna. "You ladies want to press charges? We can call the guardi."

"Yes," said Pam, "call the police!"

"No," said Donna, "we have places to be tonight." She glanced down at the semi-conscious lump at her feet. "Besides, he'll think twice about doing that again!"

"Well then," said the first man, "you'd best be runnin' on. We'll tell the cops we saw him pull a knife on some tourists who ran away. With Jimmy's record, they won't need much to put him back where he belongs."

"Great!" said Donna. "Come on girls, or we'll miss the show!" Hoshi and Pam stared down at the drunk and then up at Donna who turned and walked away. Pam didn't want anything more to do with the grungy thief at her feet, so she started to follow. Hoshi was still in shock, not so much at the drunken thief, but at what Donna had just done.

"Come on, Hosh!" Donna called. "I need a drink!"

Hoshi stared at her in utter amazement before finally shaking her head and trudging off after her friends.

CHAPTER *FORTY-SIX*

Present day...

"You're wet!" Zack stood at the top of the stairs gazing down at Flenn who was dripping on the entranceway floor.

"Nothing gets past you, does it?" Flenn groused as he headed up for a warm shower. "How about making some coffee, huh?"

"Forget your umbrella?"

Flenn dropped his clothes on the bathroom floor. "Last I saw, it was floating down the River Wear with me right behind it."

"What?"

Flenn turned the faucet all the way to the left. "Just go and make the coffee; I'll explain when I come down."

Zack couldn't stop laughing at the image of his friend taking a plunge off the bridge. "Wish I could've been there," he chortled as he poured Flenn a second cup of coffee.

"I wish you were there now! Then I could see how you like it," Flenn said, as he sat in the rocking chair, cradling the warm mug. "Run a check, will you? Make sure Connor O'Malley and his crew really do go back to Ireland."

"Will do. By the way, what's for supper? I haven't eaten anything since this morning at the pub."

"Gee, you're really shook up that I was almost drowned, aren't you?" Flenn shook his head. "I bought some stuff earlier, but I don't feel much like a salad anymore. How about we go over to the Bram and Bull?"

Zack looked away. "Um, about that… "

"Yeah."

"How about we order a pizza instead."

"Don't you want to see the fellas?"

Zack turned his eyes toward the far wall. "It has to do with what I found out at the library," he said. "When you told me how few people would have had access to the wine, it started me thinking."

"Well, that's something new," Flenn said. "Did it hurt much?"

"Ha, ha. Anyway, remember what Davy Spate told you about colocinium?"

"That it comes in a paste or liquid you mean?"

"Precisely. Well, I did some checking. Davy's right. I couldn't find anything out about the paste on the web, so I went through a few books in the chemistry section over at the university library. It took a while, but I found something. Not only does it come in a paste, but it is far more stable in that form. It can last for weeks."

Flenn stopped rocking.

"Remember how you said it was a goldish color?"

"I said it was yellow."

"Well, it's not, its gold. Antique gold to be precise. Which got me thinking. What if someone had handled the chalice?"

"A lot of people probably handled it."

Zack nodded, "That's what you would think; but not so. I found an article in the university newspaper from two weeks ago talking about the ordination of the new bishop of Durham and how this centuries-old Prince Bishop's chalice was being taken from the antiquities display. As with several objects over there, the chalice was behind secure glass with laser detection. The only time it is ever gotten out of the display case is for a bishop's ordination."

Flenn started to interrupt. Zack held up his hand. "The college newspaper didn't have anything else about it, so I looked through the Durham newspaper, but didn't find anything… at first."

"At first?"

"It was in an earlier edition from a couple weeks ago. Buried way back behind the real estate section."

Flenn leaned forward. "And?"

Zack grinned. "And, you can get a nice flat like this one over on Aidan Avenue for a steal."

"Come on, Zack!"

Zack reached inside his pocket and pulled out an envelope. Inside he'd stuffed a torn section of the newspaper. Flenn reached for it.

"This better not be a real estate ad."

Zack shook his head. "You may wish it were."

Inside the envelope was a brief story about the history of the chalice along with a photograph of four men and one woman, all smiling. One of them was holding the Prince Bishop's Chalice. According to the paper, the woman was the dean of Oxford's history department. The caption said that the others were retired scholars from nearby schools.

"Take a close look," Zack said.

"Yeah, it says these people are all retired professors living here in Durham."

"No, I mean at the photograph."

Flenn did. "Oh my God!"

Zack sighed. "That's exactly what I said when I saw it."

There, standing in the very back, smiling with the other academicians, was Charlie!

CHAPTER *FORTY-SEVEN*

11 years earlier...

Pam stared at the marquis above the theater. "No way!" she exclaimed. "I'm not going in there."

"Come on, Pammy," Donna said. "It'll be fun."

Hoshi looked at the poster of two naked males with strategically placed black rectangles. "A strip joint? Really, Donna?"

"Oh, don't you turn into a prude on me too, Hosh."

"I'm not, I'm just saying... "

Donna interrupted. "Don't say it. I expected Pam might object, but not you, girl. I seem to remember a certain fraternity party where someone was dancing on a table completely in the buff."

"Yeah, I remember it too," Hoshi said, "but it wasn't me; that was you!"

Donna shrugged. "It doesn't matter who it was; you were there." Donna desperately wanted another drink.

"I was there, trying to protect *your* honor... up until you climbed up on that table."

"I don't care what we did back then, I'm a married woman now," argued Pam.

"All the more reason for you to come with us!" Donna said before walking inside.

Hoshi turned to Pam, who was looking around to see if someone might recognize her. "I guess we sort of owe it to her," said Hoshi. "She did save our bacon back in the alley."

Pam sighed, pulling the collar of her jacket up to conceal as much of her face as she could. "Besides," said Hoshi, "if you've seen one, you've seen 'em all."

Pam couldn't help giggling, "Well, Donna certainly has!"

****

"Come on, Hosh, have a drink!" Donna said, then threw her head back and laughed.

"Yes, Hoshi, I must say it does help." Pam had scooched up as close to the back of the booth as she could.

"Waiter!" Donna called. A well-built man wearing nothing but a smile came to their table. "Bring my friend here some rum to put in that cola she keeps nursing."

The waiter glanced down at Hoshi, who, because of her height, was in a very awkward position at the moment. "No, really, I'm fine," she said, looking away. "Just another soda for me, please."

"Well, not for me," Donna called. "Bring me another one of these…," she looked at her glass, "… these… oh, whatever they are."

"And you, miss?" he said to Pam.

"Another Chardonnay please."

"So," Donna said, watching the man walk away, "are you having a good time?"

"Ugh," Pam replied. "I swear, if you tell Windsor that

we came here tonight I will never speak to you again! He'd never understand. He's gotten all holy-roly lately. I don't have anything against the Church, mind you, but that's all he wants to talk about these days."

"He's a great guy," said Hoshi; "and so is Zack," she said, turning to Donna, who was having difficulty keeping both eyes open at the same time.

"Who?"

"Zack! You know, the man you're going to marry in a few months at that castle."

"Oh, yeah... here's to whazzisname!" Donna accidentally knocked over her empty glass.

Pam shook her head. "And what about you?" she said to Hoshi. "Seems like you've landed quite a catch of your own."

Hoshi smiled at Pam just as a muscular behemoth took center stage. He was wearing a Stetson and dressed up as a cowboy... *at least he was for now!* She was growing rather bored with the spectacle. They weren't kids anymore, and none of this was making the impression that it was supposed to make. Hoshi wasn't interested in any man... other than Scott.

Donna, however, was thoroughly enjoying the show, and she *had* gone to a lot of trouble to plan the evening for the three of them. Hoshi and Pam agreed to stay another half hour and then convince Donna that it was time to go. After all, she and Donna had a plane to catch tomorrow.

"So, Wonder Woman," Pam said after the waiter brought them their drinks. "Are you going to tell us where you learned that Kung Fu move back in the alley?"

"Yeah," said Hoshi, "what's up with that?"

"It's Judo," Donna said. "Zack taught me."

Hoshi sipped her cola. "How come Zack knows Judo?"

Donna giggled, then put her finger to her mouth. "Shh, it's a secret."

"What is?" said Pam.

Donna tried to focus as the big man on stage tossed his leather vest into the crowd. "What Zack and Flenn *really* do for a living," she said, followed by a hiccup and another giggle.

Hoshi set her soda down just as a plaid shirt landed on their table. "They work for Scott's father… "

Donna tried to shake her head, but the motion made her dizzy. "That's just a cover."

Pam stared at her. "Huh?"

Hoshi's eyes narrowed. "A cover for what?"

Donna leaned closer, nearly collapsing onto the table. "You two are not going to believe this… "

CHAPTER *FORTY-EIGHT*

Present day...

Zack left early for the American Embassy in London where he would have secure access to the CIA database. He planned on running a background check on Charlie. Knowing Zack, it would be thorough. Flenn figured Zack would also look into the other professors pictured in the newspaper who had handled the Prince Bishop's Chalice that day.

As for Flenn, he needed a break from all the intrigue. He rented a car and left early for a place called Seahouses, a picturesque market town on the Northumberland coast. The car wasn't the only thing he rented. A boat was waiting to take him to the Farne Islands, where Flenn planned to spend the day alone in prayer and remembrance. *The port town known as Seahouses was not far from the island where he had been rescued from the sea years ago, right after Hoshi...* Flenn shook his head, to clear the memory from his mind.

Few cars were on the road today; most of it farm traffic. Flenn had never liked driving in the UK, but today he'd risked driving on the 'wrong side' of the road in order to go to the Farne Islands. After what had happened in Honduras, not to mention his and Zack's escapade last

December, Flenn had been longing to return to this peaceful place. It was on the innermost island that he'd first met the man who had turned his life upside down.

His senior warden, Martin Billingsly, had noticed the vicar's moodiness over the past month. "Father Flenn," he had told him, "you need a break." Flenn had protested, saying that he had just come back from a break in Honduras, but Martin had been ready for such an excuse. "You were down there doing back-breaking work. It's time you take a break from *all* of your ministries... Saint Ann's included."

"Well," Flenn had said. "We do have this pilgrimage to Ireland planned."

"Which is a good start," Martin had told him. "but you need to take some time off just for yourself."

Driving to Seahouses, Flenn remembered the rest of the conversation. "I need to be here to take care of Saint Ann's," he'd told the senior warden.

"Your parish *needs* you to take care of *yourself*!" Martin had argued. "No offense, Father, but you seem to have lost your focus lately." Flenn knew the reason why. "Try to think of a place you'd like to go; you can certainly afford it. Ask yourself where would you like to go most in the world."

As soon as Martin had said it, an image of the Farne Islands popped into the priest's mind. *He* wouldn't be there of course—Flenn knew that—but maybe just being back on the island would be balm for his spirit. The more he'd thought about it, the more excited he had become, until finally he had planned this trip. The surprising news about Windsor's ordination had come at just the right time. Flenn sighed. *Well, at least it had seemed right.*

He was sorry for Windsor, that he never got a chance to enjoy life as a bishop—if one can *enjoy* such a thing—but he was sorrier for Pam. She had lost her husband and her future as a bishop's wife. He wondered which one she'd miss more.

Pam had changed over the years. He couldn't say he'd ever really been overly fond of her, but Hoshi had been, and that had been reason enough.

Flenn sighed. Ten years, and he still grieved. Hoshi had been the love of his life. He'd vowed to her back then that he'd never be with anyone else. He didn't want another woman. He only wanted Hoshi. Even now. He said a prayer, the same one he always said when he remembered her.

The sign ahead read *Seahouses, 4 km.*

Flenn checked his watch. He was a little early, which meant that he'd have time for a coffee. He found himself wondering if Zack's train had made it to London yet, and what, if anything, his friend would be able to find out.

No, he reminded himself, *today is not for that. Today is for the sea and the sky, the cliffs and the birds. Today is for peace. The peace Cuthbert had once found on that very island.*

Of course, Cuthbert hadn't had to deal with Zack Matteson!

****

The waves of the North Sea crashed against the tiny boat as it made its way out to the innermost of the Farne

Islands. Flenn was glad he had decided not to cancel his trip after seeing that newspaper photo. Charlie hadn't mentioned anything about the Prince Bishop's Chalice to him or to the 'boys.' *If Murph had known, everyone in Durham would've known!* Flenn guessed that Murph, George and Bob didn't keep up with events at the university, getting most of their news from the 'telly' or from gossip around the pub.

So what if Charlie had access to the chalice, Flenn kept telling himself, *so had all of those other professors. It didn't necessarily make the man a suspect.*

Or did it?

If the poison had been placed in the chalice itself—and not in the wine as everyone seemed to think—then someone had to have put it there. Only a handful of people would've had access to that chalice prior to the service. Now, these six academicians would have to be added to the list of possible suspects, including Charlie.

Flenn sighed. He definitely needed this break today. After all, he'd originally come to Durham to relax. So far, his time in England had been anything but relaxing. Zack had gone to London to find out what he could. He'd told Flenn that he wasn't sure when he'd return, but that he'd call him if he discovered anything. Flenn figured Zack might have to stay in London since Wainwright had been called back to Parliament for an urgent session to discuss further sanctions against Russia. The editorialists at the *Times* and the *Sun* were clamoring for action against the Russians for yet another poisoning. The BBC was less direct, asking what motives the Russians might have for killing the Bishop of Durham. Some in parliament were publicly speculating that the Archbishop of Canterbury had been the real target.

Flenn tried to let all of that go as he sat in the back of the small boat with the sea spray washing over him. Ahead was what had forever been known as the Inner Farne. Celtic monks from Lindisfarne had lived here in quiet solitude centuries ago—the most notable of which was Cuthbert, who had resisted leaving even when the people had begged him to become their bishop. He had loved this tiny island, looking right now like a fortress against the sea, with its steep crags and formidable cliffs. The 'old man' had returned here to spend his last days after the simple Celtic Christians had been overwhelmed at the Council of Whitby by leaders from the larger, imposing Roman Church from the South.

Cuthbert had helped to keep the peace between the North and South to avoid civil war. It hadn't been easy. The Celtic Church of the North had been angry about being outmaneuvered (and outshouted) by the delegation from Rome. *No wonder the saint had sought solitude here amongst the waves.*

A squat, red and white lighthouse in the middle of the island warned sailors to keep their distance. Hundreds of shipwrecks littered these waters as, over the centuries, Danish, German, and French ships had come to tragic ends here—the more fortunate sailors having made it to one of the islands to await rescue.

Cuthbert's Island was a bird sanctuary and had been since Cuthbert himself had decreed it so in the year 676.

From out at sea, the cliffs looked like icebergs, solid white from centuries of bird waste. Flenn had wanted to return here ever since that night when he'd washed ashore 10 years ago, half-drowned. He knew now who it had been that rescued him, though he'd been clueless at the time.

Part of him wished to see that man standing on the shore of the island today, welcoming him back. Flenn sighed as he looked at the rocky beach. No one, not even the tour guides, were around today.

"I'll wait here," said the man who'd brought him. "How in Gawd's name you managed clearance to come here when the sacnt'ry is closed is beyond me," he said, helping Flenn onto the shore. "Mind the birds and the muck, and stay back from the edges; we've lost more than one wazzock who got too close to the cliffs."

Flenn climbed onto the small dock and made his way up several wooden steps to the top. The island was all grassland, no trees. Other than the lighthouse, the only other structures were Cuthbert's chapel and the ranger's office, along with separate loos marked 'Gents' and 'Ladies.'

Birds flew in every direction, tens of thousands of them. Flenn recognized terns, razorbills, gulls, and the little penguin-esque puffins. Those were the only species he knew, except for the eider ducks. Several legends abounded about Cuthbert and these ducks, all of them with some syrupy-sweet story about how the kind saint had taken to them.

"Damn nuisance," the man had called them the night

he had rescued Flenn from the sea. "Quacking all night long during mating season!" Flenn could still remember how good that one had tasted on the spit that night.

Birds, birds and more birds! It reminded Flenn of the Alfred Hitchcock movie from the 1960's. None of them seemed particularly happy at his arrival, either. Some nipped at his cap and one sat atop his shoulder and pecked at his ear. Flenn gently shooed the creature away. The birds had been quiet the night he'd washed ashore, but this morning they were everywhere. He was glad he'd taken the advice and worn the baseball cap and jacket after all.

"You came back!"

The voice behind him caused Flenn to nearly jump out of his skin. He turned, his eyes and mouth open wide. No one was there. "Is it really you?" Flenn stammered.

"Um, hello," said a young woman lying in the grass off to his left. "I'm sorry, have we met?" The park attendant was wearing a beige shirt with green pants and white cap.

Flenn was embarrassed… and a bit disappointed. "Sorry, I thought you were someone else."

"You must be Mr. Flenn. They told me to expect you." She reached out and lightly touched a bird who hopped toward a small nest. "I've been worried about these eggs, I hadn't seen the mother all morning, until just now. Sorry to give you a start."

"How can you possibly keep up with one nest? There must be thousands!"

The woman got up slowly so as not to disturb other

birds milling about. "Oh, I don't know. I just saw these eggs here this morning, and I was a bit worried. Sometimes, the mothers wander off."

Flenn smiled as he held out his hand. "I'm surprised they can find their way back at all. There's so many of them."

The woman, girl really, shook his hand. "I'm Rachel."

"Flenn, Scott Flenn." He smiled. "No need for the 'mister;' makes me feel old."

"Then you should come here more often," Rachel said. "This place will keep you young." She smiled at him. "I'm actually 62!"

"More like 16, I'm guessing," he said with a smile.

Rachel nodded. "Close. I'm 18. Me dad was going to meet you today but he took ill, so afraid you're stuck with me." The girl turned and led him toward the guide office.

"Sorry to hear about your father. I hope he'll be okay."

"Just too long at the pub last night, that's all," she said closing the door behind them. "So, what would you like to see?" she asked, removing her cap. Long, thick, red hair fell across her shoulders.

"Everything," Flenn said.

The girl smiled. "Well, that will cost extra." Flenn felt his ears turn red. "Just joking; the island is yours for the day. I have to say, we don't have many folks rent the island all to themselves. Was there something special you were interested in?"

"Well, you might say I'm a bit of a fan of Saint Cuthbert."

Rachel pulled out a brochure. "Then you came to the right place. Cuthbert spent a lot of time here, most of it by himself, according to Bede's history."

She took off her jacket and set it across the back of a chair. "Would you like some coffee?" Flenn nodded enthusiastically. "Come, sit over here. I'll pour you a cup."

Ah, to be eighteen again, he thought as he watched her walk over to the coffee stand near the wall. "Thank you," he said. "The sea was a bit chilly this morning."

"So was Sam, I bet."

"Sam?" he asked.

"The captain of your boat. He's a bit dodgy, that one. Me dad wouldn't have let me come alone if he'd known ol' Sam was bringin' you."

"Yet, he let you come alone having never met me?"

She laughed. "Yeah, well knowin' me dad, he figures someone who donated as much as you did to the National Trust to rent the island for a day might make a good husband for his only daughter."

Flenn's ears turned bright red for a second time. She placed the mug in front of him and handed him a map depicting what archaeologists thought the island might have looked like in Cuthbert's time. "When was the church built?" he asked.

Rachel sat down next to him. "They're not really sure. Sometime in the thirteenth or fourteenth century. But there was a small monastery here centuries before that. Of course, no one stuck around during the Viking invasions. They killed scores up at Lindisfarne." She looked at him. "Have you been to Lindisfarne?"

"I have," he said, remembering. "Years ago."

She smiled. "The mead there can't be beat."

Flenn raised an eyebrow. "I thought you said you were only 18?"

"Take a look around. It's lovely here, but there's not much else for a girl to do. Seals and Sea Lions don't make very grand companions."

Flenn thanked her for the coffee and studied the map, comparing it with the current landscape. The Chapel of Saint Cuthbert had been built on high ground overlooking the sea just over the original burial ground of the saint.

"Legend says when they moved Cuthbert's body to Lindisfarne years later it hadn't corrupted a bit," she said. "Course, that's impossible, I say." Flenn chewed on his bottom lip.

"You don't believe in miracles?" he asked.

She shrugged. "I dun'no. Maybe. I mean, sometimes I look out at the sea and... I don't know how to describe it. It's just a feeling, you know, like we're all part of somethin' grander." She blushed. "Listen to me goin' on, I'm sorry. You must think I'm just a silly girl."

"Not at all."

"What about you," she asked, "do you believe in miracles?"

Flenn thought back to the first night he'd been here. Rachel would have been no more than seven or eight back then. He looked down at the old map. "Absolutely."

CHAPTER *FORTY-NINE*

Present day...

"I'm sorry, Mr. Flenn, but I'll need to be going home soon." The late afternoon sun made the teenager's red hair sparkle as she stood at the doorway of Saint Cuthbert's Church. Flenn hadn't heard her come into the chapel; or known how long she'd been standing there.

He had spent the early part of the afternoon walking the island, careful to avoid stepping on birds, which had been a bit of a challenge. Rachel had loaned him the keys to the lighthouse, and even though it wasn't extraordinarily high, from the lantern room he had been able to see for miles. No one lived here anymore, the lighthouse had been automated for 20 years. At first, he'd thought that the hero who'd plucked him from the sea that night had been the keeper. It wasn't until later in Edinburgh that he'd discovered the truth.

After spending time in the lighthouse, he'd made his way to the far side of the island. He had come here to get away from the insanity of the past few months. He had planned his sabbatical to allow his spirit time to heal after Honduras. Sometimes, late at night, he could still see the trusting smiles of the village children right before... He took a deep breath and remembered the words of scripture: *Let the little children come unto me, for as such is the kingdom of heaven.* Flenn had learned to take comfort in those words these last few months, and had finally accepted that he had not been the reason for the slaughter of those innocent souls.

Standing now on a white cliff near a group of about 50 puffins, Flenn gazed across the North Sea. There was nothing he could do about the past, except to give it entirely to God, and trust that his maker could redeem any and all things. Flenn felt at peace here where Cuthbert had spent his last days. It was that peace he had originally come to England to find, and that peace which he needed now as much as ever. He closed his eyes and felt the wind caressing him. He took a deep breath; as he exhaled, he allowed the chaos of the past week to flow out of him.

Only the sound of the sea, the wind, and the roosting birds surrounded him now. Flenn opened his eyes. Soft, creamy-white clouds in the distance seemed to beckon him to join them, their golden edges promising the peace of a land far away. The cry of the birds seemed more like an invitation: "Fly away with us. " Flenn glanced at the crashing waves down below and stepped back. "Do it," a voice in his head said. "Jump! *He* will catch you. "

He shook his head, feeling as though he had been someplace else, a juncture where bliss and agony collided—one leading to paradise, the other to the abyss. The spell broken, Flenn walked back toward the tiny church wondering, not for the first time, just which path it was that he was traveling these days.

Durham had not proved the refuge he had hoped it would be. Instead, he felt as if he were trying to find his way through a cloud of chaos which made absolutely no sense. Windsor Tammerlane poisoned, IRA thugs throwing him into the river, and an old man at the end of his life, somehow caught up in all of this drama. *And to think*, Flenn told himself, *when he had come to England he'd thought his biggest problem would be Delores Dilwicky!*

He had found his way inside the Chapel of Saint Cuthbert and spent the rest of the afternoon in prayer. He prayed for the families of the slain Honduran children, for Pam and her family, and that justice would be swift so that no one else need suffer. He prayed for Charlie, who seemed to be wrestling with many demons right now. And, he prayed for Zack—the same prayer he always prayed, that Zack would one day find faith in something other than his job. Lastly, he prayed for those who would come to this island seeking the same peace Cuthbert had found here—and for Rachel, that she would find her miracle one day, and that it would bring her happiness.

"Mr. Flenn?"

Flenn crossed himself and stood, his knees aching more than they usually did. He had missed his morning run; maybe he'd go for a short one tonight. He looked at his watch, "Thank you, Rachel. I suppose Sam will be around soon?"

"Oh, he never left," she said. "He's been sleepin' in his boat all day."

"This whole time?" Flenn said.

"Nuttin' better to do, I s'pose. Pro'lly thinks me dad's here instead of me, thank Gawd."

Flenn stretched, then headed out into the daylight with the pretty redhead. Birds were flitting about everywhere. They donned their caps and walked slowly toward the edge of the island toward the dock. "Mr. Flenn, mind if I ask you somethin'?"

"Shoot."

The girl looked up at him. "Just how rich are you?"

As a kid, his family's wealth had embarrassed him. He'd long ago gotten over that. Money, he knew, was a tool, nothing more. A tool which could either be invested to amass more, or to be put to good use. Banks, the stock market, fancy cars and houses… these were nothing but fancy tool boxes. But for a tool to be any good, it had to be taken out and used. Which is what he preferred to do with his vast wealth—supporting charities and helping others in need. Flenn stopped and gazed into her green eyes. "Not so rich as you, I don't think."

The teenager's eyes widened. "Me?"

Flenn looked around the island at the tall meadow grass and the birds winging their way safely around this ancient sanctuary. He turned his gaze out to the North Sea and beyond. "I know of a girl, a couple years younger than you. She came from a wealthy family. Her name was Shelly." Flenn looked back toward the chapel. "Her stepfather abused her… her mother knew, but ignored it. Shelly had no friends; no one who cared."

"What happened to her?"

Flenn didn't go into detail, about how Shelly had

turned to a life of prostitution, or how she was brutally murdered by two power-mad sociopaths. He just shook his head and watched a little white bird fly toward the sea. "She died."

He looked at Rachel. "Rich in things is not really being rich."

The girl thought about that for a moment. "Will you ever be coming back here?" she asked.

He took a long, last look around. "I hope so, Rachel. I do hope so." They made their way toward the top of the steps leading down to the dock. "I suppose you manage that boat down there fairly well by yourself?"

She smiled. "Have since I was nine."

Flenn reached for his wallet. "Nine? Wow, that's impressive. Next time you are out there at sea, say a prayer for the Shellys of the world." He handed her five hundred pounds.

Her eyes grew wide. "I can't possibly take that!"

"Just promise me you'll have some fun with it. Someone your age needs to have fun. Thanks for today." Flenn turned and headed down the steps. Rachel waved goodbye as he climbed aboard Sam's boat.

Sam was leering up at the girl. "Gawd, I never knew *she* was here! Have some fun did you, mate?" The sneer disappeared when Flenn quickly stepped up to the man, his face inches away from the captain's own.

"I'm Rachel's friend, nothing more! And, unless you want to find yourself swimming home, you'll leave her alone from now on. Do I make myself clear?"

Sam tried staring Flenn down, but only for a moment.

Something in this stranger's eyes told him that he meant business. Finally, Sam turned away and untied the boat and shoved off. Not another word was spoken between them. Flenn turned back toward Rachel and the birds flying all around her. For the briefest of moments, he thought he caught a glimpse of someone else standing beside her.

CHAPTER *FIFTY*

Present day…

"Wotcha!"

Several patrons of the Bram and Bull turned toward the tall man with sandy brown hair as he entered the pub. "Wotcha, Father, fancy a drink?" cried Murph, Bob, and George all at once.

"Just some water," smiled Flenn. "I'm heading off for a run in a bit." He already had on his gym shorts, tee, and running shoes.

"Awfully late for a jog, Father." George said.

"Been gone all day; first chance I've had."

"Whenever I get the urge to exercise," Murph said, "I go straight for a lie-down until it passes!"

"I used to run," said Bob.

"Ah, go on," said George. "The only runnin' you ever done was from your Missus back in the day."

"That's not true," Murph said. "His nose runs every now an' again!"

Bob didn't laugh. "I'll have you know I was a star on my school's track team."

"Were you now?" said Murph.

Bob smiled and reached for his ale. "Best of the lot."

"All girls' school was it?" George chortled.

Flenn sat down next to Bob as Val handed him a tall glass of water. "Where's Charlie?" he asked.

"Dunno," said Murph. "Haven't seen the codger all day."

"I think I saw 'im," said Bob. "Early this morning, gettin' in a cab."

"A cab? Wonder where he was goin'?" George asked, offering his glass to Val. "Top 'er off will ya', love?"

Val shook her head. "You haven't paid for the last one yet."

"S'alright," Murph chimed. "The father's buyin'."

Val shot a questioning glance toward the priest. Flenn nodded his head. "I'm going to be broke by the time I leave Durham!"

"Listen to 'im!" Murph said with a grin. "Your secret's out, Father."

Bob nodded. "Your friend told us."

"Zack?" said Flenn.

George nodded. "Said ya' was loaded, he did."

Flenn shook his head. "I learned long ago, never to believe everything that comes out of Zack Matteson's mouth."

"We had Val look it up on the internet," Bob said.

George nodded. "Flenn Industries… Gawd almighty!"

Flenn stared at Val. "Gee, thanks."

She smiled, "Guess you're busted, eh Father?"

"Guess so. Next round's on me, fellas. Val, can I settle up with you tomorrow?" He pointed to his gym shorts which had no pockets.

"Course ya' can," said Murph.

Val nodded. "Have a good run, Father, but don't expect to see us out there wit' ya'."

Flenn stood up to leave. "Listen, if anyone sees Charlie, let him know I'm looking for him, would you?"

"We'll give 'im fair warnin'," said Murph.

Flenn headed down Crossgate away from the cathedral, then turned left onto Margery Lane. Rows of attached, and semi-attached, red-brick housing lined both sides of the street. There was still plenty of light, even though it was nearly 9 o'clock at night. It didn't get dark here until much later in the summer. He'd be back at the flat long before that.

Flenn rounded a sharp corner and nearly got clipped by an old man on a bicycle. "Sorry," the man called out behind him.

A sign ahead told him he was nearing a school. A drab-gray, two-story stone edifice seemed to go on forever. Someone had hung a white vinyl sign along one of the walls announcing:

Durham School, where every day is an Open Day

Flenn wondered what an open day was. He turned to look back at the sign just as a black Mercedes passed him. The car turned in front of the school and disappeared.

Flenn's thoughts turned to Zack and Pam. *Why had Pam not wanted to go to the police with that threatening note? And why hadn't it concerned Zack more than it had? Granted, he and Pam had never been that close, but there was something else going on, something odd. Zack usually came running when he had a puzzle he couldn't solve. So far, his friend had been keeping him at arm's length. It seemed as if Zack knew who the note was for. But that was impossible, wasn't it?*

If there had been any other traffic on the street, Flenn would never have heard the Mercedes creeping up from behind. He turned just in time to see the passenger window roll down…

…to be replaced by the muzzle of a semi-automatic!

Years of training kicked in as Flenn dropped and rolled backward. Most people confronted by a drive-by shooter instinctively run forward, in the same direction as the oncoming car, but Flenn rolled in the opposite direction. The car drove past him before the assassin had time to fire. By the time the driver stopped, Flenn had darted across the street and disappeared into the empty school playground to hide in the shadows. He heard the Mercedes' tires squeal as the driver sped away.

Flenn stood and brushed at his clothes, wiping the grass and dirt away. Apart from a few bloody scrapes he seemed to be okay. He found the playground's water fountain and cleaned his face and hands, while cursing himself for not paying more attention to his surroundings. *There was a time when he would have not only have escaped with his life, but would've been able to describe the color and make of the car, the license tag, and what the assailant looked like.*

Flenn made his way around the school and over a wall into a residential neighborhood. He waited to make certain his assailants weren't circling around searching for him. Eventually, he knocked at a nearby house where a family was cleaning up after a birthday party. Someone called for a taxi, and Flenn had the driver take him to the Bram and Bull.

"Whaz this all about?" Murph exclaimed, alarmed to see Flenn all banged up.

"You all right?" asked Bob.

George had already left, but Charlie had come in for a nightcap. "What on earth happened, Father?"

"It's nothing." Flenn made out that he had simply taken a tumble. "Guess I should know better than to run at night, huh?"

"Need us to ring Doc Martin?" Bob said. "He's just down the street. Val, give Isaac a call and get 'im up here."

"No, no, please, I'm fine." Just wanted to grab a cheese sandwich is all." What he really wanted was to sit by the window and keep an eye on his flat, in case the Mercedes showed up.

"Sure you're all right then, love?" Val asked before going to prepare his sandwich.

He winked. "Nothing hurt—other than my pride."

"'Ere, come join us, Father," Murph said.

"Actually, I think I need to stretch out a bit, guys, but thanks."

Charlie went behind the bar to pour a pint, then brought it over to Flenn. "Here, Father. This time, it's on us." Charlie stood by the table, surveying Flenn's injuries. He made no effort to return to his usual perch.

"Care to join me, Charlie?"

The old man pulled out a chair. "I'm sorry," he said.

"Just a fall," Flenn forced a grin. "Not my first." Flenn glanced out the window, but the street was empty.

Charlie lowered his voice. "Was it?"

"Huh?"

"Was it just a fall? It's not dark yet, and the streets here are well-lit at night; seems strange an experienced runner like you falling."

Flenn sipped the beer. "Nothing to worry about."

Charlie shook his head. "It may be, if what I think happened… "

Valerie called from the kitchen, "You be wantin' some chutney with that, love?"

"Absolutely," Flenn said, as he looked over to the bar. Murph waited for Val to disappear before reaching over to top off his own beer; he turned and winked at Flenn.

"Who was it, Father?" Charlie asked.

"Nobody, I just fell, that's all." Flenn tried changing the subject. "How about you? You feeling okay?"

Charlie shook his head. "Father, I went and talked with someone today."

Flenn nodded. "Your doctor?"

"No, not about that." He bit his bottom lip. "I think I may have made things worse." Charlie's eyes met his. "You may be in danger."

CHAPTER *FIFTY-ONE*

11 years earlier…

"This one should prove easier than the last," Davy Spate promised as he met Flenn and Zack at the elevator. They exited into an underground network of cement and tile hallways, each leading to steel-gray doors, some open, others guarded by soldiers holding standard-issue French assault rifles.

Davy led them down a long corridor into one of the unguarded rooms. A rectangular table was pushed up against the pale white wall. Folding chairs were scattered about the room and a large monitor was attached to the wall opposite the door. Underneath was a small cabinet with a coffeepot, half empty. Flenn headed straight for it.

"What do you guys know so far?" Zack asked.

"Just that this chap isn't like Yasir Kamul at all. He seems to have wandered unintentionally into all this mess. He's a warlord from a tiny Syrian village who made a small fortune off the opium trade. It looks like the bloke was simply trying to get a piece of the action when Kamul recruited him."

"Sounds like my guy Asim," Flenn said. "He didn't really understand the ideology of it all either."

"Compared to Asim, this guy's a pushover," Davy

said. "We may finally be onto something here." The Brit reached up and turned on the monitor. Immediately a picture of a room, similar in size to the one they were in, flashed across the screen.

"So," Davy said, "what's this I hear about you having a new girlfriend?"

Zack poked Flenn in the ribs. "You mean you haven't told him? I thought the whole world knew." Zack looked at Davy. "She's no longer just a girlfriend. She's his fiancée now!"

"Not yet," said Flenn, but I plan on asking her this week."

"Well, 'ol boy, congratulations are in order then! Wish I had some Champagne to offer you a toast."

"After what happened last time, I don't think I'd drink anything during this interview," Flenn said.

"Still and all," Davy offered, "I hope that you will be as happy as my next wife will be… whoever she is."

A moment later, the three of them watched two guards bring in a man in an orange jumpsuit, shackled at both the ankles and wrists. Omar Rashad's eyes darted around the room. He looked exhausted and thinner than he had when they'd last seen him trying to buy surface-to-air missiles.

One of the guards bent down and fastened Rashad's manacles to the heavy chair, which Flenn knew was bolted to the floor. The guard had Rashad sit so that he could connect his handcuffs to the arm of the chair. After that, both guards left the room. Rashad looked directly into the camera, not with the cocky self-reliance Flenn and Zack had seen in the hotel that day; it was more as if he were pleading with whoever was on the other side.

Flenn sipped his coffee and Zack reached in his pocket for a small bag of jellybeans. "You're right, Davy. We may finally find out something with this one."

Two men in dark suits walked into the interrogation room, each holding a soda can. Rashad didn't bother looking at them, but rather licked his lips as he stared at their drinks. Flenn knew why. *There were lots of techniques to get a man to talk.*

The men wasted no time in questioning Rashad about his relationship to Yasir Kamul. The interrogators were skilled in their craft and Flenn, Zack, and Davy listened as the Brits artfully led the man into describing his involvement with Kamul, what his relationship had been to Al-Qaeda, what he knew of Zamir's whereabouts, and finally... *the name they had been waiting to hear!* Flenn leaned closer to the screen.

"They call themselves *Al-Mashriq*," he said. Flenn knew Al-Mashriq was an Arabic phrase meaning to shine or to illuminate. It could also be translated as 'land of the sunrise,' the mythical birthplace of the Arab world.

CHAPTER *FIFTY-TWO*

Present day...

Flenn hung up the phone and walked outside. Summertime back home in Alabama was brutal. Here in England, it was only 65 degrees at noon. He wasn't sure what that translated in Celsius, nor did he care right now. He had a lot on his mind this morning as he made his way toward the cathedral.

He'd tried calling Pam but was told that she was not receiving visitors. Something in the manner her maid had spoken over the phone seemed odd. She'd been short, rude even. *Perhaps Pam was embarrassed that he had seen her over-medicated, and had taken it out on her maid? Or maybe the woman was in trouble for having told Flenn about Pam's drug problem.*

He'd had more success with Davy Spate. Davy had agreed to come to Durham and do some snooping around. They'd arranged to meet tonight at the Cope and Mitre, a pub just down the road from Durham Cathedral. Last night, Charlie had mentioned something about having gone to speak with his nephew, but Flenn had still been pretty shaken last night and had paid more attention to keeping an eye on his flat. Realizing that Flenn wasn't in a listening mood right after his 'fall,' Charlie had agreed to talk more about it later.

After Flenn was reasonably certain no one was watching the flat, he'd left the Bram and Bull, but he'd piled up chairs and furniture against both doors and slept on the floor by the fireplace last night. He had considered calling Zack to tell him what had happened, but thought better of it. His friend was here on an official assignment. He wasn't in England to babysit him, or even to figure out who'd killed Windsor Tammerlane for that matter. Somehow, however, Flenn couldn't escape thinking that the two events were connected.

The next morning he made his way down Neville Street on his way to purchase a do-it-yourself alarm system from electronics store he'd seen near Tesco. He wanted something loud enough to wake the neighbors should someone break through either of the doors or the downstairs windows. He'd need to warn Zack, in case he returned from London unannounced.

He and Zack hadn't said goodbye. *No need—Zack would be back; Zack always came back.* Flenn sighed. He'd seen more of Zack Matteson in the past year than he had in the previous five put together. That wouldn't necessarily be a bad thing, except that every time Zack came, trouble soon followed.

After purchasing a door alarm system and promising to pick it up later in the afternoon, Flenn made his way to the cathedral. He wanted to spend some time alone in Cuthbert's shrine. *He'd come to Durham for a reason, well two reasons. The first was to relax. The second was to visit and pray at this shrine. He'd at least try to accomplish the latter.*

Damn!

The man Zack referred to as Rip Van Winkle was waiting for him just outside the shrine. *What's he doing here?* Flenn wondered.

"Mr. Beamish, I didn't know you were a fan of Saint Cuthbert." Flenn walked past him and up the steps to the chapel.

"May I have a word?" said the British agent.

Flenn sighed. "I suppose, but it will have to be in here."

Beamish seemed surprised. "What? In the shrine? I'd prefer we went outside."

Flenn turned; he'd had enough. "Look, I came to Durham for some R&R, and so far I've been mugged, thrown in a river, shot at, and had a friend murdered in this very cathedral. I came here to pray; whatever you have to say to me will just have to be said in front of the saint!"

Flenn turned and disappeared into the shrine.

"Shot at?" Beamish bounded the steps after him. "I didn't know anything about that."

Damn. No one else was inside; he'd hoped there'd be enough people to make Beamish reconsider and just leave. Flenn sat down across from the tomb. "No one actually ever fired. I slipped away before they could."

Beamish stood over him. "Who was it?"

"Drive-by, I didn't get formally introduced." Beamish

grunted as he sat beside him. Flenn shook his head. "Beamish, why are you here?"

"I understand Matteson is back in Durham."

"Not to my knowledge." Flenn figured he'd see Zack again, but didn't feel particularly motivated to tell Beamish that.

"What is your business with David Spate?"

Flenn raised an eyebrow. "You know Davy, do you?"

"Not on a personal level, no."

Flenn wasn't about to tell Beamish what he wanted with Davy, at least not anytime soon. Not until he and Davy had managed to find out something out about who had tried to kill him.

"He's an old friend. He helped me with a tour group I brought over from my diocese." Beamish made a face, similar to the one Delores Dilwicky made anytime someone asked her for a favor. "He's a tour guide, you know."

"Spate's a lot of things," Beamish said. "Why is he coming to Durham?"

"I owe him money." Flenn wasn't above lying, but only if it was for the right reason.

"What money?" Beamish was persistent, Flenn gave him that, at least.

"Five-hundred pounds. Down payment for the next trip. Though, if it doesn't go a lot better than this one, I'll just stay home."

Beamish looked him directly in the eye. "What does Spate have to do with Elton Wainwright?"

Flenn shrugged. "Nothing. At least, not that I know of? Why?"

"Did he mention anything to you about a certain property Mr. Wainwright owns in the Yorkshire Dales?"

Flenn shook his head.

"Are you certain?"

Flenn glanced across the room toward Cuthbert's tomb. He was tired of this. "Look, would you mind leaving me to my prayers? I don't know anything about Elton Wainwright, other than he is apparently in line to be your next prime minister, that he seems to have some inside connection with Sinn Fein, that he likes the ladies and doesn't let a little thing like a wedding ring get in his way… oh, and that Windsor Tammerlane couldn't stand the man."

"Well, do you blame him?"

"For what?" Flenn said.

Beamish cocked his head. "Matteson didn't tell you?"

"Tell me what?"

"About Wainwright and Pamela Tammerlane?"

Flenn didn't understand. "Wainwright and Pamela what?"

Beamish winked.

Flenn's eyes grew twice their normal size.

****

Thunder pealed outside as Flenn finished installing the alarm system late that afternoon. He wasn't sure who'd tried to kill him last night, and he wasn't at all happy that Beamish had somehow known about his meeting with Davy Spate tonight. At least the alarm would offer a modicum of protection.

The unexpected storm had hit Durham right as Flenn had returned from the cathedral. Incredibly, someone knocked at the door just as Flenn set the stepstool back in the closet. *Who could possibly be knocking in this downpour?*

Zack Matteson, who else.

"Damn it, Zack! You could've told me!"

Zack rushed inside, shaking the lapels of his trench coat, relieved to get out of the rain. "Sorry, you know me. I just show up."

Flenn was furious. "That's not what I mean! I'm talking about Pam having an affair with Elton Wainwright!" Zack hadn't seen his friend this angry in a long time. Lightening illuminated the tiny flat a split second before being followed by a deafening roar.

"Wow, that was close!" Zack said.

"I thought *we* were close!" Flenn yelled over the storm. "Didn't you think I deserved to know?"

Zack took off his jacket and shook off the water. "Well, hello to you, too."

"I'm not fooling around. You owe me an explanation. Pam and Windsor were friends of mine!"

"Hey, they were my friends too, you know." Zack countered.

"Still, you could've… "

"Could have what? Ruined your friendship with the Tammerlanes? How the hell did you find out?"

"Beamish told me."

Zack shook his head. "That jerk never did know when to keep his mouth shut."

Flenn paced back and forth; not an easy task in the

tiny living room. "Damn it, Zack, that has nothing to do with it."

Zack got an ale out of the little refrigerator. "It has everything to do with it. Beamish didn't need to tell you. He obviously discovered that we were all old friends and just wanted to mess with you." He took a swig from the bottle. "What business is it of yours in the first place? The only reason I knew was because I followed him to his summer house in Yorkshire a couple of weeks ago."

Flenn stopped pacing. "Beamish mentioned something about that place; he wanted to know if Davy had some sort of connection to it." Zack cocked his head. "I'm having dinner with Davy," Flenn explained. "Beamish wanted to know why."

Zack didn't ask how Beamish had known about Flenn and Davy meeting tonight. Spies have their ways. "Probably wants to know if Davy had anything to do with the place burning down last week."

"Wainwright's house burned down?"

"Gas leak. At least that's what it's being blamed on."

"Why would he think Davy knew anything about that?"

"Davy spends a lot of time out in the Dales these days." Zack shook his head. "Davy's not the same guy we knew back in the day. Since leaving MI-6, he's managed to get himself in with some not so very nice people. He's been known to dabble in some things."

"What things?"

"Illegal gambling, mostly. He's thrown in with a

bunch of small-timers in the Dales. They pay him to help find ways to work around the police."

"*Davy*?"

Zack nodded. "Drinks a lot, too; not sure you need to be telling him anything important."

Flenn stared out the kitchen window. "What the hell is going on? Someone poisons Windsor in a grand spectacle, the IRA throws me off a bridge, Pam's having an affair with a member of parliament, MI-6 is trying to protect their golden boy, someone threatens Pam, Davy's thrown in with hoodlums, and I'm nearly killed in a drive-by."

Zack almost sprayed ale across the room. He wiped his mouth. "What?"

"I was going to get to that—eventually. Somebody tried to shoot me last night while I was out running."

Zack leaned over and grabbed a towel from the table to wipe the ale from his lap. "Any idea who?" he asked as he tossed the towel toward the kitchen counter, missing it entirely.

Flenn reached in the cabinet for a glass. "I think I do now."

"Care to enlighten me?"

Flenn stared at the towel on the floor until Zack picked it up. "Elton Wainwright."

"Why would Wainwright want to off you?" Zack threw the towel at him.

Flenn poured himself a double. "Makes sense to me now. He probably thinks I know about his affair with Pam. Can't have something like that leak to the press; it'd ruin his bid for prime minister."

Outside, a clap of thunder rolled down the cobblestone streets.

Zack shook his head. "He's not the type. He's a cad, but Wainwright's not violent."

"Oh? What about his ties to the IRA?"

"There are no ties," Zack said. "He's catholic, so he gives a nod to North Ireland. Sinn Fein listens to him; he's been one of the people helping keep the treaty working all these years."

Flenn thought for a moment as he swirled the liquor in his glass. "Okay, what about his public feud with Windsor? I understand that it made all the papers over here." Zack didn't respond. "On top of the affair with Pam, and Connor O'Malley and his boys just happening to be at the ordination, it all looks pretty damn convincing to me!"

Zack set his glass on the table. "Okay, I'll check it out; but I don't believe it. In the meantime, I don't like you staying here alone anymore."

"Well, so far I haven't been. You've been in and out so much I'm thinking of charging rent."

Zack reached in his pocket and tossed him a penny. "Seriously, a hotel might be safer."

Flenn shook his head. "Hotels are too easy. At least here I can sleep downstairs and keep an eye on both doors."

Zack sighed. "Still as stubborn as you ever were. Well, at least some things never change." He finished his ale and headed for the door. "I'll be back."

"You're not going out in this weather, are you?" As if to accentuate the point, lightning lit up the block, followed immediately by a huge explosion of thunder. "My Lord! That was close!"

Zack stuck his head out the door. A pungent aroma of burning plastic filled the room.

"See anything?"

"It hit the pub!"

"Not the Bram and Bull!"

"The other one!" Zack ran out the door and around the corner with Flenn close behind. A small crowd of patrons stumbled out of the Death Angel into the pouring rain. Zack and Flenn could see flames rising inside the building.

"Somebody call an ambulance!" a man yelled. "Bluto's not breathing."

Flenn pushed past the fleeing customers into the pub. Two scantily dressed young women were dragging a third woman toward the entrance.

Flenn stopped them and put his finger to the unconscious woman's neck until he felt a pulse. "Get her under the awning and try to keep her dry," he told them as the angry flames flashed from the back of the pub.

"Somebody needs to get Bluto!" one of the women screamed.

"Who's Bluto?" Zack had followed Flenn inside.

"Doesn't matter," yelled Flenn over the noise. "Where is he?" he asked the woman.

"He's in the back, behind the bar!" she yelled as he and Zack made their way to the door.

A small explosion came from their right. "Kitchen!"

said Zack, "I'll see if anyone's in there; you go find Bluto!"

Smoke was thick as the flames began to make their way forward. Flenn found his way to the back where he nearly tripped over a man on the floor. Even though Bluto seemed as if he weighed a ton, Flenn managed to hoist him upright and place his right leg between the big man's legs. He grabbed Bluto's right hand and pulled his arm around his shoulder. With his head under the man's armpit, Flenn wrapped his arm around Bluto's right knee, squatted down, and let the man fall across his shoulders.

The smoke made it difficult to breathe and Flenn only made it halfway to the door before collapsing. Zack had managed to find an extinguisher and was busy trying to fight the fire, but he dropped it as soon as he saw Flenn struggling with the big man. He rolled Bluto off of Flenn, and together they carried him out to the street where Flenn started CPR. Zack ran back inside to see if anyone else needed help.

The rain began to let up as a crowd formed a semi-circle around Flenn.

"My Gawd!" cried one woman.

"Is 'e goin' to be a'right?" asked another.

Flenn paid little attention as he pinched the man's nostrils and blew air into his lungs. He didn't even hear the fire truck or ambulance coming up Neville Street.

"My Lord, that's the Father, that is!" Murph and Bob bounded across the street toward Flenn. Murph had a fire extinguisher in one hand and a beer in the other. George and Charlie weren't far behind. Murph handed Bob the beer and ran inside the Death Angel.

"Come on, damn it... Breathe!" Flenn yelled as he compressed Bluto's chest several times before blowing more air into his lungs. The firemen quickly unrolled their hoses and began attaching them to a nearby hydrant. When a paramedic took over for Flenn, the priest stood, wiped the soot from his face, and stood over the man. His eyes were closed in prayer.

"Zack! Are ya' in there!" Murph called.

"Back here!" Zack was working his way back out. "Is that you, Murph?" The ceiling suddenly began to groan and a beam fell between the two men. Flames shot up to the ceiling, trapping Zack behind them. He turned his extinguisher toward the beam, but it was empty; he'd used it all. Murph aimed the one he'd brought from the Bram and Bull and started spraying flames.

"Aim at the base!" Zack yelled.

Murph did, and the flames abated enough for Zack to jump across. The firemen were coming through the door just as Murph and Zack found their way back outside. Flenn was grinning from ear to ear. The big man they called Bluto was sitting up and coughing.

"The Father saved 'im!" George called out with a grin.

Zack patted Murph on the back. "And Murph here saved me!"

"Did I?" Murph said, scratching his head. "I suppose I did at that!" Murph looked around, "Where's Bob? Bloke's got my beer..."

CHAPTER *FIFTY-THREE*

11 years earlier…

"Beer?" Zack held up a bottle as Flenn sat down across from him at the café.

"No thanks." Flenn was more in the mood for Champagne. Even if they hadn't caught Zamir yet, they at least now had a name for the barbaric new group emerging from the bowels of Al-Qaeda. American and British intelligence could now track the group by following monetary transactions and monitoring cyber-traffic.

Flenn tried signaling the waiter, who simply ignored him. "You'd best take me up on the beer; it took me half an hour to get that guy's attention," Zack said.

"Serveur, un bouteille de votre meilleur Champagne," Flenn called loudly. *Asking for his best Champagne would certainly bring the man over.*

It did.

"So," Flenn asked, "you contact Langley yet?"

"I thought you would."

Flenn knew his friend's propensity for waiting until the last minute to notify their superiors. "God, Zack! Davy has probably filled in everyone at MI-6 by now!"

Zack reached into his pocket for a jellybean and

grinned. "Then what is the point? Langley already knows."

"They don't *always* share everything with us, you know."

"Who is talking about sharing," Zack said. "You know how things work as much as I do."

Zack was right. Leaks between the intelligence agencies were common. "Still," Flenn said, as the bottle of Champagne arrived along with two glasses and a tray of cheese and fruit, "you need to call Langley."

"Why don't you do it? They don't like talking to me." Zack reached for a strawberry.

"Because I have a date tonight. Hoshi's flight is coming in at eight."

"Yeah I know." Zack said. "Donna's coming with her."

Flenn raised an eyebrow. "I thought Donna was heading back home."

"She changed her mind." Zack opened the second beer. "How about we all go out for a late dinner tonight?"

Flenn shook his head. "Thanks, but we have plans."

Zack chuckled. "Plans, yeah right. I know what you're planning." He pointed at the bottle of Champagne. "You drinking that all by yourself?"

"You can't order just a glass of the good stuff; you have to order the whole bottle. Finish that beer and you can help me."

Zack pushed the beer aside, reached over, and poured the glass to the brim. "I'll say this much, when you finally fell, you fell hard." A breeze stirred the blue-and-white umbrella above their head.

Flenn grinned. "Well, Hoshi's a special girl. I've never met anyone like her. She's funny, smart, beautiful, and sweet."

"And 12 years old, don't forget," teased Zack.

Flenn sighed. "We do get some odd looks from people, but I don't care anymore. I mean, what more could a guy ask for, she's funny, smart, beautiful…"

"You said that already."

Flenn refilled his glass. "Well, it bears repeating."

Zack tasted the champagne and then peered into his glass, watching the bubbles make their way to the top, never seeming to stop. "Not bad."

"Glad you like it. It's $400 a bottle."

Zack's jaw dropped. "Not bad, I said, but not worth 400 bucks! Are you crazy?"

Flenn leaned back in his chair and smiled. "Nah; I just have an appreciation for the finer things in life… like Hoshi."

Zack shook his head. "Since when have you ever cared about the 'finer things in life'?"

"I'm just happy, that's all. Sheesh, give a guy a break, why don't you. She's funny, beautiful… "

"And sweet; don't forget sweet." Zack picked up the dark green bottle to read the label. "Can't say as I blame you. You and Hoshi seem great together. Donna was saying just the other day that she's never seen Hoshi so happy."

"I think we both are," Flenn said. "Strike that. I *know* we both are! And tomorrow I have the day all planned… "

Zack interrupted. "That's when you're proposing?"

From Flenn's grin, Zack knew that it was. He raised his glass. "Well then, here's to another match made in heaven!"

Flenn accepted the toast readily. "Well, I may not believe in heaven, but I think the only response to that would be, 'Amen'!"

CHAPTER *FIFTY-FOUR*

Present day...

The fire yesterday hadn't caused as much damage as first appeared. Flenn had ventured around the corner to survey the damage at the Death Angel where he found Bluto talking with a short man dressed in a blue shirt and gray tie. Zack had left last night after a quick shower, saying something about checking on Elton Wainwright, who was back in Durham.

"There 'e is! Me savior!" The big man wrapped his arms around Flenn and nearly squeezed the life out of him.

Flenn turned red. "Well, I do work for him... "

"Oh, that's right! Ol' Murph told me you were a man of the cloth." Bluto turned to the man in the tie. "This 'ere's the one who pulled me out of the grim reaper's clutches. Father, this is me insurance man. Says we can have the pub up an' runnin' in a month!"

"A month or *two*," the short man corrected.

"Can't have two, else I'll be givin' all me business to the Bram." Bluto turned to the priest. "If yer' still in Durham, Father, all the drinks will be on the house!" Flenn thanked the man and left them to their business. He wandered across the street into the Bram and Bull.

"Wotcha!" Flenn called out.

Only Charlie and Colin were in this morning, each with a steaming mug of coffee. "Wotcha, Father!" Charlie said. "I was just about to have some eggs and toast, fancy joining me?" Flenn looked across the bar at Colin. "I'd love some. Add a couple of sausages; oh, and put Charlie's on my tab."

Colin shook his head. "Not today, Father! Breakfast is on me. What you did yesterday was a miracle."

Flenn waved the compliment away. "No miracle, just CPR."

Charlie shook his head and grinned. "That's not what he means. You just sent a ton of business over here until the Death Angel opens back up."

"Aw, listen at 'im, will you now," Colin said as he disappeared into the kitchen.

Charlie picked up his mug and moved from the bar to a table. Flenn joined him. "Seriously Father, that was pretty impressive yesterday. And the way you went about it... didn't seem like your first time."

Flenn shrugged. "It wasn't. When I was in the Air Force, I saw a good bit of action overseas."

Charlie leaned forward. "About the other night. That nephew I spoke of..." Charlie paused, staring down at his coffee. He took a deep breath before continuing. "I think he might know something about what happened up at the cathedral."

Flenn raised an eyebrow. "Know something? Like, maybe who did it?"

Charlie nodded, but didn't look up. "Maybe more than that."

A crease formed across Flenn's brow. "Charlie, are you saying your nephew may have been involved?" The look on the old man's face reminded Flenn of one of his parishioner's, when the doctor told him that his wife hadn't made it through surgery last year.

After a moment, Charlie nodded. Flenn couldn't recall if Charlie had ever said just who his estranged nephew was. "Why do you think that?" Charlie turned and gazed out the window as a gentle shower began to fall on the other side of the pane. The old professor reached in his pocket for a handkerchief and blew his nose.

"My sister's boy. Never had anything to do with the rest of us. Hadn't heard from him in years until he called a few weeks ago." He looked over at Flenn. "You have to understand, it's hard on a pensioner. There are bills to pay, accounts to settle, whether you're healthy as a horse or dying of cancer."

Flenn wasn't following. "Who is this nephew of yours?"

Charlie turned to look out the window again; his bottom lip quivering ever so slightly. Small drops of rain trailed slowly down the pane; a soft tapping against the glass the only sound. After a moment, Charlie took a deep breath and said, "His name is Tobias Love."

****

Charlie didn't show up the next morning to share a cup of coffee with the guys at the Bram and Bull. Instead, he'd been invited to the flat to talk with Flenn, Zack, and an older man who said he was from York. The priest had told Charlie that the man used to work with British intelligence.

"I didn't know what Tobias had planned, and I don't know for sure that he's involved," Charlie told them, "but it's been nagging at me for days now." "He's my sister's kid. Some kid—he's 50 years old!?

"Hadn't heard from him in years; then, somehow he gets wind that I'm one of the professors who's been invited to see the Prince Bishop's chalice. He said he had a dear friend who was a history buff and would pay me 10,000 pounds just for a look. I originally said no; it just didn't feel right, but Tobias kept calling. Finally, at £50,000, I agreed. You know, Father, a pensioner doesn't make very much, but his widow makes even less. I was just thinking of Nancy is all, and my granddaughter. She'll be wanting to go to university soon."

Flenn got up to refill his mug. "Just tell us exactly what happened."

"They gave each of us a half-hour to take photographs, make studies, whatever. It wasn't very scientific really, none of us brought any equipment with us; it was just a way to make some of us coffin-dodgers happy. The dean from Oxford brought gloves, magnifying glasses and a few other things we were free to use. Each of us was allowed to bring along one companion. I brought my nephew's friend."

"His name?" Zack asked.

"Potter. Like that kid in those books. I don't remember

his first name. Sorry. He was a short fellow, kind of pudgy, and bald."

"That's okay, Charlie," Flenn said, reassuringly. "Just tell us what happened next."

Charlie took a breath. "Well, we were the last two to get to see it. They made sure we had gloves on and wore masks. Potter brought his own, in fact, which I thought kind of odd." Charlie shook his head. "Something else bothered me: He handled the chalice roughly, not at all like a professional. You'd think someone with his interests would have known how to handle an ancient artifact. I had to tell him at least twice to be careful with it.

"About ten minutes in, he asked if he could have a moment alone with the bloody thing." He shrugged. "I figured since Tobias was paying me fifty thousand quid for his friend to have this opportunity I'd excuse myself to the loo for a few minutes. When I came back, the chalice was on the table and Potter said he was ready to leave."

Flenn raised an eyebrow. "Your time wasn't over?"

"No, we still had another ten minutes. Potter thanked me and said he was ready to leave. Just like that."

Zack leaned closer. "Did you notice if he'd done anything to the chalice?"

Charlie hesitated. "No, it looked… well, now that you mention it…"

"Yes?"

Charlie wiped his brow with the back of his hand. "The cup did seem a bit duller at the bottom of the well. Could've been the way the light was reflecting off it.

Funny… I never thought about it at the time, not until you just asked."

"And you were the last ones to see the chalice?" Flenn asked.

"That's right," Charlie said. "After we were done, they locked it back up until the day of the ordination."

Flenn turned toward Zack. "That's when it happened."

Charlie took a breath. "Potter did it, then? He poisoned it while I was gone?"

Davy nodded. "Looks like it. Colocinium can come in a golden paste which is safe to handle, until you add liquid. Then it becomes highly toxic."

"So… it was never in the cruet?" Zack was confirming what he had already surmised.

"No," Davy said. "It would have lost its toxicity by the time they used it. I mean you can still identify it in a laboratory and all, but its relatively harmless after just a few minutes. You remember that guy in Iraq? He must have mixed the poison in the juice right before he brought it inside."

"What about that doctor, then?" Zack asked. "The one who died trying to save Tammerlane."

"Any scratch or cut on his skin would have let it into his bloodstream when he was trying to help the bishop." Davy nodded toward the priest. "Flenny-boy here is a very lucky man."

Flenn nodded. "I got to the sacristy and washed off immediately. No cuts on my hands, I guess."

Zack turned toward Davy. "The color of that stuff, is it about the same as the chalice?"

"Nearly identical, I'd say. You would have had to be looking for it to see the paste at the bottom of that gold cup."

Flenn shook his head. "And nobody was looking for it."

Charlie put his head in his hands. Flenn reached over and patted the old man's shoulder. "It's not your fault, Charlie. You had no idea that Love and Potter were planning something like this. How could anyone? You were just trying to help your family. Nobody blames you."

Charlie didn't respond. When he did look up, his eyes were moist, but his face was rock hard. Flenn had seen that look before.

"Whatever you're thinking, Charlie, don't do it. Let Davy handle it. He's a professional, like I told you. I'm sure his friends with British intelligence are on top of this."

Zack rolled his eyes.

"And, if not," Flenn was staring at Zack now, "Zack will make sure that they are!"

Charlie stood and headed for the door, but stopped half way there and turned toward Flenn. "I'm sorry, Father, I truly am. I never meant for any of this to happen."

Flenn followed him to the door; he hadn't noticed until now just how frail Charlie truly was. "Don't you worry about any of this. It wasn't your fault."

Charlie didn't seem convinced, but he shook the priest's hand and bid the other two farewell. He looked across the room at Zack. "And don't worry, Zack, your secret is safe with me. I must say, I never figured you for a New York City police detective."

Flenn glanced at Zack.

"I don't tell too many folks about it when I go out of town," Zack said. Charlie nodded before shutting the door behind him, leaving Flenn, Zack and Davy to figure it all out. "Well, gents," Zack said, "we know the what and the who and the how of it all. Now all we have to figure out is the why."

CHAPTER *FIFTY-FIVE*

11 years earlier...

Flenn and Zack waited impatiently to catch sight of Hoshi and Donna as passengers from Flight 815 filed past them. Charles de Gaulle Airport was busy tonight with flights arriving from all over the world.

The hour-and-a-half flight from Scotland had been delayed, giving Flenn time to buy a dozen yellow roses from a nearby kiosk. He stood holding them as they both caught sight of Donna. Instead of her usual bubbly self, Donna's face was drawn, her lips pressed tightly together. She didn't look at Flenn, only at Zack, who grabbed her in his arms and gave her a hug.

"Donna," Flenn said, "where's Hoshi?"

Donna turned, although she refused to make eye contact. "She's not coming."

"What?" Zack said.

"Not coming?" Flenn said. "Why not?

Donna brushed her hair behind her ears and looked up at Zack. "I tried to call you, really I did! You didn't answer."

"What's happened?" Flenn said. "Is Hoshi okay?"

Zack looked down at his phone and then back up at Donna. "Sweetheart, what's going on?"

Donna began to cry.

"My God, Donna, what's happened to Hoshi?" said Flenn.

She turned and looked at him. "Me! I'm what happened! God, I'm so sorry Flenn, I didn't mean to… I just had too much to drink."

She looked up at her fiancé. "You know me, Zack, when I drink I say things… stupid things."

"What did you say?" Zack asked her.

"I told her… you know, about what you two do."

"You didn't!" Zack said.

"I'm so, so sorry, Flenn." She looked down at the floor. "I told her you were both in the CIA."

Flenn's eyes narrowed, "Donna, that was for me to do!"

"I know," she cried. "I'm so sorry."

Flenn took a breath. "She's mad, right?"

Donna nodded. "Furious."

"That's why she didn't come with you?"

Donna fished in her purse for a balled-up tissue and then wiped her eyes. "I begged her to come, but all she kept saying was that you had lied to her, and that she couldn't be with another liar."

Flenn reached for his wallet. "Which way do I go to book a flight to Scotland?"

"It won't do any good," Donna said. "Hoshi exchanged her ticket for one to New York. She's on her way home."

Flenn glared at Zack. "This is why we're supposed to get clearance first!"

Zack pulled Donna close. "Hey, come on, it's not Donna's fault… "

"No, it's not. It's yours!" Flenn turned and walked away, "I'm going to New York!"

Zack called after him. "You can't! We have work to do."

Flenn turned. "No, *you* have work to do. I quit!" He dropped the flowers into a waste bin and kept walking.

CHAPTER *FIFTY-SIX*

Present day...

Flenn sat alone in the coffee shop working on his second Americano of the morning. Zack and Davy had each gone separate ways to track down information on Tobias Love.

He finished reading the *Times* and pushed it aside. There had been another article about the poisoning, but it was buried inside, under a report about a downed train line in New Hampton. He sighed. *It's nothing but old news now.* Flenn despised the way people chucked the victims of yesterday's tragedies aside, always eager for the next big calamity. *But hadn't he done the same thing to Pam?* He felt a twinge of guilt for not insisting to Pam's maid that he be allowed to see her again. Flenn sipped his coffee, disturbed by what he'd read. The newspaper article had claimed that there was no hard evidence linking the Russians to the assassination attempt against the Archbishop of Canterbury—*that's what the media had decided to call it*—and that security remained tight around Canterbury Cathedral.

Anyone who had gone to such great effort to cleverly disguise colocinium would have gone over every aspect of the ordination service in detail. He, or she for that matter, would know that the newly consecrated bishop always became the chief celebrant and would be the first to drink from the cup. No, Windsor had to have been the intended target. But why? What possible vendetta could Tobias Love, a billionaire oil magnate, have against Windsor? There were still no answers to that.

Flenn understood why people were pointing a finger at Russia. The Russians had a reputation here in England. When they'd poisoned the double agents near Salisbury, they'd sent a message to all their spies: "Don't double cross the homeland!"

A thought crossed Flenn's mind: *What if Windsor had only been a pawn in all of this? What if something else was going on?*

Tell him he will be next, unless...

It hit him like the beam crashing down at the Death Angel...

CHAPTER *FIFTY-SEVEN*

11 years earlier…

Flenn walked around the terminal for hours, pondering whether to fly to New York or not. *What now?* He asked himself.

There were so many things he needed to say to her, so much to clear up. He had wanted to tell her the truth about what he did for a living, and he was going to eventually… just not yet.

Damn Donna for opening her big mouth! Zack had said she couldn't hold her liquor, and he'd been right. One night out… 'a girls' night,' Hoshi had called it. Why hadn't he just taken her with him to Paris; this could have all been avoided!

Or could it?

Flenn thought about what agents had to go through with their families. Absent sometimes for months at a time, never knowing what the next assignment would be, or when you would come home… or even whether you *would* come home. The CIA could be brutal to families. The divorce rate far exceeded the norm, as did the amount of substance abuse and alcoholism among agents and their spouses. *Maybe this is for the best,* he thought.

The hell it is!

****

Hoshi stood alone in her empty apartment next to her suitcase. She hadn't been able to sleep at all on the flight home; she was way too angry for that. Now, standing here where only a few weeks ago Scott had been with her, the anger morphed into sadness.

She gazed into the kitchen, where Scott had prepared her an amazing Middle Eastern feast one night… at the table where he had served it… at the television where they had watched a stupid comedy but couldn't quit laughing … at the sofa where they had fallen together after coming home from a play and had given passion a whole new meaning. Everything here reminded her of Scott.

Her phone rang. It was Scott… again. She turned it off.

The CIA! Of all things for him to have been involved in! Scott worked for the CIA, an agency with a reputation of violating many of the things she held dear. Hadn't they sponsored coups and assassinations around the world? Or, had she just seen too many movies? Hoshi couldn't imagine Scott doing any of those things. *But he had lied to her!*

Hoshi had never told Scott a lie. She thought for a moment… *well, she hadn't been completely honest with him either.* She ran her hands across her belly.

She picked up her suitcase and walked into the bedroom. She looked around the room until she saw the bed, where he had held her so tenderly afterward, then walked into the bathroom where the opened box still lay on the counter. Hoshi picked it up and read… *98 percent accurate.*

CHAPTER *FIFTY-EIGHT*

Present day...

Flenn sat across from Davy Spate at the Bishop's Finger, an out-of-the-way pub on the edge of Durham. "So, you're telling me all this was about a bloody affair?" Davy signaled the barmaid for another ale.

"No, it's much more than that," Flenn said. "Pamela and Elton Wainwright were having an affair; Tobias Love discovered it somehow and was trying to use it to his advantage."

"What the hell for?"

"Leverage."

A young woman with dyed white hair and a Union Jack tattooed on her neck brought them both a fresh brew. "Love wasn't interested in Pamela or Windsor," Flenn said after she'd left. "It's Wainwright he wants, or at least his support once he's prime minister."

Davy cocked his head, not understanding. "I think you're way out on a limb on this one, Flenny-boy."

"If I am, it's a short one." Flenn explained, "As prime minister, Wainwright would stand in the way of Love's building his pipeline. Right now, labour opposes it. But, with Love threatening to ruin his political aspirations, or

297

even kill him, Wainwright would convince his party somehow to support English Petroleum's interest."

"Good God, man. There's got to have been a simpler way!" Davy blew the foam off of his ale. "I mean, kill a bloody bishop right in front of the whole bloomin' nation?"

Flenn nodded. "From what I hear, Tobias Love is a cocky son-of-a-bitch. He's the narcissist's narcissist. Probably didn't think he would ever be caught. What better way to send a dramatic message to Elton Wainwright? Kill his lover's husband in front of everyone, knowing that the entire country would blame someone else."

Davy shook his head. "The Russians have supplied Britain with oil for decades. He aimed to get rid of the competition and his chief roadblock all in one fell swoop. Brilliant!"

Flenn nodded as he reached for his ale. "One thing I haven't figured out."

Davy grinned. "Only one?"

"Who was it that tried to shoot me? I doubt Love would risk something like that."

"Maybe personally, but he could have hired a thug—someone like that Potter fellow."

"Potter's probably not his real name," said Flenn.

"I'm still working on figuring out who he was. The description the old man gave wasn't all that helpful. There are a lot of short, fat, middle-aged, bald men in England, you know."

"But not that many who would know how to handle colocinium," Flenn reminded him.

"My guys only know the local riffraff. Seems to me this bloke likely runs in posher circles than the chaps I deal with."

Flenn's brow furrowed. "Why are you dealing with them anyway, Davy?"

Davy gazed into his ale. "It's easy for you Flenny, you coming from money and all. Plus, you're still young." He shook his head. "Our pensions aren't very grand; that's why a lot of us keep working as long as we do." He grinned. "I've got a lot of ex-wives to feed."

Flenn couldn't help but grin. *Davy had been a friend for a long time. It wasn't about the money, no matter what Davy said. It was about the thrill. Throwing in with some small-time gamblers probably made Davy feel like he was still at work, living in the shadows.*

"Find out all you can," Flenn said. "I'll talk with Zack about how to rattle Love's cage. I'm working on an idea."

*****

Zack stood outside the massive glass-and-granite structure that housed the offices of English Petroleum. "You know I don't usually get to see you in your holy suit," he said to Flenn who was wearing his clericals and a black suit. You look like a tall penguin."

"God, Zack, not a penguin joke! Can't you come up with anything original?"

Zack shrugged. "You know, seeing you like this reminds me of that time in Rome… "

"I remember." Flenn said. "So... remind me what I do if I get into any trouble in there?"

"Simple," Zack said, pulling out a small bag of jellybeans from his blazer pocket. "You pray."

Flenn raised an eyebrow.

Zack brushed some lint off his friend's shoulder. "I'll be listening in; just don't mess with the microphone behind your lapel."

"And then you and your imaginary army rush in to save me?"

"Exactly," Zack said.

Flenn made a face. "Thanks, but praying sounds like a better idea."

"Besides," Zack said, "Love isn't going to do anything in his own building."

Flenn relaxed, "I suppose you're right."

"No, he'll wait and try to whack you later, when you're least expecting it."

Flenn adjusted his collar. "Tell me again, why is it that I like you?"

Zack simply smiled and walked to a nearby bench where Flenn watched him insert an earpiece and fiddle with a controller in his pocket. He nodded at Flenn for the sound check.

"Our Father, who art in heaven..." Flenn began.

Zack rolled his eyes.

"Well, it wouldn't hurt for you to learn at least one prayer in your life," Flenn said. Zack pretended to snore. Flenn tapped his lapel hard, causing Zack to wince and reach for his left ear. "Serves you right," Flenn said, as he turned and headed toward the visitors' entrance to English Petroleum.

The lobby was full of men in suits and white lab coats busily heading in various directions. The only women Flenn saw were the ones sitting behind a reception desk. Four other men, wearing identical black suits, stood near the elevators watching everything in front of them. *Guards.*

Everything here was functional and bright. There was no artwork on any of the walls, but the silver-and-blue trim encasing the pale-yellow desk provided a focal point for the large room. Flenn wore his biggest smile as he stepped up to the desk. "I'm Scott Flenn; here to see. Tobias Love," he announced to the good-looking, young woman sitting behind a steel-and-glass information desk.

The woman checked her screen. "I'm sorry, Father, but I don't have an appointment listed for you."

Flenn feigned surprise. "Are you certain?"

The woman checked again. "I do apologize."

Flenn nodded and turned as if to leave, then turned back to the woman. "Perhaps you should call his office. I'm sure that he'll want to see me. Tell him that Father Flenn has the Prince Bishop's Chalice for him."

"Father," the young woman said politely. "I hate to say no to a priest, but I simply cannot call up to Mr. Love's office. It's against protocol."

Flenn leaned in and whispered, "It is a present from his uncle. Tobias is dying to see it. Perhaps you could just call his secretary? He'll be very disappointed if he knows I was here, and you didn't let me in."

She thought for a second, then pointed to a group of cream-cushioned chairs with silver trim. "I will have to speak with my supervisor."

"Of course," Flenn said with a smile. He sat as directed and watched as the woman leaned over and spoke softly to another receptionist, who glanced at him. The second woman whispered something to the first and then picked up her telephone. Less than two minutes later, a tall, smartly dressed woman in a gray, woolen business dress approached him.

"Father, may I help you?"

Flenn stood. "Yes, Mr. Love is expecting me."

The woman frowned. "We have nothing on our schedule about such an appointment." Flenn smiled; he loved how the British said 'schedule.'

"Oh, but he does want to see me, I assure you. Please, would you call up to his office at least? He'll be very upset if he knows you didn't let me see him." Flenn leaned in and whispered, "You know how he is when he's angry."

The tall woman drew a breath. "Please, wait here," she said before walking back to the receptionist's desk and picking up the phone. The look on her face told Flenn he would either be heading up the elevator or out the door in the next few minutes. *Either way, he would have succeeded in rattling Love's cage.*

The woman hung up the receiver and walked over to one of the black suited men at the elevator who then accompanied her back to Flenn. "This is Jerome," the woman said. "He will be escorting you to Mr. Love's office. Have a good day, Father." She walked away quickly as Flenn and Jerome headed for the elevator. Flenn smiled at the two curious receptionists as he passed. Jerome inserted a keycard into the elevator and then pressed an unmarked button. Flenn had counted 16 floors from outside, but the elevator pad only listed 15. The doors opened on the top, unmarked floor and the guard led him down a long, carpeted hall to a suite of offices. A muscular man with a mustache opened the door. Several other burly men were also standing in the secretary's office, all staring at him. The young woman behind the desk looked uneasy. "Mr. Love is waiting for you."

Mustache opened the door and Flenn walked inside. Beautifully tiled floors interlaid with cream-colored carpeting led to a circle of leather sofas in the middle of a massive office. At the far end, a large desk made of English walnut was encircled by two large bookcases with various memorabilia and photographs. Flenn recognized several celebrities in the photos, all standing with Tobias Love, including a past President of the United States; the one who was now serving time in a federal prison.

Tobias Love stood and walked toward Flenn. Mustache also came in and closed the door behind him.

"Ah, Father Flenn," Love said, offering his hand. "The man who saved us all from being poisoned at Durham Cathedral." Love slowly lowered his hand when Flenn refused to shake it. "What's this I hear about a chalice?"

Flenn smiled. "The Prince Bishop's Chalice. The one you had your man tamper with."

Love wasn't very good at pretending to look surprised. "I'm afraid you've lost me."

Love glanced toward Mustache. Without turning around, Flenn said, "Young man, stay where you are; there's no reason for anyone to get hurt."

Tobias Love forced a grin. "No one is going to hurt you, Father."

"I was talking about *him*."

Love gestured toward the man. "Look Father, I don't know what it is that you've come for, but I can assure you that you are—what is it you Americans say—barking up the wrong tree."

"And I can assure you, sir," retorted Flenn, "that you won't get away with this. Colocinium is a byproduct of treating sulfur, something your company has been doing in Middleton for years. It won't take MI-6 long before they put it all together."

Tobias Love's cheeks were turning bright red, which is exactly what Flenn was hoping for: *Make the man lose his temper, say something for Zack to record!*

"Father Flenn," Love said, enunciating every word. "I mean no disrespect to the collar which you wear, but it is time for you to leave."

Flenn felt a hand firmly grip his shoulder. "Not yet," Flenn said. Without taking his eyes off Tobias Love, he reached up and grabbed Mustache's pinky finger, bending it sharply. The man cried out in pain as he fell to his knees. Flenn didn't let go, nor bother to even look behind him. Instead, he stared Love directly in the eyes. "I'm here to tell you to leave your uncle out of this. If you come after me again, or him, it will be the absolute worst day of your life."

The door swung open as the guards from the outer office rushed inside. Flenn let go of Mustache's little finger. Tobias Love held up his hand and the guards stopped. "I have no idea what you are talking about, Father... but you will find that threats do not easily scare me."

Flenn smiled. "I understand," he said. "Rest assured, however, this was no threat; simply a promise. And I'm a man who keeps his promises."

Love's face flushed again, but he managed to restrain himself. He looked at the guards. "Show Father Flenn to the door. Gently, please, gentlemen. I wouldn't want anything painful to happen to a *meddlesome priest.*"

The reference had been clear. Henry II had once remarked to his ambitious knights, 'Will no one rid me of this meddlesome priest?' right before they rode out to murder Archbishop Thomas Becket.

Flenn cocked his head. "I, too, know what happened to Becket." He glared at Love. "Despite what you may think of yourself, you, sir, are no king!"

Love couldn't let the comment go. "I would be careful if I were you. Doesn't your good book say that pride goeth before a fall?"

"Don't try me, Tobias," Flenn warned as he turned and walked past the guards. "Or you will most certainly find out."

CHAPTER *FIFTY-NINE*

11 years earlier…

Scott Flenn sat alone on the flight back from New York. He had hoped to talk to Hoshi, to convince her that he was going to tell her about being a spy as soon as he had clearance from his superiors. He was also going to tell her that he would quit the CIA, that she was worth more to him than anything else. But she had refused to speak to him, even after he'd camped out in front of her apartment.

Hoshi had opened the door only once; her eyes red and swollen. She'd handed him a small envelope, and then slammed the door. Inside it she'd written two words: *Get Lost!*

Flenn sat next to an empty seat in First Class. He had bought both seats so that he wouldn't have to carry on a conversation with a stranger on his way back to Paris… and back to work.

The flight attendant had offered several choices for dinner, but Flenn refused, sipping Scotch until he finally fell asleep. Zack was waiting for him when his plane landed at the airport. Flenn didn't say a word; just handed him the envelope.

Zack drove to Flenn's hotel. Flenn got out; still silent.

Zack lowered the window. "I'm sorry," he said, as gently as he knew how.

Flenn stopped for a second but didn't look back. He took a breath. "I know," was all he said before heading inside.

****

"I've got an idea," came Zack's voice over the phone. "Why don't we *both* go to New York and talk to Hoshi? That way, she can… "

Click.

Zack didn't call Flenn's hotel again; instead, he finished getting dressed, then took a taxi to the embassy where he pored over new intel from the Egyptians. It turned out that Al-Mashriq had been trying to get a foothold in several countries, but, so far, the most receptive had been Iraq and Syria. Al-Qaeda had broken with the group, saying that its tactics were too brutal.

From what the Egyptians had told him, they expected that Al-Mashriq would likely just fizzle out and go away. Zack knew better. Davy Waite had passed on his own intel—that MI-6 had traced massive amounts of money which were being funneled into the new organization.

"Damn," Zack said to the walls. "This just isn't going away."

"What's not going away?"

Zack turned to find Scott Flenn standing behind him. Flenn crossed to the other side of the table and pulled out a chair.

"Before you ask, no, I didn't quit."

Zack smiled. "I knew you wouldn't." He pointed to the dossier in front of him. "Once this stuff gets into your blood, it never goes away."

Flenn sighed, wondering if Zack was right. *Was nothing going to matter except King and Country for the rest of his life?* He pointed to the folder. "So, what's next?"

Zack slid the dossier across the table. "The Egyptians think Zamir and this other terrorist group will simply fade away on their own. They say that they're too far outside the mainstream for Al-Qaeda to put up with for long."

Flenn skimmed through the reports. "What do you think?"

"It's not just me, but Davy, too."

"Okay, what do you and Davy think?"

Zack shook his head. "It's not good. Al-Mashriq seems to be gathering steam, not losing it. Judging from a group that was just rounded up in Cairo, they're attracting losers, dropouts, criminals, the disillusioned… all sorts. Most of them young."

"How young?" Flenn scratched his beard. He hadn't shaved in three days.

"Teenagers and young twenties. You know, the ones whose brains aren't fully cooked yet."

Flenn looked through the file in silence. Finally, Zack couldn't stand it anymore. "Heard anything from Hoshi?"

Flenn turned a page. "Nope, and I won't, either. Hoshi and I are over. She's made that abundantly clear."

"Did *she* say it was over?"

Flenn didn't look up. "I don't want to talk about it, okay?"

Zack repeated himself. "Did she *say* it was over?"

"No, she didn't *say* anything. She wouldn't talk to me."

Zack smiled and leaned back in his chair. "Then it's not over!"

Flenn glared at him.

"No, seriously," Zack said, "it isn't over unless she used those exact words: 'Flenn, it's over,' or 'Flenn go to hell, or go jump in a lake of fire, go slide down a razor blade into a vat of alcohol' even. But, until she says 'it's over,' it ain't over!"

Flenn looked back at the dossier. "Can we just get back to business?"

"Sure, but for the record she didn't say it, right? I mean, sometimes women… "

Flenn looked up. "Stop! You may have more experience with women in general, but I know Hoshi, okay?" He lowered his voice. "It's over."

Zack sat quietly for a moment, unsure of just what to say, before offering to go out for coffee.

"Great," Flenn said, staring at the report. "Make mine a large."

CHAPTER *SIXTY*

Present day…

"Wotcha!" Flenn called out as he entered the Bram and Bull.

"Wotcha, cocker! Fancy a drink?"

Flenn called across the bar to Val, "Got any good Scotch back there? Single malt?"

"Aw, listen to Mr. Darwin, would you now?" Murph said. Flenn looked at Charlie for an explanation.

"Means a rich man; Darwin's face is on the ten-pound note."

Val held up a bottle. "Will this do?"

Flenn smiled. "Absolutely, and pour one for the rest of the guys, too, while you're at it."

Val seemed surprised. "Are you sure, Father, this stuff is expensive!"

"In that case," Murph said, "make mine a double!"

"No worries, Val, pour up," Flenn said, handing her his credit card.

"Make sure to put all my other charges on there, too," he said. "Charlie, could I speak with you a minute?" Bob, George and Murph were too engrossed in sampling the Scotch to pay much attention as Charlie walked out the door with Flenn.

Outside, Davy Spate was waiting. "You remember Davy, don't you?"

Charlie held out his hand. "Yes, good to see you again, sir."

Flenn put his hand on Charlie's bony shoulder. "Davy's going to be watching over your place for a few days. Just as a precaution."

"A precaution," Charlie said, "against what?"

"Your nephew. I'm afraid I may have ticked him off yesterday."

Charlie scratched his head. "Tobias? That wasn't very smart, Father. But I'm not worried about me... it's you he'll come after."

Davy and Flenn exchanged glances. "I'm counting on it."

Charlie's eyes narrowed. "Are you sure you know what you're doing?"

"Don't worry about Flenny-boy," Davy said. "It's your nephew that ought to be doin' the worryin'."

Flenn opened the door. "Come on guys, let's go sample that Scotch before Murph drinks it all!"

"Scotch, you say? That sounds grand!" said Davy.

Flenn shook his head. "Come on, there's someone you need to meet." Flenn smiled. "You and Murph are going to get along just fine."

****

"Anything you're not telling me?" Flenn stared at Zack from across the small room on the main floor of his flat.

"Let's see," Zack held up his fingers one at a time.

"Pam and Elton are having an affair, Wainwright's place burned down, O'Malley and his boys have gone home to Ireland, there's likely a team of Love's hit men gunning for you… no, that's it. Oh, wait; there is one thing I haven't mentioned."

Flenn raised an eyebrow. "What's that?"

Zack lifted his right hand. "My glass is empty."

Flenn rolled his eyes. "You know where I keep it. Pour me one, too, while you're at it."

"What's the latest from Davy?" Zack asked.

"He's been sticking to Charlie like glue. Charlie's wife has gone to visit their son and granddaughter, so Davy's staying with him."

Zack handed Flenn a glass. "And what about the fellas' over at the Bram?"

Flenn laughed. Charlie's got them convinced that Davy's an old friend from university staying with him for a few days."

"I bet Davy fits right in over there," Zack chuckled.

Flenn nodded. "Especially with Murph; they're like two peas in a pod."

A knock came at the door. Both men stiffened. Zack drew his pistol and went to cover the back door, while Flenn looked out the peephole at the front. He relaxed when he saw who it was. He nodded to Zack before opening the door and Zack slipped the gun underneath a kitchen towel.

"Speak of the devil, and there he is," Flenn said to Murph who stood sheepishly on the front stoop. "Come in."

"Sorry to bother you, Father, but we haven't seen you all day, and well," he licked his lips, looking a bit like a leprechaun today for some reason. "The fellas' were wondering... well you see, now it ain't just me mind you, but George and Bob too... well, we were just hopin' you might be comin' over for another nip of that fancy Scotch we had yesterday. It's too pricey for us you see, and well... "

"Don't say another word." Flenn looked back at Zack. "You see? Some folks appreciate good whisky." Zack rolled his eyes. "Sorry, Murph," Flenn said, "I may not be at the Bram today. Tell Val to put a bottle of it on my tab, and I'll pay her tomorrow."

"Really, Father, a whole bottle?"

"You guys enjoy."

"Blimey, this might just make a churchgoer of me yet!"

Zack called out, "You, Murph? Why, because of Father Flenn's generosity?"

Murph shook his head. "No, not that. It's just what I might do once I'm thoroughly pissed." He winked. "I figure I might have some confessin' to do when it's all over and done."

Flenn closed the door and chuckled. "I'm going to miss those guys when I leave."

Zack reached under the towel for his pistol. "Well, let's make sure that neither one of us leaves prematurely." He lifted his glass. "Now, about this plan of yours... "

CHAPTER *SIXTY-ONE*

11 years earlier…

Donna got up to hug Flenn as she spotted him making his way to their table in the crowded restaurant. "It's good to see you, Flenn."

"Sorry I'm late," Flenn replied. "The cab driver had a hard time finding this place."

"He must be new to Paris," Zack said.

"She," Flenn corrected. "Yeah, said she was from Romania." Flenn looked around. The restaurant was modestly decorated, but the aromas from the kitchen were intoxicating.

Zack kept looking at him and grinning.

"What?"

"Nothing," Zack said, but he kept grinning.

The waiter came to take their drink order. Flenn ordered a single-malt Scotch, Zack a bourbon, and Donna a white wine.

Flenn turned to Donna. "So, how was your flight?"

"It was fine; got in late last night," she said.

"Yeah, Zack told me. He's been looking forward to you coming all week." He glanced at Zack, who looked like the proverbial cat who'd just swallowed the canary. "What is with you?"

Zack looked at Donna. "Are you going to tell him, or am I?"

"Tell me what?" Flenn said. "No! You guys are expecting, aren't you?"

"No!" Zack said, a bit too loudly, causing Donna to shift uncomfortably in her chair.

"So… what is this big secret?" asked Flenn.

The waiter returned with their drinks. Donna downed half of hers before answering.

"Hoshi came with me."

Flenn could hardly believe what he'd just heard. "Hoshi is here… in Paris?"

"She's at the Sheraton," Donna said.

"But how, when… no, why?"

Zack reached across to put his hand on Flenn's shoulder. "Isn't it obvious? She misses you! After all, it has been a month," he said. Donna sent him a cautioning glance.

Flenn jumped to his feet. "I'm going over to the Sheraton! Wish me luck."

"Flenn!" Donna called. He turned, grinning from ear to ear. She looked down at the table and then back up again, not quite meeting his eyes. "Nothing. Good luck."

Flenn sprinted out the door, leaving Donna and Zack alone. "Donna?" Zack said, inquisitively. She reached for the menu.

"Come on, what's up?"

"I don't think she's here to kiss and make up."

"Why do you say that?"

Donna hesitated. "There's more to this story, a lot more."

Zack smiled and squeezed her hand. "There always is. Tell me."

"No, I've said too much already," she said.

"Aw, come on, sweetie; is she going to take him back or not?" Donna ignored him and surveyed the menu.

"Come on," Zack said as sweetly as he could. "Say something."

"All right," she said, looking at him and then at the menu, "I'll have the chicken."

****

"You lied to me!" Hoshi said angrily as Flenn stood in the hallway in front of her hotel room door holding a bouquet of yellow roses.

"You told me you worked for your father!"

"I do, I mean I did, I mean... " As soon as he said it, he regretted it.

"Oh my God!" Hoshi said. "I told you in the beginning that the one thing I cannot tolerate is a liar! How could you be so… so cruel?"

"Can I at least come in?"

She shook her head, her face growing redder by the second. "No! No, you cannot."

"Hoshi, you didn't come all this way to tell me that you don't want to talk to me."

Hoshi bit her bottom lip. *He was right, that was not why she had come.* "The CIA, Scott? Of all things; the bloody CIA!"

Flenn glanced around the vacant hallway. "What?" she exclaimed loudly. "Is the spy afraid someone will hear, someone will find out that Scott Flenn is in the C-I-A?"

"Hoshi, listen, let me in; I can explain."

"The hell you can!" she said.

"Hoshi, if you will just let me in, I will tell you everything! I was going to just as soon as they gave me clearance."

"*Clearance*? You have to get permission to talk to me?"

"Yes," he stammered, "I mean no. Come on, please just let me in. I can explain all of this."

Hoshi had planned on confronting him on her own terms, but Donna had obviously spilled the beans about her being in town. "No, you don't get to 'explain.' I get it, you're a spy and can't tell anyone your precious secret. Not even me! Well, don't worry, Mr. CIA, your secret is safe! Hoshi slammed the door in his face before he could see her break down and cry. She fell against the door, furious that he'd lied to her, but even more furious with herself for exploding like that. *This was not why she had come to Paris! She had wanted to have a civil discussion, hear him out, tell him how she felt, then tell him about the...* but all the anger and frustration had just poured out of her the moment he'd knocked on her door.

Damn it, Scott! she thought. *You're supposed to knock, then I let you in, then I let you have it all over again and then we fall together and make up. Just knock, damn it!*

She waited for him to at least call her name from the other side of the door. *This was far from over, but she'd at least let him explain. As angry as she was, it was more at having found out about the CIA from Donna instead of Scott.*

As she was leaning against one side of the door, she was sure that he was doing the same on the other.

Men! Why do they have to be so... so damn... male!

She wiped her eyes, took a breath, put her hand on the doorknob. *Okay, I'll be the bigger person,* she told herself.

She opened the door.

The hallway was empty.

CHAPTER *SIXTY-TWO*

One month later...

"Hoshi Takamura?" said the voice over the phone. "No, she no longer lives here. She moved out last week." Flenn had called the landlord after having tried Hoshi's cell phone for the past three weeks before finally getting an automated reply that said the phone had been disconnected.

"Did she leave a forwarding address?"

"No sir, but even if she did we aren't allowed to give that out."

"I understand," Flenn answered, "but I'm her fiancé."

"You might try the U.N.; she works over there as a translator, I believe."

"Thanks," was all Flenn said. He'd already tried calling the U.N. He was told Hoshi had taken a leave of absence.

He didn't want to do it, but he was desperate now; he'd have to use his connections to find her. *Somehow, using the CIA database to locate his girlfriend seemed wrong. After all, it was his work as a spy that had caused this mess. He couldn't let it go any longer; he needed to talk to her, at least once more. They were going to see each other in a couple months anyway, at the wedding. If he could just reach her, he'd tell her that they owed it to Zack and Donna.*

319

He retrieved his phone and placed the call. He waited for a beep from the other end. "Locate," he said. "Sending image." He clicked a button on his phone and a picture of Hoshi's face came up. It was the one that contained the most detail, which would make the computer's job easier.

He waited for several minutes until an automated voice came over the phone. "Preliminary facial recognition complete. Subject not found. Continue search and return call?"

"Yes," Flenn said with a sigh.

He hung up as Zack Matteson came into the office, a bag of jellybeans in one hand and a cup of coffee for Flenn in the other. He held them up. "Thought I'd feed both our addictions."

They spent the morning cross-checking satellite photographs of known Al-Qaeda camps who were reportedly sheltering several Al-Mashriq leaders. By noon they had been able to identify at least six Al-Mashriq commanders hiding in two different camps. "So," Zack said pointing to the map, "these camps are probably the ones most likely to be training grounds for Al-Mashriq?"

"That's for Langley to decide," Flenn said. "Our job is to put together as many of the pieces of this puzzle as we can."

Zack dug out the last two jellybeans from his pocket. He offered the licorice one to Flenn, who refused. "Well, I suppose someone could infiltrate one of these camps and see how far Al-Mashriq has gotten," he said.

"Fine. It's your turn this time," said Flenn.

Zack grinned. "Nah, you look better in a dress; besides, my Arabic isn't that great."

Flenn's phone buzzed. He glanced at the caller ID, but the screen was blank. He pulled out a pen and reached for a piece of paper before answering.

"Hello?"

The automated response simply said: "Location discovered. Tokyo. No further information available."

Flenn pocketed the phone. *What was Hoshi doing in Tokyo?*

"Seriously," Zack said, "these are terrorist camps either way. Whether they are Al-Qaeda or Al-Mashriq doesn't really matter, does it?"

Flenn didn't answer; instead, he was staring off in space. *Was it something to do with her job? If it was, then why had she moved out of her apartment? And why had she changed her phone number?* Flenn knew the answer to that... to avoid him.

No, it won't be that easy for you, Hoshi!

"Does it?" Zack asked again.

"Does what?"

"Earth to Scott Flenn, are you out there?"

"I'm sorry. I zoned out." Flenn looked down at the maps. "Any sign of Zamir?"

"Maybe... someone that looked like him was seen at this camp a few days ago." Zack pointed to the smallest of the encampments.

Flenn picked up his coffee and stood. "Can you report what we've found?" He retrieved his jacket from the back of the chair. "I've got to go."

Zack looked puzzled. "Go? Go where?"

"Seattle."

Zack looked at the maps of terrorist camps in Pakistan and Syria and then back at Flenn. "What's in Seattle?"

"Hoshi's parents."

Zack shook his head in disbelief. "Can't you just call? We have work to do."

"Tried. Didn't get anywhere."

"And you think showing up on their doorstep will help?"

"Yep," Flenn said as he walked out the door.

Zack got up and followed him into the hallway. "And why is that?"

"Because I'm not leaving that doorstep until I know where Hoshi is!"

****

The flight to Seattle was long, especially to someone who hated flying as much as Flenn did. There'd been no openings in first class so he'd had to squeeze his tall frame into coach—the dreaded middle seat. He sat between a large Portuguese woman even more terrified of flying than he was and an evangelical preacher who kept trying to convert him.

"How was your flight?" asked the taxi driver as they pulled out of the lot.

"I don't want to talk about it," was all Flenn said.

They drove to the Loews Hotel where Flenn crashed for 10 hours. The next morning, he reconsidered dressing in the suit and tie he'd brought along, but he didn't want

Mr. and Mrs. Takamura to think that he was flaunting his wealth. People in Seattle dressed practically. *What was it Hoshi had called it... 'Frumpy.'* Flenn decided on khakis and a blue button-down instead.

The address for Ren and Rueko Takamura had been easy enough to find. The taxi pulled up to 1312 Woodland Drive, an attractive ranch home surrounded by spruce trees and large Cypress shrubs. A path of lavender-blue aster led to the front door. He told the taxi driver to keep the meter running, as he had no idea how long he'd be here.

He had rehearsed exactly what he was going to say to Mr. and Mrs. Takamura: *Hello, I'm Scott Flenn, Hoshi's boyfriend. I came here from Paris because I wanted to apologize to her for not having told her about my work. I was hoping that perhaps we could talk and once you see that my intentions are honorable, perhaps you would tell me how to contact her*

He had gone over the speech time and time again on the flight, when he wasn't peeling the frightened woman off his arm or having to pretend to listen to the religious zealot.

Flenn stood on the curb, staring at the house. *Why was he so nervous? He had faced drug lords and mullahs, kidnappers, and terrorists. Mr. and Mrs. Takamura were likely understanding, compassionate people. They would see that he loved their daughter. That he had flown all the way from Paris...*

It suddenly hit him... they might think he was unstable! What kind of lunatic flies halfway around the world to chase down an ex-girlfriend? *A stalker, that's who! Oh my God, they're going to think he is one of those crazies you read about in the papers!*

He stopped halfway up the sidewalk, took a deep breath, and forced himself to run through his speech again, *Hello, I'm Scott Flenn…* he decided to leave out the part about Paris.

Flenn made it to the steps of the front porch, going over the amended speech one last time, moving his lips just a little as he did. *Good God,* he thought, *what if they're watching from the window?*

The steps felt as though they were leading to the guillotine. *So, this is how Louis XVI and Marie Antoinette felt!*

Flenn summoned all of his courage, took a deep breath, and knocked on the door. He saw the blinds from a bay window part and then waited for what seemed like an eternity. "Hello, I'm Scott Flenn, Hoshi's boyfriend," he whispered as he knocked a second time.

The door finally opened and a distinguished, Japanese gentlemen with gray hair and soft features answered the door.

"May I help you?" Mr. Takamura said politely.

"Um… "

A middle-aged woman, looking a lot like an older Hoshi, joined her husband at the door.

"Hello?" she said.

"Um, yes," Flenn stammered.

Mr. and Mrs. Takamura waited.

"Eh… "

The couple looked at one another then back at him. "Yes?" Hoshi's mother prompted.

Flenn finally managed to speak.

"I want to marry your daughter!"

Flenn turned beet red. "Oh my God, I didn't... I mean I wasn't... I mean..."

"You must be Scott." Mrs. Takamura smiled and took him by the hand. "Won't you come in?" Mr. and Mrs. Takamura couldn't have been nicer. They served him tea and sugar cookies. As he'd expected, they had already heard much about him, even that he was in the CIA, which they both promised they would keep to themselves. Throughout the conversation, Mrs. Takamura kept excusing herself and disappearing into the back. *Perhaps,* Flenn thought, *she was giving the two men time to talk...* which they did, at length. Mr. Takamura seemed sympathetic.

"You have to understand," he said, "our daughter is everything to us. We only want her to be happy."

More at ease now, Flenn spoke freely of his affection for Hoshi. He explained how he had wanted to tell her about his work but that policy required him to have clearance from his superiors first. Mr. Takamura seemed to understand. Flenn also said that he was willing to give all that up for Hoshi if he could convince her to come back to him. Mrs. Takamura returned again and looked at her husband. Flenn thought he saw her shake her head slightly. He knew that he should probably leave.

"Mr. and Mrs. Takamura, I'm not usually an impulsive man, but I came here in the hopes that you might tell me how to contact your daughter. I want to do nothing more than apologize to her and see if we can work things out." He swallowed. "I understand that she may be in Japan?"

Mr. Takamura raised an eyebrow.

"She went for a job interview with the Japanese consulate," Mrs. Takamura said. Her husband said something to her in Japanese. It was too fast for Flenn to understand. He thought he heard the words *deserving* and *truth* in there somewhere. Mrs. Takamura didn't respond.

"Scott, my daughter has very deep feelings for you, but you must understand, she also had feelings for her last boyfriend." Her eyes narrowed. "That man was a liar and a cheat. Hoshi needs to be able to trust the man she marries." She tried to smile. "Do you understand?"

Flenn did. "I don't suppose you would give me her new number?"

Mr. Takamura nodded to his wife, but she gently said, "No, dear, but I *will* tell her that you came by. If she chooses to contact you, then my husband and I will be very supportive. I'm afraid that's all we can do for you."

Flenn stood. "Thank you," he said. "I'm sorry to have troubled you."

Outside, the sky was clouding over. The taxi driver was asleep until Flenn opened the door and climbed inside.

Mrs. Takamura walked slowly back into the kitchen;

her husband sat at the table and pushed his tea away. "You should have told him," he said.

Mrs. Takamura gazed sympathetically toward the slight figure emerging from the bedroom hallway.

"No, she shouldn't have, Daddy."

Hoshi ran into her mother's arms and sobbed her heart out.

CHAPTER *SIXTY-THREE*

Present day…

"Val, you got any pizza back there?" Murph was hungry. "The good Father just arrived and I suspect he'd fancy a bite."

Flenn sat between George and Murph. "No thanks, I'm not hungry. A cup of coffee would be nice, though."

"Shh! Val might hear you."

Flenn laughed. "Where's Bob?" he asked.

"Gone to the dentist," George said, "goes every six months, though for the life of me I don't see why. I ain't been since I was 12."

"Pizza?" Murph called.

"Give me a bloody minute, will you?" Val stuck her head out from the kitchen. "Oh, sorry Father."

"No need. My congregation is used to my swearing."

Murph looked surprised. "You, Father? A man of the cloth?"

"I learned a long time ago not to try and pretend to be something I'm not," Flenn said. He winked at Val. "I think Murph's hungry; you might want to make that two pizzas. My treat."

"Splendid idea!" said Murph.

Val disappeared back into the kitchen, but not before

calling out, "Would you keep an eye on him for me, Father? I'm running low on Irish Whiskey."

"And she's all out of that fancy Scotch, too," complained Murph as he reached behind the bar for a bottle of American bourbon.

"Have a nip with me?" he asked Flenn, pouring himself a shot.

"Wotcha!" The door shut behind Charlie and Davy.

"Wotcha, Cocker! Fancy a drink?" Murph called out, holding up the bottle.

"I know I certainly do!" said Davy. He rubbed his hands together, "Jack Daniels? Brilliant!"

Flenn sighed. "Set them all up, Murph. I'll square it with Val and Colin when I settle my bill." He sat by the window and looked outside toward his flat. Tobias Love had yet to make his move. "Oh, and pour one for Zack. He's supposed to be here in a few minutes."

Murph rubbed his hands together as the pizza arrived. They all grabbed a slice, even Flenn. *He was going to get fat! He hadn't jogged since the drive-by attempt, and probably wouldn't again until after all this was over.*

The door opened. "Is that pepperoni I smell?" Zack said.

"Fancy a slice?" Murph called out. "The Father's buyin'!"

"Charitable fellow, our Father Flenn," said Zack. He reached for a slice as Murph handed him the bottle of Jack Daniels and a glass.

Murph reached across for some ice, but Val slapped

his hand. "One of these days I'm lettin' Colin loose on ya', Murph," she said.

"Ah, he'd never have a go at me," Murph said. "Colin's me mate!"

George laughed. "The whole bloomin' world's your mate if they're buyin'."

Davy grabbed another slice and brought his glass over to the table where Flenn was sitting. Zack followed.

"Still nothing?" Flenn asked.

"Not quite nothing. I did some checking on Pam's maid. Seems she has a new boyfriend. I managed to get a name from the neighbor's housecleaner who's taken a fancy to me. She thinks I'm from the cathedral, checking up on Pam."

"Why does she think that?" Flenn asked.

"Your shirt's a bit long on me, but the collar fit nicely."

Flenn rolled his eyes.

"The boyfriend's got a record it seems."

"What's the name?" asked Davy.

"Soren. Clive Soren."

Davy nearly spilled his whiskey. "Good God!"

Flenn raised an eyebrow, "You know him?"

"Wish I could say I didn't. He used to work in the Dales. Caused too much trouble so he moved on to Liverpool."

"What's he known for?" Zack said.

"Slitting throats, mostly. He used to run a numbers game in the Dales until some Russians hired him to kill a friend of theirs."

Flenn raised an eyebrow. "A *friend*?"

Davy nodded. "Yeah, wouldn't want to see what they do to one of their enemies these days, eh?"

Zack took a bite of pizza. "No, you wouldn't."

"So, Pam's maid is hanging out with a gangster?" Flenn turned toward Zack. "Sounds like Tobias Love is using Soren to keep an eye on Pam."

Zack nodded. "And Wainwright. What's this Soren guy look like?"

"Let me guess," Flenn said. "Short, pudgy and bald?"

"That's him," said Davy. "Wait a minute, isn't that how Charlie described Potter, the guy who was alone with the Prince Bishop's Chalice?"

Flenn nodded.

"So," Zack said. "I guess we're going to go have a talk with this Clive Soren."

"How do you propose we do that?" Davy asked.

Flenn pulled out his cell phone. "Like this." He pressed a few buttons and then waited for someone to answer. "Hello? Yes, this is Father Scott Flenn, I'm coming over to see Mrs. Tammerlane tomorrow at noon... Oh, I'm sorry to hear that, but I'm still coming over. See you then." He hung up before the maid could reply.

"You think the maid's in on it?" Davy asked.

"Doubtful, but I do think she'll tell her boyfriend about the 'cheeky priest' who's coming over even after she told me not to come."

Zack nodded. "And Soren will then tell Love... "

Flenn pushed his diet soda aside and signaled Val for an ale. "You guys will be there, right?"

Davy glanced at Zack. "Wouldn't miss it for the world."

****

Pamela Tammerlane seemed alert as she stared at Flenn across the dining room table. "Honestly Flenn, I'm afraid I don't know what you are talking about." Pam ran her hands across her lap and smoothed the creases in her black skirt.

"I'm afraid you do," Flenn said. The concern that had been in his voice a few days ago was absent now. "How long has it been going on, Pam?"

Her eyes flared. "How dare you suggest… "

"No, Pam; how dare *you*! You sit here pretending to be in mourning for Windsor when all along you've been planning to divorce him and marry the next prime minister. When did it start, Pam… not the affair; I don't give a damn about that; I mean your quest for status?" He didn't give her time to answer. "It wouldn't do to allow Win to just be a priest. No, I suspect you pushed him to become bishop. But even that wasn't good enough for you, not when Elton Wainwright came along!"

"Flenn, I… "

"Was it before you started taking the opioids? Couldn't live with yourself anymore? Frankly, I don't blame you. I couldn't live with you either; I'm surprised that Windsor could."

"Winnie loved me!" she protested.

Flenn nodded, even as his eyes shot holes through her. "Yes… yes he did. God knows why. How do you sleep at night, Pam?" Flenn glanced at the prescription bottle on the buffet behind her. "Oh, that's right; never mind."

Before she could protest further, Flenn stood. "By the way, you should fire your maid. Her new boyfriend is a hitman working for Tobias Love." Pam's eyes widened at the revelation. "If I were you, I'd do it quickly."

Flenn stormed out of the dining room, through the kitchen, and past the maid, who he was sure had overheard everything. He walked out the front door to the car he'd rented for the day. He had purposefully left the windows down even though it was threatening to rain.

He climbed into the driver's seat but before he could put the key in the ignition, he felt something hard pressing against the base of his skull. He looked in the rearview mirror and saw a bald man grinning at him.

"Looks like you made a stupid mistake, Father," said Clive Soren.

"No, the mistake is yours," came a voice to Soren's right.

"Yes, and a very stupid one, indeed," said another voice on his left.

Soren gasped as he saw two .45s, one at each side window and both pointing at him.

"If you don't mind," Flenn said. "Hand one of these gentlemen your weapon before someone gets hurt. I have to return this car in a couple of hours, and I don't want to pay a cleaning fee."

Soren cursed as he handed Davy his pistol. Flenn

started up the car and Davy and Zack climbed in on either side of Soren. "Mr. Soren," Davy said as Flenn pulled away from the curve, "you have a choice. You can either talk to us, or we can head over to the Yorkshire Dales. I happen to be friends with some blokes over there who aren't too happy with you. I'm certain they'd enjoy a few hours alone with you."

Soren slumped in the seat. "What is it you want to know?"

CHAPTER *SIXTY-FOUR*

11 years earlier…

"Hoshi, sooner or later you are going to have to tell him." Mrs. Takamura sat across from her daughter at her favorite Japanese restaurant in Seattle after having spent the morning window shopping at baby stores.

"I know, mom. I've come close several times. I keep picking up my phone to call him, but then I chicken out."

"You can't hide forever, sweetheart."

Hoshi glanced down at her plate. "I'm not hiding."

Mrs. Takamura reached across the table and squeezed her daughter's hand. "You are a strong woman; what are you so afraid of?"

"I don't know. Maybe that he won't have anything to do with me."

Hoshi's mom shook her head. "So, you break up with him, yet you are afraid that once he finds out about the baby that he will break up with you?" She threw up her hands. "Do you know what your father would say to that?"

"Yeah. He'd tell me that I'm crazy."

Mrs. Takamura mixed a small bit of wasabi into her soy sauce. "And he'd be right. Listen, sweetheart, you can't hide out with us forever. We've raised our child, it is time for you to prepare to raise yours." She knew that Hoshi had sent out resumes and had already been offered two lucrative jobs, both of which she'd turned down.

Hoshi reached for her chopsticks. "I know," she said, rearranging the dumplings on her plate. "I really appreciate you and dad putting up with me, but I guess you are right, I have been acting like a baby lately. Can't we just blame it on the hormones?"

"Please! If had a dollar for every time your father wanted to blame something I did on hormones… " She poured them each a cup of green tea. "Your dad wants you to stay and have the baby in Seattle." Hoshi's eyes darted up, hopeful. "You and I both know that is not what is best for you. You have a bright future ahead of you in New York. You need to ask for your old job back." Mrs. Takamura lifted her teacup. "Your boss has been calling and asking for you. Apparently, your father has been telling him that you are not at home because your dad wants you to stay."

Hoshi pouted. "But you don't?"

"It isn't what is best for *you*, dear. You cannot rely on others to take care of you. You must take care of yourself. What is it your grandmother always said… "

Hoshi finished the sentence. "We are not that kind of people."

Mrs. Takamura nodded. "They endured much, your grandparents; but they were strong and independent. So are you. Your father and I raised you to be able to take care of yourself. You can do it, Hoshi. You have to."

"So… you're kicking me out?"

Her mom gave her a knowing smile. "I am pushing you out of the nest... again, little bird. Call your old boss. Get your job back. Go to New York."

Hoshi sighed. "I know you're right, but I just wish Scott could be there with me."

"Then call him!"

"But he might reject me... "

Mrs. Takamura reached over and poked her daughter with a chopstick. "Crazy!"

****

"Crazy!"

Flenn stared at Zack. "Look, I tried, okay! I called her a billion times after she left Scotland, but she wouldn't answer. I even flew to Seattle to her parents' house, remember?"

Zack stepped over a piece of broken tile on the floor of the Charles de Gaulle Airport. He and Flenn were flying to London to coordinate with British intelligence for an upcoming mission to take out Col. Zamir. The past two ventures had failed. He and Flenn had spent the past several weeks in the desert outside of known Al-Qaeda camps waiting for Zamir to show. Each time the intelligence had been wrong.

"Well," Zack said, "I happen to have something that might turn that all around."

"What?"

Zack held out a slip of paper which Flenn reached for, only to have Zack pull it away. "Not unless you say, 'Please.'"

"Not if my life depended on it."

Zack tucked the paper into his blazer pocket. "Fine. Have it your way." Neither said a word as they walked past a kiosk selling mobile phones.

"Okay, I'll bite," Flenn finally said. "What is it?"

"Hoshi's new telephone number. Donna gave it to me."

They rounded a corner on their way to their gate. "Keep it," Flenn said.

"You're kidding, right?"

Flenn stopped. "On second thought, give it to me." Zack grinned, but shook his head. "Fine, have it your way," Flenn said. "*Please*."

Zack handed him the note. "You're too easy." Without looking at the number, Flenn tore the paper in half and tossed it in a nearby trash can and headed for the gate. "Hey!" Zack called, running to catch up. "What'd you do that for?"

"I just have to accept that it's over. She's not ever going to take me back."

"You don't know that."

Flenn shrugged. "You've found a good thing with Donna, Zack. Cherish it. And don't let this damn job get in your way."

Zack tried again. "Go back there and get that damn note. Hoshi is perfect for you…"

"Drop it, Zack," Flenn said as he picked up the pace. "Just let it go. I have."

Zack turned to look at the trashcan, then at Flenn as he walked toward the gate. He shook his head. "Yep. Crazy."

CHAPTER *SIXTY-FIVE*

Present day...

It didn't take long for Clive Soren to figure out that the priest's accomplices weren't policemen. He didn't have a clue about who the men were, only that they both had .45s pointed directly at him. The one with the American accent asked most of the questions.

"None of it was my idea," he kept saying, "I'm just the middleman, you see."

"It's not you we're interested in," the Yank told him. "Who else is in this with Love?"

Soren never varied in his telling of the story. Tobias Love hired him from time to time when something needed tending to, such as when someone at English Petroleum needed to be taught a lesson or to have an 'accident.' Soren had worked for Love on and off for the past three years. Love had approached him a couple of months ago with a peculiar job. He was to accompany Love's uncle to Durham Cathedral and pretend to be a scholar.

"Mr. Love gave me one of them plasticine envelopes with a small strip of clear tape," Soren said, eyeing the guns trained at his torso. "It 'ad a golden dot in the middle. I 'ad strict instructions not to touch the tape with me bare hands, or to let anyone else see it." Once alone with the Prince Bishop's Chalice, Love had told him to carefully remove the tape after the dot had affixed itself to the bottom of the chalice. Soren had been amazed at how closely the color of the dot mimicked the gold of the communion vessel.

"That was it. He gave me fifty-thousand quid, more than he had paid for anything I'd ever done before."

Flenn glanced back from the driver's seat. "What was I worth?"

"A grand," Soren said. "I didn't collect."

Flenn looked back at the road. "Lucky me."

Zack asked, "Why did Love want you to kill the priest?"

"I reckon he's sore. Love figured everyone would automatically blame the Russians again." Soren shifted in his seat. "Plus, he said the Father was, how'd he put it… 'too blasted cocky to be a priest.'"

Zack couldn't keep from grinning. "Well, I can't argue with him there."

"*Hrumph.*" Flenn snorted, glowering out the window.

Soren searched the American's eyes. "What's to become of me, then?"

No one answered. "Come on mates, I've told you everything!"

He looked at Davy. "You're from the Dales; surely you'd let a fellow Yorkshire man off the hook, right?" Soren looked toward the front seat. "Father, I'm sorry about what happened on the road; just doin' me job, that's all. I admit it's lousy work, but… "

"Will you shut him up?" Flenn snapped. Davy pushed the pistol into the man's ribcage and Soren went quiet. Zack pulled out his phone and made a call. Ten minutes later, they pulled off to the side of the road where a black Mercedes was sitting with the engine running. "Come on, chaps, have a heart. I told you everything I know."

Flenn got out and opened the door to let Davy climb out of the backseat. Zack pushed Soren, forcing him onto the gravel road. Two men exited the Mercedes, both wearing black suits and dark ties. Flenn recognized one of them.

Beamish and the other man walked up to Soren, who looked up and began to tremble. "We'll take it from here," Beamish said.

"Happy to give you a hand," Zack said, "again."

Not another word was spoken as Beamish handcuffed Soren and escorted him to the car. As Beamish climbed into the driver's seat, Zack called out, "See you later, Rip!"

Beamish raised his hand only to give Zack the finger.

"Well, now that wasn't very nice," said Zack, dusting off a jellybean from his pocket. "Here I am giving an ally a leg up on an investigation and he does something like that!"

"Knock it off, Zack," Flenn said. "We still have work to do."

Zack snapped back, "What did I do to you?" He looked at Davy as they all three climbed back into the rental car. "He's just sore because they only offered a thousand pounds for him." Zack patted Flenn on the shoulder as Flenn started the car. "Cheer up. Why, with the exchange rate and all, that's more like thirteen hundred. Much more than you're worth, if you ask me."

"*Hrumph!*"

CHAPTER *SIXTY-SIX*

10 1/2 years earlier...

The skyline of New York from the air looks very different than the paintings ofen done of it. For one thing, rooftops are not very attractive. That seemed especially true to Hoshi as she looked out the window of the 737 as it prepared to land at LaGuardia. Somewhere down there was her new apartment. She'd found it online, had a friend check it out, and was meeting the movers tomorrow. Her things had been in storage since she'd left for Scattle.

A new apartment... her old job. Hoshi was aware of the contrast of past and future as she rubbed her belly. She had put off calling Scott, despite her mother's advice, but then decided to contact him through Donna in order to test the waters. As soon as she got settled she would let Donna know about the baby, but only if she swore not to tell Zack, at least not yet. She figured Zack would just tell Scott and her baby's father deserved to hear it first from her.

"Ladies and gentlemen, this is your captain speaking. We will touch down at LaGuardia in five minutes. Please remain seated with your seatbelts securely fastened."

Five minutes.

Hoshi took a deep breath. She would return to her old job on Monday. She had three days to unpack and settle into her new life. *But was it a new life?* Working at the United Nations again, with all of the same people, going through the same routine day in and day out. *Not so bad, really,* she told herself. *There can be comfort in the familiar.* She thought of Scott. How she would love to have his familiar presence beside her now.

Five minutes.

Things weren't *all* going to be the same. A new apartment, new subway trains to catch, new supermarkets to find… and daycare facilities to investigate, not to mention interviewing obstetricians and pediatricians. Hoshi reached into her pocket and touched the Omamori her mother had given her. The tiny brocade bag contained an amulet that her mom had intended for good luck. Hoshi didn't believe in such things, and neither did her mom, really, but they both reasoned that it couldn't hurt.

Hoshi sighed. There was so much to do, so many new things she'd have to figure out. Fortunately, her mom had promised to come stay for a few weeks when the baby was born, until things settled down a bit. *Settled down?* Hoshi wondered if things would ever settle down. Life as a single mom in New York City… what would grandma say about *this,* she wondered.

Five minutes. That was all it would take to call Scott and tell him that they needed to talk, that they needed to meet and discuss things… *good Lord, did they ever!*

She'd tried so many times to pick up the phone and

call him. She regretted having changed her number after coming back from Scotland. She hadn't even given Donna the new number at first, figuring that Donna would just pass it along to Scott. She'd been so angry back then. Later, she had relented and finally given her new number to Donna, but now in the hopes that she *would* pass it along. However, Donna either hadn't, or Scott no longer wanted to talk to her. *God, what a mess!*

In a few weeks, she'd be off to Scotland for the wedding. She couldn't wait until then before talking to Scott... *could she?* She was angry at herself for not calling him, but also was angry that he'd quit trying to contact her. *The man is with the CIA,* she reasoned, *couldn't he have just done some spy mojo thingy to find out my new number?* She wafted between blaming herself and blaming Scott. Her mom kept telling her how strong she was, but Hoshi didn't feel strong. Right now, she felt like a baby herself. Scared, vulnerable, and most of all, alone.

Five minutes.

She willed the plane not to land. *Couldn't it just hover here for eternity?* She had seen a late-night television show once about a plane that got stuck in limbo, forever circling the airport and never landing. All the passengers and crew were forced to learn how to get along with one another, despite their many differences. Hoshi looked around the plane: white, black, Asian, Latino, Middle-Eastern, Hasidic, young, old, fat, thin—America truly was a melting pot of cultures. Not only cultures, but experiences.

She reminded herself that she was not the first single parent to make a new life for herself. *Others had done it, so could she!* She took a deep breath. *And she would… in just five more minutes.*

CHAPTER *SIXTY-SEVEN*

Present day…

It was over at last. With Clive Soren in custody and Tobias Love soon to be, Zack and Flenn agreed to allow Davy to show them around the Yorkshire Dales the next day. Flenn would be leaving Durham soon for two weeks in Edinburgh before heading home to Alabama. Zack, who figured that he now had enough information on Elton Wainwright to make his report to Langley, would also be returning to Washington in a few days.

Flenn found the Dales stunningly beautiful. Davy drove them through lush vistas of wind-swept hillsides formed by ancient glaciers. They stopped at a creamery for what Zack proclaimed to be the best cheese he had ever tasted. They drove through valleys, past slow-running streams, and by pastures populated by recently shorn sheep and lambs. They stopped at Bolton Castle which once housed Mary Queen of Scots when she'd fled to England shortly after her defeat at the Battle of Langside in 1568.

They'd all enjoyed the day. Flenn especially liked seeing Davy take such pride in his homeland. *Whoever these shady characters were that he'd aligned himself with on occasion, Davy was a man who knew right from wrong and would never allow himself to get in over his head.* At least, that's what Flenn told himself.

That night in the Holtz and Claw, a German restaurant near York Minster, Davy had insisted upon treating everyone to dinner. "Your money's no good here tonight," Davy had said, looking at Flenn, "no matter how bloomin' rich ya' are."

Flenn ordered accordingly, but not Zack, who chose the most expensive item on the menu. It wouldn't matter. Flenn was going to send Davy a generous bonus for helping him with Love and Soren… and with the pilgrimage tour earlier.

"So, this is it, is it chaps?" Davy said as they walked out onto the street. In front of them, York Minster was bathed in soft yellow light. Only a handful of people were out this late. Zack checked his watch. He and Flenn had only a few more minutes if they were going to catch the last train to Durham.

"How about a quick picture over by the statue of Constantine?" suggested Flenn.

"Brilliant!" said Davy. "Just be sure to email me a copy." The three men sauntered over to the statue of the emperor in full military dress, reclining in his seat of power, sword in hand.

"Let me get one of you and Zack first," said Flenn, standing in front of the bronze figure.

"How about I get one of the three of you together," said an approaching stranger.

"Lovely," said, Davy.

Or not," added Flenn as he turned to hand the man his phone and saw a revolver pointed straight at him.

CHAPTER *SIXTY-EIGHT*

10 1/2 years earlier…

In the end, it had been Donna who'd told her. Flenn and Zack were on assignment somewhere in the Middle East. That was all Zack had been able to say, other than there would be no way to reach them for the next several weeks. "He promised they'd be back in plenty of time before the wedding," she said over the phone.

Hoshi looked into the mirror. *Great,* she thought, *I'll be eight months by then and the first Scott will know about the baby will be when I walk down the aisle!* "Are you sure there isn't a way to get hold of them?" Hoshi said. According to Donna, Zack had said they'd have to leave their phones behind.

"I wish there were. I promise I'll let you know as soon as I hear from him. I'm sorry, Hosh. I really am."

She'd be even sorrier if she'd told Zack about the pregnancy. Donna was a blabber mouth, but at least this time she'd managed to keep the secret.

"So, did you get the dress I sent you?" Donna asked. Hoshi had. It was hideous. Even worse, she'd have to find someone who could let it out so that she'd be able to wear it. She sighed as Donna prattled on. *Maybe she could get to Edinburgh early, meet with Flenn, try to make up with him.*

Although, by now he might have moved on, maybe he wouldn't want her anymore...

"Isn't it divine!" Donna said. I've decided that everything will be in red and green for Christmas. The castle people said that they would take care of all the decorations. Apparently, they don't let brides have much of a say as to how they'll fix up the castle other than to select a color scheme… some historical thing, I guess. Anyway, red and green. I've already picked out Zack's kilt!"

"Sounds… Christmassy," was all Hoshi could think to say.

"Just another month!" Donna said. "Can you believe it?"

Hoshi sighed. "No, I can't." *A whole other month before she could try to patch things with Scott.*

She felt her belly. *Forever!*

CHAPTER *SIXTY-NINE*

Present day...

Flenn stared at the revolver. "If it's money you want, son, here, take my wallet."

"Before you reach into your pocket," said the voice of another man approaching the small group, "you should know that Cecil here is an excellent shot."

"I don't have a weapon," said Flenn, knowing full well that Zack and Davy did. "I was simply reaching for my wallet."

The second man stepped out of the shadows.

Tobias Love!

Love signaled and another man joined them. *So much for thinking that Love would no longer be a problem!*

"Now, let's all go somewhere where we can talk, shall we?" Love said.

"I don't think so," said Zack. Tobias Love looked down at his chest and saw a red laser dot. "At this range, I never miss."

The first man looked to his boss. Love didn't seem concerned.

"Ah, Zack Matteson, I presume. My sources tell me you are a man to be reckoned with."

"Try me and you'll find out," Zack said.

Love simply smiled in return. "I think if you will just look to your right you will see that I do indeed still have the advantage."

"Good God!" exclaimed Davy.

Zack turned. Rip Van Winkle was aiming his weapon directly at them. "Beamish, what in God's name are you doing?" Zack said.

"I warned you to stay out of this, Matteson. You should have listened to me."

Tobias Love's smile turned into a smirk, rivaling that of the gargoyle just above him. "You Americans are so bloody full of yourselves! You think you own the world." He looked at Flenn. "And you, what excuse do you have, priest? You should have left well enough alone. I suppose I'll have to take care of my fool of an uncle now!"

Even if Flenn had been armed, he wouldn't have been able to turn and squeeze off a shot before Love's two goons took him down. Zack and Davy still had their weapons pointed at Love's henchmen, but the arrival of Beamish gave Love the upper hand.

"Now, Father, if you will instruct your friends to lower their weapons."

Flenn fixed his gaze upon the man who had murdered Windsor Tammerlane in the very home of the blessed remains of Saint Cuthbert. He wasn't afraid; he was angry! "I'll do no such thing!"

"I understand that you have acquired a certain affinity for my uncle's drinking companions," Love said. "It would be a shame if they also suffered for your stubbornness."

Flenn was filled with the same explosive rage as when he'd discovered that Eric Scudder had murdered the innocent children in Honduras. He wanted to tear Tobias Love limb from limb.

"Perhaps you are deaf as well as meddlesome. I won't ask you again. Tell your friends to lower their weapons!"

"Like hell we will!" Davy shouted. Flenn turned toward Davy just as he fired at the oil magnate. Love screamed and grabbed his arm as he fell against the stone edifice. Both of Love's goons fired simultaneously at Davy. Zack managed to quickly take out the one on the left, then dropped to his knees to fire at the one on his right... only to have his Glock jam! Love's henchman aimed at Zack but Flenn jumped between them. They both heard the shot...

"No!" screamed Zack... but Flenn didn't fall. The man stood wild-eyed, blood trickling from his forehead. He crumpled to the ground a second later.

Beamish!

"Damn it, Matteson," he said, "I had this! Love thought I was on his payroll, now you've blown a year's investigation!"

Stunned, Flenn turned to Davy, who lay on the ground, both hands pressed against his abdomen. Flenn and Zack rushed to Davy's side where both knelt beside him. Flenn took off his jacket and pressed it against the gaping wound.

"Love!" Beamish shouted. "He's gone!"

"Go after him!" yelled Zack. Beamish disappeared around the side of the church in hot pursuit.

Flenn peeled back one of Davy's hands to find the man's insides in shreds. He took off his jacket and pressed it tightly against the wound. Whether it was bravery or from the abundance of alcohol from dinner, Davy didn't make a sound.

"Don't you worry, old man," said Zack. "You'll be dancing again in no time."

Davy's lips, now covered in blood, began to move. "I... I... "

Both men leaned closer. "What, Davy; what is it?"

A flicker of light flashed from Davy's eyes. "I don't dance."

Zack forced a grin. "Well, I'll just have to teach you." He glanced at Flenn, who shook his head ever so slightly.

A shot rang out in the distance, then another. Zack looked toward the church, then down at Davy and finally over at Flenn. "Go!" said Flenn. Zack picked up one of the pistols from Love's henchmen, both lying lifeless only a few yards away, and tossed it to Flenn before disappearing around the back of the Minster. Flenn glanced down at the weapon briefly before casting it aside.

Davy reached for Flenn's hand, clasping it feebly with both of his. "Well, well, lad, looks like this is the end, eh?"

Flenn squeezed Davy's bloody hand while continuing to press his jacket against the wound, for all the good it would do.

"I won't lie to you, Davy, it's not looking good."

"Ach, at least I went out in a blaze of glory, not sitting

on some bloody barstool waiting for my next pension check." He smiled. "Thank you, Flenny-boy."

"What for?"

"For helping an old man feel useful again," He winced. "Now leave me be, and go get that bugger!"

Flenn reached for his phone to call for help. "I'm not leaving you."

"Go, damn it! Your friend needs you." Suddenly, Davy's eyes darted to the left. Flenn looked up but no one was there. "What's this, then?" Davy said to no one. "Wait a minute, I know you! Flenn, look who's here… My Lord!… it's bloody well *him!*"

Flenn looked, even though he knew it was the loss of blood causing Davy to hallucinate.

"You know, the chap from the shrine in Durham; he says he knows you…" Davy's eyes dilated then closed as his hands fell limp. Flenn felt for a pulse. Nothing. He murmured a prayer as he made the sign of the cross on Davy's forehead.

Flenn got to his feet and ran toward the Minster. Zack and Beamish had gone to the right so Flenn went left, hoping to catch Love if he tried circling around. Flenn could hear sirens in the distance as he ran around the massive stone structure. *Someone must've reported gunshots.*

He heard a door close off to his right, near the south transept. He found it quickly; the door opened and he slipped inside.

Moonlight shone through the stained-glass windows onto the statues of England's great kings adorning the 1,000-year-old choir screen. A shadowy figure moved off to his right. Flenn's foot slipped in something dark and wet on the floor. He reached down to touch it, rubbing it between his thumb and index finger.

Blood!

****

Outside, Zack had caught up with Beamish. The British agent was sitting behind a bench, pressing his hand tightly against his left leg. "You okay?" asked Zack, crouching next to him.

"Do I bloody-well look okay?" Beamish snapped.

"Aren't you supposed to say, 'I'm fine, go get Tobias,' or something like that? Zack gently tugged Beamish's hand away. "Here, let me see." Zack checked to make sure an artery hadn't been nicked while Beamish kept an eye out for Love.

"How's Spate?"

Zack frowned. "Not good… Flenn's with him." Zack risked using the flashlight on his cell phone to examine the wound. "You're okay."

"Still hurts like hell."

"That's cause you're a wimp… here, take this." Zack pulled out a handkerchief from his pocket and handed it to Beamish. "Press on the wound with this until the paramedics arrive. There's no exit wound; the bullet's still in there. Afraid you're going to need surgery."

"Just my luck. First you muck up a year's investigation, then I get shot by that blasted idiot. If you had just kept out of this… "

"So," Zack interrupted, "which way did he go?"

Beamish sighed. "Around the north end. No telling where he's got off to; but I think I may have winged him."

"That should slow him down. Zack squeezed the man's shoulder and asked, "You okay?"

"Would it matter if I said no?" Beamish answered. Zack grinned in response. "That's what I thought. Alright then, I'm fine, go get the bad guy."

Zack nodded. "I will. Guess the CIA is going to wrap this one up too, Rip." He saluted. "As you Brits say: 'Ta-ta'."

"One day, Matteson... one day."

Zack smiled. "Just not today," he called as he ran off to find Love.

CHAPTER *SEVENTY*

10 1/2 years earlier…

"Donna's going to kill you if we don't get back soon," Flenn warned. The mission had taken only a day to put together but weeks to implement. He and Zack had been entrenched with a number of marines in an underground base camp for the past two weeks.

The hidden base wasn't far from the terrorist encampment where Zamir had been reported coming and going. Days had been used for sleeping and the nights were spent making their way through the desert to the edge of Al-Mashriq base waiting to catch sight of Zamir.

Wearing night vision goggles, the two agents crept silently alongside the special forces unit just as they had done every night. Their mission was simple: observe the terrorist camp up close, then—once Zamir arrived—call in an airstrike and stand back while the marines did mop-up and reconnaissance, which Flenn knew meant killing any survivors and making off with all of the electronic equipment.

War was a horrible reality, and America was at war. President Bush had declared this the 'War on Terror' only to admit, when a reporter tripped him up, that such a war could never be truly won. The media had made much of that, but Bush had only meant that terrorism had always been and would always be an ongoing reality... as long as there are crazy ideologues in the world with access to weapons.

When they were out at night, trudging through the bitter cold of the Afghani desert, Flenn and Zack seldom spoke—no one did—but tomorrow was when Zack had promised Donna he'd be home. The wedding was just two weeks away, and so far, there had been no sign of Zamir. The only communication allowed out was a cryptic message sent at 3 a.m. each morning. The message was sent as a numeric code, meant to tell the chiefs back home whether Zamir had arrived.

"This will all be over soon," Zack whispered, hopefully. Donna wasn't the only reason why he wanted to get back. He'd run out of jellybeans days ago, and the only other sweet thing the combat unit had was dried fruit. "Maybe tonight will be the night."

It wasn't. Nor was the next night, or the next. But four days later, as Flenn Zack, and six marines lay camouflaged in the night sand, a Jeep drove into the encampment.

"Zamir... " Zack whispered excitedly. A stocky man wearing a dark shirt and a bandana of some sort was sitting in the back seat. Flenn's night binoculars were equally powerful, but Flenn wasn't as certain.

"You sure that's not just wishful thinking, Zack?"

"Zoom in on his face... the scar under his right eye; that's Zamir!"

Flenn still couldn't tell. He waited for the man to turn,

which at last he did. "Bingo!" Flenn said. "That's Zamir. Let's go back and call it in."

"No need," said the lieutenant as he pulled a radio from his vest. "You guys positive it's him?"

Zack nodded. "Without a doubt."

The lieutenant powered on the device. "Then we don't need to worry about them intercepting our transmissions anymore. He toggled a switch, "Rover One this is Rover Two."

What seemed like an eternity went by before they heard a soft, crackling noise and then, "Rover Two, go ahead."

"Santa Claus has arrived. Say again, Santa Claus has arrived. Notify the North Pole to deliver the presents."

"Roger that," said the voice, "…and Merry Christmas, boys!"

Less than 12 minutes later, the sky lit up as a series of Tomahawk Cruise Missiles from an American ship anchored somewhere in the Gulf struck the terrorist camp.

Flenn and Zack watched the spectacle as two Humvees, which had previously been camouflaged with netting back at the marine's hidden base, came rushing across the sand. Both vehicles pulled up alongside them, and 15 heavily armed men jumped out. They waited for a second round of missiles to strike before entering the camp.

"I don't know what we're going to find in all that mess!" yelled Zack over the explosions.

"You'd be surprised what actually survives after one

of these attacks," one Seal shouted. "Last year, outside of Kabul, we found an entire set of antique china still intact, inside what had been somebody's kitchen."

"The somebody? Who was it?" Flenn asked.

"Don't know," the ensign responded. "Could have been Taliban, or someone in the wrong place at the wrong time. Anyway, I sent the dishes back home. My wife had them appraised; said they were worth a small fortune."

Flenn exchanged a disapproving look with Zack.

Just then someone opened up on their position. As one, the marines returned fire. There was no further response.

"Okay, spread out!" ordered the lieutenant as they reached the edge of the camp. "Groups of two; watch your back, and for God's sake don't shoot me!"

Flenn, Zack, and the lieutenant waited for several minutes before entering the camp. Occasionally, they heard weapons-fire; Flenn knew what that meant. *There had been survivors.*

Charred bodies made it impossible to distinguish one man from another, although Zamir couldn't possibly have escaped. Zack's job was to take photographs while Flenn searched for computers, telephones, and any other electronic equipment that might have valuable information. They'd have roughly an hour before Afghan troops arrived to survey the situation. By then, they would all be long gone.

"Looks like I'll make it back for the wedding after all," Zack said. "I can't wait to call Donna!" Small fires lit the sky as the smell of sulfur and burning flesh permeated the air. Flenn gazed at the carnage around him and wondered if maybe it had been a good thing that he'd lost Hoshi. *How could someone as sweet and wonderful as her be tied up with someone who does… this… for a living?*

Flenn comforted himself with the fact that he knew he was where his country needed him to be. Al-Mashriq was morphing into something far worse than Al-Qaeda had ever been. This new group had no rules. The sand farmers were outnumbered now by murderous thugs willing to torture women and children simply for their own pleasure. At Flenn's feet were a half dozen dead terrorists. He stared at them; his jaw like stone as he thought: *The world is a little safer tonight.*

"Flenn! Get over here!" Zack was standing by an overturned Jeep. "Take a look." He pointed to a corpse on the ground. "Is that Zamir?"

Flenn looked down at the body. "I can't tell, the man barely has a face left."

"Yeah, but look at his neck."

"What about it?"

"The bandana. It's him."

Flenn looked around; nothing was moving. "I'm sure he wasn't the only one wearing a bandana."

"I don't see anyone else wearing one; plus, he was right here by this Jeep when the missiles landed. I'm calling this one a success."

Flenn looked at the mangled bodies surrounding them. "Seems like there ought to be a different word for it."

"Whatever," Zack said, taking several photographs of the dead man.

In the dark, fifty meters away from the edge of the camp, a man, very much alive, collapsed in pain and shock. Colonel Zamir turned to watch the horrific scene play out in front of him. In the distance he thought he recognized two men he'd once known well... Scott Flenn and Zack Matteson!

CHAPTER *SEVENTY-ONE*

Present day…

York Minster was eerily quiet. The dim light from the towers above cast silvery shadows across the marble floor. Flenn made his way silently in front of the rood screen to the north transept, where the Five Sisters, a quintet of towering slender glass, had kept a centuries-long watch over this house of God. Flenn turned to his right and followed the aisle that ran along the north end of the choir.

Nothing.

He considered waiting for the police to arrive, but that might allow Love to slip away. With Love's money and vast network, he could convince someplace like Ukraine or Venezuela to hide him away. Flenn set his jaw: *No; this ended here, tonight!*

Flenn crept slowly past the tombs of the great church to the east end, then back around until he had circled the entire chancel. *Love must be hiding inside the quire!*

During worship, York Minster's clergy and choir sat inside the walled inner structure surrounding the high altar. In the dark, however, the hallowed quire seemed closed in and foreboding. Cautiously, Flenn made his way through the medieval chancel. A narrow aisle separated the two-bay choirstall on either side. In front of him, the largest single expanse of medieval glass in the world— the magnificent Great East Window—towered above the altar and wooden spires.

If Tobias Love *was* in here, he was either cowering in one of the stalls or behind the altar itself. Enraged that the man who'd poisoned Windsor at his own consecration might be seeking refuge behind a similar altar, Flenn made his way boldly down the aisle.

He stopped to listen for any sound that might betray Love's whereabouts. Flenn glanced at the small statues towering above. He felt as though the saints themselves were cautioning him to leave the quire.

"If you move another inch, I will shoot."

Flenn froze. *Damn, Love was behind him!*

"Stay where you are," said Love as he made his way closer.

"It's over, Tobias," Flenn said. "My friends will be here any moment, and the police are on their way."

"Which is why you're my ticket out of here," Love gloated.

"Taking a hostage won't help you. They're never going to let you out of here!"

"Who said anything about taking a hostage? I'm simply going to shoot you some place where it will really hurt; your screams should be enough to distract the police while I get away. Oh, but I'll be back, don't you worry. I have a few scores to settle, thanks to you!"

"When is it going to be enough for you, Tobias?" Flenn turned to face him. Love was not three feet away; his shirt was bloody, a bullet having grazed his left shoulder. "You poisoned Bishop Tammerlane, involved your own uncle in your hellish plans and now you want to manipulate the next prime minister. Have you no shame?"

Tobias Love's eyes narrowed. "The shame is that I let the likes of you and my blasted uncle stand in my way! Now, turn around."

"Hell no."

"I said, turn around!"

Flenn saw something move near the chancel entrance. Then, quick as lightening, a silhouetted figure sacked Love from behind, sending the pistol sliding across the marble floor. Flenn jumped into the fray, managing to help whoever it was pin the murderer down. He looked up, expecting to see either Zack or Beamish… it was neither.

A fresh-faced kid with red hair smiled and said, "Halo Father!"

It was the boy from the wall! The very one who'd tried to rob Flenn just over a week ago. "Fancy seeing you at the Minster tonight! 'E're, what's this all about?"

"Ow, you're hurting my arm!" Love shouted.

"Shut up, you! How dare you bring a gun into this holy place and threaten the good Father here. Why I oughta… "

"You're hurting me," Love complained.

Flenn eased his grip on Love's wounded shoulder. "Edgar, how did you…"

The young man grinned. "Got the job, just like you said. Already promoted to night watchman in less than two weeks!" Despite the current situation, the kid was beaming from ear to ear.

"Congratulations, Edgar. Well done!" Flenn stood to retrieve the gun. "Watch him; don't let him up."

"No worries;" said Edgar, "this 'un ain't goin' nowhere!"

Love whined, "Be careful, you fool; I'm injured!"

"Not 'alf as injured as you're gonna' be if you don't stop thrashin' about!"

Flenn picked up the pistol with two fingers and set it gingerly on a prie-dieu behind him. "So Edgar, how's your sister?"

"She's comin' along just fine, Father, just fine. Gettin' better health care too now, thanks to you!"

"Me?"

"Don't play coy, Father. Dean Jackson told me what you did for us. I don't know how we can ever thank you."

"I think you just did!" Flenn said.

"If you two are quite finished," Love snapped, "I'll make you an offer, kid."

"Oh yeah, what's that?" Edgar said.

"Let me go and hold off Mr. Goody Two Shoes here and I'll see that you and your sister each get a million dollars."

"Too late, mister." The boy looked at Father Flenn as the York Police poured through the same side door that Love and Flenn had found open. "Plus, the Father's given me something worth a lot more."

"What's that?" Flenn asked, raising an eyebrow.

"Me self-respect."

CHAPTER *SEVENTY-TWO*

10 ½ years ago...

Hoshi looked at herself in the hotel mirror. "I'm not going," she said.

Donna was busy straightening her hair. "What? Of course, you're going." She reached for some hairspray.

Hoshi stared at her belly. "No, I'll just stay here in your room. I won't even go across the hall... he might see me."

"Well, duh... he has to see you; he's the best man." Donna set the hairspray down and searched for her lipstick. "And as for staying here, you can forget that. Zack will be staying here tonight."

"Whatever happened to waiting until the wedding night?"

Donna turned and snickered, "Yeah, you're the poster child for that, aren't you?"

Hoshi turned to look at her profile. "God, why didn't I tell him? I'm such an idiot. I've had all this time. I must've picked up the phone a hundred times and put it right down again. This isn't right. I should have *told* him, not waited until now and *shown* him!"

Donna leaned into the mirror to apply her cherry red

lipstick. "Well, honey, you're showing the world now. Nothing you can do about that."

"Yes, there is. I can hide out here."

Donna shook her head. "Not happening. You're my maid of honor."

Hoshi shrugged. "Some maid. I lost my honor a long time ago."

"You worry too much." Donna stepped around her and into the bedroom. "Now finish getting ready. The rehearsal is in a couple of hours."

"I'm not going."

"Get ready!"

Hoshi stuck her head out of the bathroom. "You're sure he's here?"

"Room 333."

Hoshi started to brush her hair. "Maybe I should go talk to him."

"No time. You're not dressed and you haven't touched your makeup… hop to it, girl!"

Hoshi opened her makeup bag and started rummaging through it. "I should at least call his room."

"Makeup!"

Hoshi stared at her image in the bathroom mirror. "What good is makeup going to do. I look like a walrus!"

"You do not."

"I do so."

Donna slipped on the dress she'd bought in Paris for tonight, and then searched for her hoop earrings. "Have you seen my gold earrings?" she called.

"They're in here on the counter, next to my pearl ones."

Donna walked into the bathroom. "Good Lord, Hoshi, do something with that hair, it's a mess!"

Hoshi glanced in the mirror, shook her head, and sighed. "Nope, I'm not going."

****

"I'm not going!"

"Come on, Flenn. You have to," said Zack, setting his bag of jellybeans on the bureau.

"I can't go up there and just knock on her door and say, 'Hey, remember me?' What if she still hates me?"

Zack turned up the sound on the television to hear the game. Manchester United was playing Scotland. "She doesn't hate you."

"How do you know that? She certainly did the last time I saw her."

Zack tried to focus on the game. "She was mad, that's all."

"Have you seen her?"

Zack shook his head. "She just got in last night. Besides, Donna sent me down here to be with you—said we weren't going to see them until the rehearsal at the castle."

"Probably planning how to throw me in the moat," Flenn groused.

"Would you stop, I'm trying to watch the game."

Flenn reached inside the minibar for a Scotch. It was a

blend, but right now he didn't care. "Since when did you get interested in soccer?"

"It's called *football* over here… and just now when you started whining about my not going to test the waters with Hoshi for you."

Flenn shot him a look. "I am not whining."

"Oh, yes you are," said Zack. "Look, you'll see Hoshi in a couple of hours. After the rehearsal, you two can go somewhere and talk."

"Yeah, right. If you'd just go up there, then I would at least know what my chances were."

Zack turned up the TV. "You know what?"

"What?"

"I should have left you in the desert with what was left of Zamir."

"Why didn't you?"

Zack turned off the television. "Hell if I know. Come on, time to go." They headed downstairs where Flenn stopped in front of a mirror in the hotel lobby to check his hair. Zack nudged him toward the car. "The groom's the one that's supposed to be nervous, not the best man. Come on, the limo's waiting. You know how Donna is; if I'm not there on time she'll find a bottle of something and start the party before we even arrive." Flenn took one last swipe with his comb and then headed toward the waiting limousine.

"I just want to look my best for your rehearsal, that's all," Flenn said, climbing into the back seat.

"Yeah, right," Zack scoffed. "I know who you want to look your best for, and it ain't me, buddy boy."

Whether Flenn's anxiety was becoming contagious, or Zack was finally coming to terms with what was happening, Zack's neck and palms began to perspire. He adjusted his tie three times as he glanced around the back seat of the limousine. "God, there's room for eight people back here! I don't know why the girls couldn't go with us."

"I'm sure Donna wanted to make sure everything was set up and ready at the castle, that's all."

Zack rolled his eyes. "You're kidding, right? Donna was over there all morning with her mother." He quit fumbling with his tie and checked the buttons on his cuffs. "No telling what it looks like. Those two aren't the best at decorating. I love Donna, but you should see her folks' place— French provincial meets backwoods West Virginia."

Realizing he sounded unappreciative, Zack gave Flenn a friendly nudge. "Not that I'm ungrateful. We couldn't have done any of this without you. We still can't thank you enough for renting Edinburgh Castle for us for two days. That had to cost you tens of thousands." The bill had been in the six figures, but Zack didn't need to know that. Money was nothing other than a tool to Flenn. His mother had taught him her own personal philosophy: 'What's the point in having money if you can't use it?'

"What else are friends for," Flenn said, turning to watch the ancient city roll by. Picturesque 16th-century buildings graced both sides of the street, giving the old town a Dickensian feel, though that wasn't what was occupying Flenn's mind at the moment. Zack felt awkward not telling Flenn about Hoshi, but Donna had made him promise.

"Look, bud, I know you're nervous. It's been six months... things change."

Flenn turned toward Zack. "What do you mean? What things?"

"Huh?"

"What things change?"

Zack shrugged. "I don't know, just *things*, that's all. The car slowed and came to a stop. The driver came around to open the passenger door for them.

Flenn's eyes narrowed. "What are you not telling me?"

Zack stepped out onto the sidewalk. "Nothing." *Everything.*

The bridge to the castle was festooned with gigantic red-and-green ribbons, and splashy red bows were tied to the lampposts on either side. Zack sighed. "Yep, Donna's mother has definitely been here."

Edinburgh castle has stood atop a high crag overlooking the city for centuries. During Scotland's wars for independence, the castle had fallen countless times but each time it was rebuilt stronger and grander. Both the English and the Scots believed that to control the castle, was to control the country. Three thousand years of history could be traced to the top of this mountain, but none of it mattered right now to Flenn. His stomach was churning and a lump was beginning to develop in his throat. He was about to see Hoshi for the first time in nearly six months, and now Zack was saying that things may have changed. *Was Hoshi with another man now?* Flenn sighed. *It was entirely possible. In fact, why wouldn't she be?*

Flenn looked over the rail of the bridge to the sharp rocks below. "What's he like?"

Zack turned. "What's who like?"

"Hoshi's new boyfriend?"

Zack rolled his eyes. "Just come with me; you'll see."

Ahead, the entrance to the castle courtyard was flanked on either side by foreboding statues of William Wallace and Robert the Bruce inset into the massive stone wall. Both statues were festooned tonight with holly and red ribbons, and neither appeared happy about it.

The guard at the entrance was waiting for them. He signaled someone inside and cheers sounded from every corner as Zack entered the courtyard. Flenn realized that he should have walked through first and allowed the groom to enter last, but right now he was fantasizing about leaping over the side of the bridge— *which might be better than seeing Hoshi on the arm of another man.*

Tall, red-and-green banners lined the courtyard where for centuries knights and warriors had defended the land. Over in a corner, enormous balloons were being inflated by a small band of exhausted workers.

"Oh, good Lord. What are the balloons for?" Zack asked Flenn.

"You're asking me?"

I thought you were paying for all this," Zack said with a scowl.

Flenn shrugged, peering through the crowd to find

Hoshi. "I'm just the guy with the checkbook. You'll have to ask your bride about the, um... decor."

"Probably her mother's idea. Where is Donna, anyway?" asked Zack. To the right and left were large cream-colored tents, which had been set up for the wedding party tomorrow. The one on the right was marked "Bride and Bridesmaids." The one on the left wasn't marked at all.

The crowd separated the groom from the best man as well-wishers came over to shake Zack's hand. Flenn wandered over to a bar that was being set up for later in the evening. Drinks and heavy hors d'oeuvres would be served inside the castle as well as out in the courtyard. A dozen or so wait staff were busy filling up glasses of Chardonnay and Merlot. Flenn had his best man's toast memorized; he just hoped he wouldn't be standing anywhere near Hoshi's new beau when he gave it—it would be nearly impossible not to throw his drink in the man's face.

Flenn took a breath as he realized how childish he was being. *Didn't Hoshi deserve to be happy? If Hoshi had someone new, then... well... good for her.* He knew that he was lying to himself, but he needed somehow get through the evening.

****

Inside the bridal tent, Hoshi tried putting her nervousness aside as she helped Donna with her hair. She gazed into the large standing mirror and couldn't help but chuckle. "Don't we make a pair? You looking gorgeous, like a model off the runway, and me like a bowling ball with legs."

"Stop that, Hosh; you're beautiful, and anybody that says differently will just have to deal with me." Donna searched the tables nearby, "Has anybody seen my wineglass?"

Hoshi stepped back. "Has *anybody* said anything?"

"What, about you being pregnant? No. Not to me, at least."

"Not even Zack?"

Donna found her glass on a table a few feet away and hurried over to it. "Oh, you know how men are! Especially those two. Zack and Flenn are always making jokes."

Hoshi straightened. "They are making jokes? About me?"

"No, no," Donna said, sipping her wine. You're too paranoid. I don't think Flenn even knows yet. I told Zack that you said not to tell him." Donna finished the wine and asked an attendant for a refill. Hoshi thought about what Donna had said. *She was right; Zack and Scott made light of just about everything when they were together.* She could just imagine what they would have to say tonight after all this was over. *Phrases like 'knocked-up,' 'bun-in-the-oven,' 'bacon-in-the-drawer'—that's what men joked about with one another.* Deep down Hoshi knew that Scott wasn't like that, but she couldn't help the anger that was welling up inside of her.

****

About 50 or 60 well-wishers encircled Zack, but Donna and her bridesmaids were still in the tent, preparing to make their entrance. A spindly, balding man with only a few wisps of grayish black hair stepped up to Flenn. "I was told you're the best man." Flenn nodded in response. "I'm Reverend Campbell. I assume you will have the rings tomorrow?"

"Nope," Flenn said. "I was told there would be a ringbearer. About four years old, I think."

The pastor scowled. "Children? Oh heavens!" With a look of disgust mixed with resignation he turned and oozed away. *Ministers,* Flenn thought, *what a lot!*

"Everyone! May I hav' yer attention please?" A tall, slender woman with short, coiffed, platinum-blonde hair stood in the center of the courtyard and clapped her hands. "May I have your attention?" she asked a second time. "Ach, everyone, please gather round."

People gathered in a semicircle where tomorrow there would be rows of white folding chairs. "I am Mrs. Shrewsbury, the wedding coordinator. May I have the groom and his groomsmen up front, please?" Zack and Flenn stepped up with three other men. "Gentlemen," she explained, "the ladies will be out in a moment. I understand that one of them is pregnant and catchin' her breath. In the meantime, I'll need you here early tomorrow for the photographs. Please bring your tuxedos with you and take them to your pavilion when you arrive."

"Pavilion?" Zack asked.

"The tent on the left," Flenn whispered.

"Oh. Ok, sure."

The woman peered across the top of her glasses at the groom. "That's where the men will be changin'. Oh, and please, no drinkin' till after the ceremony. I canna' tell you how many grooms we have had to try and sober up before their wedding."

"Won't be a problem," Flenn said.

"At least not with *us*," Zack added with a low chuckle.

"Well, see that it isn't," the woman grunted, turning toward the ladies' pavilion. "Let me go see what's keepin' them." Just as she said it, the flaps of the tent rolled back and the crowd pushed in front of Flenn to catch a glimpse of the bride. Even as tall as he was, Flenn couldn't see Donna and the bridesmaids for all the people.

Everyone gushed and nodded approvingly as Donna made her way through the crowd. Flenn thought he could just make out the top of Hoshi's head following behind. As people stepped back to let the bridal party join the groom and groomsmen, Flenn could see Donna but not Hoshi. Donna was wearing an emerald green, sequined, floor-length gown with a slit all the way up her right thigh. She was walking a bit unsteadily and clutching a glass of white wine. Her hair was pulled back behind her ears and topped with a silver and gold crystal tiara. Her face was slightly flushed, but Zack didn't care. He'd be joining her with a few drinks of his own soon.

The bridesmaids began to peel off one-by-one and gather around the coordinator until, at last, Flenn saw her. Hoshi was standing behind two other bridesmaids and staring right at him. Her eyes, usually soft and warm, were glaring angrily at him. It wasn't what he had expected. Neither was what he saw next.

The two bridesmaids parted, one to the left, the other to the right. Flenn's eyebrows both shot straight up.

CHAPTER *SEVENTY-THREE*

Present day…

"Quiet everyone, 'ere he comes!" Murph had been watching the window half the morning, waiting for the priest to arrive. He took his place beside the bar with the rest of the gang.

The door opened.

"Wotcha!" Flenn said as he entered the Crown and Bull. He hadn't expected to see balloons and streamers, or Murph leading Val and the gang in a cacophonous round of: 'For He's a Jolly Good Fellow.' Flenn grinned and shook his head.

"Guys, I don't know what to say… yes I do… that was awful!"

"Ach, he's a music critic now!" George said.

"Doesn't know quality when he hears it," added Val.

"I thought it was rather nice," said Bob.

Charlie reached for his coffee. "No, the good Father's right; we're terrible." He raised his mug. "The sentiment's what counts, right Father?"

Flenn smiled as Val handed him a cup of steaming black coffee. "Sentiment is never off-key," Flenn said.

"Where's your chum this mornin'?" Colin asked.

"Zack? He's never been great at goodbyes," Flenn said. He left last night. He didn't tell me where he was heading."

"Well, that means more for the rest of us," Murph said, smiling. "Colin and Val here cooked you up a grand farewell breakfast." Murph winked at Val, "By the way, love, where is it?"

Val and Colin both turned for the kitchen, "Comin' right up!" Murph waited for them to get out of sight before reaching behind the bar for a bottle.

"We're gonna' miss you, Father," said Bob.

"Yeah, you kinda gave the place some class." George held his mug out to Murph for a shot.

"What? Ain't I classy enough?" joked Murph.

"Seriously, Father," Charlie added, "we've really enjoyed having you around here. The place won't seem the same once you're gone."

"I'm going to miss you guys, too, but I'm off for the next leg of my sabbatical."

"Charlie told us," Bob said. "Sounds grand! I haven't been there in years."

"I ain't never been," said George.

"Ah, what's Edinburgh got that we ain't got?" Murph said, pouring a little more whiskey into his cup. "Fancy a bit, Father?"

"Why not?" Flenn said, holding out his mug as Val entered with a platter of sausages and English bacon. She spied the bottle in Murph's hand and shook her head.

"I can't leave you boys alone for a second, can I?" She

set the platter down as Colin brought fried eggs, beans, and scones with apricot jam. Murph reached for a plate straight away.

"Wait a minute everyone," said Flenn. "I think today I'd really like to offer a prayer first."

"Sound idea," said Bob.

"Jolly good," agreed George.

Charlie leaned forward to see past Bob and George. "What about it, Murph?"

Murph set his plate down on the bar. "If Father Flenn here wants us to pray, then I say we pray."

Charlie smiled. "Well Father, looks like miracles do still happen!"

The door opened and Charlie stood as a beautiful teenager with red hair breezed into the pub. "Sweetheart! It's great to see you. He went up to the girl and gave her a hug. "Rachel, I'd like you to meet… "

"Mr. Flenn!" The girl crossed in front of the bar. "So, you're the priest me granddad's been goin' on and on about! I had no idea you were a member of the clergy. And me flirtin' with you and all."

"What's this?" Charlie said.

Flenn felt his cheeks turn warm. "Rachel, I can't believe it! *You* are Charlie's granddaughter?" He gave her a hug. "It truly is a small world!"

"Oh, that reminds me." She turned to her grandfather. "I heard from Cambridge. They accepted me!" she squealed.

Her grandfather gave her another hug. "Sweetheart, that's fabulous! I'm so happy for you."

She turned to Flenn, "I guess you were right, miracles do still happen!"

"Rachel, you know the guys, go have some breakfast with them, I want to talk with Father Flenn a moment." Charlie looked over at Murph. "And no whiskey in her coffee this time! Understood, Murph?" Murph winked. Charlie took Flenn by the arm and led him over to the corner out of earshot of the rest of the gang.

"What about the prayer?" Flenn said. Charlie glanced at his granddaughter and the crew digging in.

"Can it keep just for a moment?" Charlie said.

"Honestly, Charlie, the kid was just teasing about flirting with me."

"What?" Charlie brushed the comment aside. "Oh, that. She's always goin' on… just like her grandmother, she is. No, 'tis something else."

Flenn raised an eyebrow. "Is something wrong?"

"No, no… just the opposite. My grandbaby is driving me to London for that appointment you made for me. He took out a blue-and-white checkered handkerchief and wiped his nose. "I just wanted to thank you for all you've done."

Flenn shrugged. "I've checked those London doctors out, Charlie; I think they can really help you."

Charlie nodded. "They certainly have all the credentials… and quite expensive, too. You really didn't have to do that for me, although I'm deeply grateful. But, I mean the other thing... not telling anyone about my nephew or my part in what happened."

Flenn placed his hand on the old man's shoulder. *Everyone expected the best from their family, even the most incorrigible members. Charlie had been no different.* "You were taken advantage of, Charlie. None of what happened was your fault."

A tear formed in the old man's eye. "I don't know... this whole thing. Well, I'm still trying to wrap my brain around it."

Flenn pretended not to notice the tear. "Your nephew was accustomed to getting what he wanted, and what he wanted was that pipeline. Controlling Wainwright was his ticket, and to do that he killed the bishop."

"Why? What did the poisoned chalice have to do with all this?"

Flenn figured that Charlie deserved to know, and explained Pam's involvement as delicately as he could, but only after first swearing him to secrecy.

Charlie's jaw dropped. "Go on! You mean, the bishop's wife was...?"

"Afraid so; just don't tell anyone, okay?"

The old professor shook his head. "You've kept my secret, so I'll keep yours... but, blimey!"

Flenn raised an eyebrow. "So, the fellas' don't know anything about what happened?"

"The chaps read about it in the paper of course, and it was all over the telly, but no, they don't know about my family connection."

Flenn smiled warmly. "Well then, why don't we just keep it that way." He nodded toward the bar. "Shall we join them?"

Charlie nodded, and with a wry smile said, "I suppose we should... after all, *you're* buying."

Glossary

Alb: White wrap-around garment worn by clergy and lay leaders during services which include the Eucharist.

Celebrant: A priest or bishop, authorized to preside at a religious service which includes Holy Communion.

Chalice: A cup used during services of Holy Communion.

Chancel: The area closest to the altar, often where a choir or attending servers sit.

Chimere: An open garment sometimes worn by Anglican (Episcopal) bishops resembling an academic gown.

Choristers: Singers in a choir.

Credence: Small table or tables used to hold the elements of bread, wine and water to be used during communion.

Cruet: Container holding wine or water.

Eucharist: Refers to a service of Holy Communion. Greek word meaning an act of gratitude or thanksgiving.

Mitre: Pointed hat sometimes worn by bishops in worship services.

Nave: The area in a church or cathedral where the congregation is seated.

Paten: Plate used to distribute the bread during communion.

Piscina: Sink which leads into the ground instead of a sewer system. Used most often to dispose excess blessed wine left over from communion.

Prince Bishops: Bishop in Durham who presided over Durham Cathedral from 1075 until 1835. Their powers were equal to the King throughout the surrounding countryside.

QUIRE: Old English for choir or place where a choir is seated.

Rector: Head priest of a parish.

Rochet: Linen vestment worn by bishops and abbots underneath a Chimere.

Rood Screen: A screen inside a church, often elaborately decorated, separating the nave from the chancel.

Sacristy: A room where the communion vessels and altar hangings are kept and where communion is prepared.

Sanctuary: In an Anglican (Episcopal) church, the area immediately surrounding the altar.

Thurifer: A person appointed to carry the incense (inside a thurible) during a worship service.

Transept: An arm of the church on either side of the central aile.

Verger: An official who serves as general attendant before a bishop, dean or other church dignitary.

Vicar: A priest appointed by the bishop to serve in a mission church.

Acknowledgements

Where would we be without friends? Many thanks to my dear friends in England—David Waite, Leigh Waite, Freda Jackson, and Valerie Chadwick—for their inspiration and hospitality while in Durham, Middleton and York. A little closer to home, thank you to Margaret Shaw, my editor; and to Larry Vinson for his invaluable assistance. Thank you also to Win Schepps, Sandra and Paul Ash and to all the fans of the Father Flenn series. I owe a huge debt of gratitude to my wife, Diane, for a final (albeit sometimes painful) review and edit. Love always to Heather and Sean. Also, to Amy, Saya, and Aaron...and to my little Dominic for always believing in his papa. Lastly, thank you to the people of my parish, Saint Mark's Episcopal Church, for their support and encouragement over the years.

Follow Father Flenn at:
www.fatherflenn.com

Finally!

What did happen to Father
Flenn in Edinburgh?

Find out in:

SHADOW
of the
SAINT

A FATHER FLENN ADVENTURE

FARNE
PRESS

About the Author...

Scott Arnold is author of *The Father Flenn Adventures*. He is past vice-president of Homewood Counseling Associates and formerly the editor of two Tennessee newspapers. Arnold resides in Alabama with his wife, Diane, and grandson, Dominic, where he is rector of Saint Mark's Episcopal Church.

Printed by Amazon Italia Logistica S.r.l.
Torrazza Piemonte (TO), Italy